DEATH IN VELVET

PARTNERS IN SPYING MYSTERIES: BOOK ONE

ROSE DONOVAN

Moon Snail Press

To my lovely and hard-working beta readers:
Anne, Barbara, and Mara

Cast of Characters at the Hôtel D'Escalier

Ruby Dove – Student of chemistry at Oxford, fashion designer, and amateur spy-sleuth. On a mission to right (clothing) injustice.

Fina Aubrey-Havelock – Student of history at Oxford, assistant seamstress to Ruby, and her best friend. Ready to defend Ruby, at any cost.

Pixley Hayford – A shameless journalist on the hunt for a scoop. Always game for a Ruby and Fina adventure, especially if it involves Paris.

Mathilde Lafitte – Owner of House of Lafitte, designer extraordinaire, and a recluse.

Henriette Giroux – Madame Lafitte's niece and an aspiring model. Almost as clumsy as Fina.

Yvonne Jourdain – Madame Lafitte's business partner. Not to be trifled with under any circumstances.

Omar Abelli – Hotel manager with a distinct *laissez faire* attitude.

Berthe Dumont – Maid of all trades, with a plain style of speaking.

Elizabeth Ryland – An over-eager fashion buyer from New York.

Dr Leo Fischer – Husband of Madame Lafitte, and a German archaeologist. Loves adventure of all kinds.

Maurice Neuville – Virginie Corbin's boyfriend. Research assistant to Dr Fischer, with a special interest in Ruby Dove.

Virginie Corbin – Maurice Neuville's girlfriend and model for House of Lafitte.

Reggie Barrington-Loftus – Snappy dresser and *bon vivant*, visiting from England.

Inspector Edouard Toussaint – An inspector with flair, and a penchant for eccentricity. Possibly a naturist in his spare time.

Sergeant Albert Coste – Inspector Toussaint's pernickety assistant.

Attila – The hotel's curmudgeonly cat.

1

"May I help you, miss?"

I ignored the question, running my finger against the silky tangerine suit. Though sceptical of the skirt's stitchwork, I admired its design.

For good reason, too. I had already seen this copied suit elsewhere.

The rail-thin shopkeeper glared at me, her severe brown shingle swinging across her pale cheeks. Her pursed lips hid the angry carmine slash lining her mouth.

"Thank you." I sighed dreamily. "It's a smashing suit, but how much is it?"

The shopkeeper moved between me and the tangerine suit, defending it against possible defacement.

"Perhaps you'd prefer to peruse the aisles of Woolworths for...something more suitable." She raked her eyes over my serviceable red frock, halting only at my shabby shoes for additional scrutiny.

I shook my head, fighting an urge to wipe her lipstick from her smug face. "I don't wish to purchase the suit, though I am curious about its provenance."

"Provenance?"

"Where did it come from? Who designed it?"

The shopkeeper sniffed. "All our designs are Madame Mathilde Lafitte's creations. From Paris, of course." She fluttered her arm in a semi-circle around the shop, pointing to burgundy, sapphire, and emerald bias-cut silk gowns lining one wall, whilst velvet gowns with daring V-cuts hung on the other.

My shoulders scrunched up in rising anger. "Well, this suit isn't one of Madame Lafitte's creations."

"Are you a designer, then?"

Her query wasn't a question at all. It was a challenge.

"No, but my best friend is, and I'm her seamstress. And I can detect a copy when I see it." I waved the sleeve of the tangerine suit at her. "The colour, cut, and design are all the same."

"Copy?" She arched her over-plucked eyebrows. "I know who you must be. You're one of those tawdry little seamstresses from House of What's-it. You're trying for a bit of extortion, aren't you?"

I countered by lifting my own less-than-perfectly thin eyebrows. "Extortion?" My face must have been scarlet by now – it certainly felt hotter than Hades. "You're just a toffee-nosed cow, or even worse, someone wanting to join the ranks of toffee-nosed cows. I wouldn't ever stoop so low as to take your money or your poorly plagiarised designs."

A few heads popped out from behind the curtains at the rear of the shop, gasping and giggling.

Grabbing my arm, the woman marched me towards the door. Her cloying sandalwood perfume and firm grip made me struggle, but the shopkeeper had apparently maintained her muscles by regularly accosting her customers. To make matters worse, I had an audience now, even if they were only the silly shop assistants peeking through a clothing rack.

"Let me go!" I jerked my arm. "I'll take this story to the newspapers. They'll be delighted to uncover a fashion scandal and extortion. Extortion of your clientele at these utterly ridiculous prices for copied frocks. And shoddy frocks at that. The stitching is second-rate. No, I'm wrong – more like fifth-rate."

The shopkeeper let my arm drop, whilst her mouth did the same. Perhaps it was just my imagination, but people had begun to gather outside the shop. The front bow window made the shop into a fishbowl, so it was scarcely surprising that pedestrians should notice any drama unfolding inside.

Now with an audience both inside and outside, I marched down the stone flag steps, only missing one along the way.

A woman with gooseberry eyes goggled, whilst a man leaned against a lamppost, pretending he was reading a newspaper. Over my shoulder, I saw the shopkeeper fling her head back and stalk off, right past her snickering minions.

Although my mother would undoubtedly have disapproved, I stuck out my tongue at the shop window.

Then I strode into the meandering West End crowd, feeling a mixture of triumph and foreboding.

I TURNED the corner of Ludgate Circus and yanked down the brim of my green felt hat, turning it from a fashion statement into a rather dated cloche. But gusts of wind would not defeat me, and neither would that dreadful shopkeeper. Even after walking two miles from Grosvenor Street, my mind played the horrid scene in a perpetual loop. Perhaps I had imagined the gowns were imitations. Perhaps the shopkeeper was right to show me the door?

I wrinkled my nose at the fluffy Pomeranian scuttling past me, and she responded with a short yap, bounding after her light-footed elderly owner.

"Fina!"

I lifted my eyes and puffed on my fringe. Ruby Dove dashed up to me, as lively as the Pomeranian. She'd swept up her raven hair under a jaunty emerald beret, and not a strand was out of place. The circles under her eyes, a likely product of end-of-term late nights at Oxford, had vanished since I'd last seen her, and her cheeks glowed, complementing her favourite opal pinprick earrings and raspberry lipstick.

"It's been only a month, but it seems like a year." I squeezed her arm. "You look absolutely marvellous. What makeup are you wearing, and where can I purchase it?"

Ruby giggled. "You know they don't carry makeup for my skin-tone. No, I owe my dewy complexion to rest and relaxation at my auntie's, mixed with a dash of good news."

At the words 'good news', I gulped. With a dawning sense of dread, I realised I had to tell her about my troubling discovery in that blasted shop. After all, Ruby's dress designs were fast becoming popular, and I was her seamstress, after all. But my news could wait, surely. Perhaps we'd discuss it after tea and a nibble…

"Tell me all about it over tea." I pointed to the bustling Lyon's Corner House where we had agreed to meet.

Harried waitresses held their trays high above their heads as customers thronged around them, clinking their spoons against their teacups and chattering away. I inhaled the luscious smell of bread, sticky buns, and tea.

"There's a table in the corner." Ruby marched through the crowd of squawking children and a feisty, barking terrier. A small child patted the dog, shrieked, and then wobbled backwards, right into my knee. The little blighter grabbed my leg and wiped her pastry-covered mouth on my frock, gleefully seeking my approval as she did so.

"Lizzie, darling, now don't be afraid of the darling doggie," admonished a sturdy woman, clearly little Lizzie Borden's mother. I shivered, remembering the story of the axe murderer recounted by a distant American cousin of mine. Still, I waited patiently for an apology from the mother.

However, she just chewed her currant bun in a slow, bovine manner, ignoring my sullied frock.

"I say—" But before I could finish my forthcoming tirade on her lack of courtesy, Ruby tugged me away.

"It's not worth it, Feens," Ruby hissed. "Besides, I have something that will remove the stain from your frock."

Reluctantly, I followed Ruby to the corner table and plopped down. Despite myself, I grinned.

"What's so funny?" she asked. "You looked like you were about to clobber that frightful child with your bag."

"Oh, nothing. I was just remembering how many times you've had to remove various stains from my clothing. I'd be a positive walking nightmare without you. And not only because of your smashing laundering abilities."

"What are you having, dearie?" The welcome wheeze of a waitress interrupted my reverie.

Her crisp, starched collar and apron strings were tighter than a whalebone corset. But her soft, wrinkled smile showed she hadn't let the uniform – or the lunchtime bustle – drain away her good humour.

Ruby removed the grey jacket of her favourite suit and carefully arranged it on the back of her chair. "I'll have tea and a biscuit."

"Tea and a biscuit," the waitress parroted.

I stared at Ruby. Was she on a slimming regime? Even when she'd claimed she'd gained a stone once over Christmas, I never detected any real change. Other than a happier Ruby.

"I'll have a cream tea. With lashings of cream, please."

"Right you are. Tea and a biscuit and a cream tea."

"With lashings of cream, please," I repeated.

The waitress finished scribbling and sailed towards the kitchen as if she were strolling through a sunny, quiet meadow.

"Aren't you hungry? Are you slimming?" I asked.

"Pish." Ruby waved a hand. "Slimming regimes are not for me...except that one Christmas. No, I'm far too excited to eat. But do tell me how you've been keeping after an entire month!"

Peering out of the window, I let my eyes rest on the blur of jostling bodies outside. I simply couldn't stomach telling her about what I'd seen at the dress shop. Why spoil our tea and Ruby's good mood? "I'm too hungry to remember – and I'm certain it's tiresome compared to your news," I said.

Ruby slipped her hand into her black clutch and removed a brown envelope. She slid it across the table, tapping it with a perfectly manicured finger.

"Go on. Read it."

It was a cheque. For £87! Triple that amount would buy a house in London. Or, even more appealing, thousands of Melba chocolate bars. I unfolded the accompanying letter and read it aloud.

Dear Miss Dove:

Thank you for submitting your designs to the House of Lafitte. We've selected two items for inclusion in our new summer-autumn line. Though we are unable to fund travel, we'd be most honoured if you joined us for our private event on April 30th. If you are able to join us, we will forward the relevant details.

Yours sincerely,

Yvonne Jourdain
Executive Partner

House of Lafitte

I looked up from the letter and blinked, unable to take it in. Travel? A private event?

Ruby squeezed my hand. "Don't you see, Feens? We're going to Paris!"

2

Ruby hummed an unrecognisable tune as our taxi sped through the gates of Le Bourget airport. Despite a delightful speaking voice, her singing often resembled a brooding hen. Far from being irritating, this endearing quality of my otherwise perfect friend cheered me. As did leaving behind the dreaded ordeal of the aeroplane crossing the Channel.

"What are you humming?" I asked.

"*Puttin' on the Ritz*. Don't you recognise it?"

A deluge of mud against the taxi window rescued me from answering. Even through the dirty glass, thrilling sights still met my eye. Notre Dame floated by, with its majestic buttresses and gargoyles rivalling those of the Oxford colleges. Parisians perused Rue de la Paix's varied shops and jammed outdoor cafes as ardent springtime sunworshippers. My mood lightened, though I expect I still looked rather pensive.

"Whatever is the matter, Feens? Ever since that day at Lyon's, something's been eating you."

I groped for an excuse. "It's those low marks for my political history of North Africa paper. They feel like a little raincloud hovering over me."

"But I already told you about my colossal biochemistry and electrochemistry failures, and you claimed that news pushed away your little raincloud." Ruby's eyes narrowed. "No, it's not that. It's something else."

"Is it so obvious?" I croaked.

"You're a dear, Feens, but I'd never play poker with you. Spill the beans."

"Dash it, I suppose I ought to tell you. Right before we met up at Lyon's, I'd been perusing the new designs in Mayfair." This was a tiny fib, since my real wish had been to see how my sewing skills compared with the stitching on display.

"Quite proper, too. Must keep up with the style of the moment – though I avoid those shops when I'm creating my own designs. I'm terribly afraid I'll copy them, unintentionally, of course."

"Of course." I gulped.

A spate of French erupted from our driver, made unintelligible by the fact his lips were wrapped around his Gauloise cigarette. Our driver had already proved a highly excitable chap when we'd told him how much we could pay for the ride to our hotel. This trip would certainly cost a mint, but Ruby and I had become adept at stretching our shillings, or francs, rather.

"Pardon?" we said in unison.

We both spoke enough French for a simple though unsophisticated conversation. Our devilishly handsome French tutor at Oxford had distracted us enough to ensure we had retained nothing of our Advanced French course. Little had we known we'd be travelling to Paris so soon.

The driver peered into the mirror and removed his cigarette, all whilst turning the corner and shifting into gear.

"Which street?" he said in French.

I glanced at the folded paper in my hand. "Rue de le Garance. It's near Champs-Élysées." I stretched out my hand with the note, but the driver didn't take it. So I leaned forward and held it up higher.

"*Merde!*" Bits of spittle flew onto the windscreen.

Through the rear-view mirror, I watched the results of my handiwork unfold. The driver hadn't grasped the paper because he'd been lighting another Gauloise with a match. Unawares, I had shoved the paper near his face, setting the note alight instead of his cigarette.

In a blur, I spotted a large lorry bearing down on us from the opposite direction.

I squeezed my eyes shut and braced myself against the front seat. Beside me, Ruby gave a tiny gasp.

The taxi screeched to the right, then to the left. I opened one eye and watched our car careen towards a streetlight. The tinkling of shattered glass followed a loud thud, shattering what was left of my insides along with it.

The driver then leapt from the taxi and jumped up and down, shouting French obscenities that I would have loved to learn under any other circumstances.

Slowly, I unbent my frozen fingers from the door handle and caught my breath. Everything was fine, I told myself. Everything is fine. If I repeated it enough times, perhaps it would be true.

"Feens! Look!" Ruby pointed at the front seat, where a small conflagration glowed. Clearly, my address paper had set light to the detritus of wrappers and cigarette packets on the passenger seat. The fire crackled away merrily, as if it were proud of its growing force.

"Selkies and kelpies!" I stared at the flames. Though my body wouldn't move, my brain still functioned, albeit like churning butter.

"Do we have water?" I spluttered. "Or something else to douse the flames?"

Ruby rummaged in her brandy-coloured, clip-framed bag. She opened a silver tin and dumped the contents over the fire.

"Spiffing!" I clapped my hands as the last of the flames licked ineffectually against the pile of white powder. "What was in the tin?"

"Bicarbonate. I take it everywhere I go. It makes a brilliant on-the-spot stain remover."

"Thank goodness for that, since I don't foresee our driver taking any constructive action." I waved at the driver, who was now too engrossed in his outraged-driver role to appreciate Ruby's crisis remedy.

But as we exited the taxi, the reason for the driver's dismay became clear. The taxi's front end had wrapped itself around the streetlight, and shards of glass from the former headlamps scattered like sparkling diamonds over the cobblestones.

A small crowd gathered as shopkeepers and passers-by stopped to gawk at the chaos created on this side street. I checked my watch. "We told the hotel we'd be arriving by now." I felt irrationally responsible for being late.

Ruby put a hand on my shoulder. "You needn't worry, Feens. It's a hotel, so they'll be accustomed to late travellers. Besides, we can enjoy the beauty of Paris for a moment." She pointed to the tip of the Eiffel Tower, peeking over the roofline of nearby flats, and the coterie of fashionably dressed ladies drinking tiny cups of coffee at a cafe, blissfully unconcerned about the world around them.

"I do smell fresh bread," I said. "And there is an adorable cat up there." I gestured towards a wrought-iron balcony over-flowing with a riot of pink primroses. A calico licked her paw, occasionally deigning to glance at the humans below.

"Another taxi will toddle along any minute, and we'll—" Ruby was interrupted by another taxi splashing slowly through a puddle as it turned onto our street.

We tentatively stretched out our arms, hoping it would halt. It did.

The side window rolled down, and a brunette's head popped out. A rather ridiculous black hat covered one side of her face, resembling an oozing stream of treacle. The visible side of her face lit up as she spotted us, her mouth grinning and eyes blinking at a rapid pace.

"Say, weren't you two on the plane?" The twang of an American accent was unmistakable. She waved us over with a swooping arm.

Ruby hesitated and then glided towards the taxi. I followed.

"Come on, I won't bite." Though the forty-ish woman's thin face indicated she had a gaunt frame, she gave out an enormous belly laugh. Like Father Christmas – or the rumbling noise I imagined Father Christmas would make. "I'm headed to the Hôtel D'Escalier," she said, her "escalier" sounding like "es-scallion".

"That's where we're staying," said Ruby cautiously.

"Hop in, gang. There's plenty of room in here, and I can see you won't be going anywhere in a hurry." She stuck her forefinger out at our taxi driver, who had transformed from an irate buffoon to a sad man, head drooping. I pulled out a bundle of francs from my handbag and hurried towards him, whilst Ruby heaved our luggage from the boot of the car.

As I pressed the bills into his still-shaking fist, he gave me a wan smile. "Be careful, mademoiselle," he breathed in English. "Be very careful."

3

Before I could contemplate our driver's parting words, our American friend ushered me inside the taxi. She held out her gloved hand again as we pulled away from the kerb.

"I'm Elizabeth Ryland, a buyer from New York. Do call me Elizabeth. I cannot stand that Mrs and Miss nonsense." She took my hand in hers and crushed it in a vigorous handshake. I surveyed her military-style navy jacket, all angles and gold embroidery, with matching gold buttons lining the front and the sleeves. It enhanced rather than softened her tight, wiry frame. The only softening element was her perfume, a somewhat incongruous mixture of jasmine, creamy peach, and cardamom.

Rather abruptly, Elizabeth leaned over me and grabbed Ruby's hand. Ruby rewarded her with a weak smile and a handshake. "Pleased to meet you," she said. "We're grateful for the lift. I'm Ruby Dove, and this is Fina Aubrey-Havelock."

"You two must be headed to Mathilde Lafitte's show, right?"

Ruby opened her mouth to respond, but Elizabeth rattled on. "I've been just dying to see her new line – and I have the money to scoop up everything this time. Last time I came to her show, I was a poor fashion journalist in Paris at the time. She's such a recluse that I didn't want to miss this opportunity."

"You said you were a buyer?" I asked. "What do they do?"

"Aren't you cute," she said in a patronising though not unkind tone. I half expected her to pinch my cheek.

"A buyer—" Ruby began to explain.

"A buyer buys a group of designs," said Elizabeth, "which is really the right to reproduce them. A particular line of, say, thirty to seventy garments will go for anywhere between thirty thousand and fifty thousand dollars."

I let out a low whistle.

"Once my employer back in New York buys the designs, the fashion houses or stores we represent will reproduce the designs for a broader group of shoppers. It's very fun."

"Delightful," I responded, though what was delightful remained unclear. "Ruby is an up-and-coming designer, and Madame Lafitte is planning to purchase some of her designs."

"Is that so? I thought Madame Lafitte did all her own designs."

"Oh, I–I–I'm certain she does," I stammered.

Ruby coughed and grimaced. "What Fina means is I've come to learn from the great one. Madame Lafitte appreciated my designs, so she invited me to her show."

I blinked an *I'm sorry* expression at Ruby.

Apparently oblivious to my gaffe, Elizabeth purred along. "The show will be great, I'm sure, but the food…! I'll be having oysters for lunch today, see if I don't."

As the taxi lumbered to a halt, Ruby pressed her head against the window. "The hotel is glorious, Feens. Not gauche. Proper and perfect."

The small hotel's cream-colour exterior hosted twelve windows with balconies, each holding geraniums and peonies. A woman stood on one balcony, pensively smoking a cigarette from one hand and sipping a cup of coffee from the other. It was all very Parisian.

Elizabeth brushed past us and hurried up the steps. Ruby held up a gloved hand to her mouth, just out of earshot of Elizabeth. "Pssst...what was it you wanted to tell me?"

"It'll keep. For now." Surely there'd be plenty of time to chat over tea.

THE HÔTEL D'ESCALIER sat on a sedate side street off the Champs-Élysées, but the hotel's interior buzzed with energy. A mound of luggage covered the brown and white marble floor under the lobby's beautifully arched ceiling. I watched a middle-aged couple follow the bellhop upstairs, stopping only to glance back as Elizabeth Ryland's loud twang echoed around the room. "I must have room 12. Yvonne understood it was a non-negotiable requirement of my stay here. It's the only large room with two windows. I need it for my nerve condition."

Her demands seemed peculiar. In the taxi, she'd made her visit seem like a coolly professional attempt to snap up a bargain, but her room negotiations made it appear as if she'd been invited – or would even be playing a central role in the show. And did she actually have a nerve condition? Being in her company for any period of time might make me develop such a condition, but I couldn't see her having one.

The man behind the registration desk leaned on one elbow and lit a cigarette, blowing a cloud of pungent smoke. "Madam, as I explained, the hotel is small, and room 12 is already occupied." His languid drawl matched his heavy-lidded eyes and casual lean against the desk. I pictured him as a piano player in a delightfully dodgy nightclub, rather than as a hotel manager. If he were, it would explain his fatigued face.

Elizabeth's back stiffened further, emphasising her almost military bearing. "I'd like to speak to the manager, please."

"I am the manager, madam." He held out a hand. "Omar Abelli at your service."

Ignoring the gesture, she huffed, "Well, I must speak to Yvonne about this!"

Omar slid his cigarette to the other side of his mouth. "I'm terribly sorry, but Mademoiselle Jourdain is attending to urgent business at the moment. I will leave a note for her if you wish."

A cacophony of guttural French consonants ricocheting off the double doors drowned Elizabeth's frustrated cry.

The words 'aunt' and 'model' were all I could pick out from the unseen women's conversation.

I whispered to Ruby, "Did you hear anything of that? You're closer to the corridor."

"Something about a missing model for the show."

"Oh dear, trouble in paradise."

Ruby suppressed a chuckle as a tall woman with long dark hair flounced her floor-skimming brown skirts into the room.

"She's like a heroine from a scandalous French novel," said Ruby.

As if to complete the look, the woman held up a hand to her furrowed brow and cried, "*Laissez-moi tranquille.*" She turned towards the assembled scene, eyed us sceptically, and swept out of the room.

"Exit stage left," I murmured. Though the woman did resemble a French heroine, Joan of Arc was a more apt description – before she cut her long hair.

The second woman stepped through the doorway.

"Yvonne!" As if she had finally met her long-lost twin, Elizabeth marched towards the tall blonde sauntering in her direction.

Ruby held a gloved hand over her mouth. "Yvonne Jourdain is Madame Lafitte's partner – she runs the business."

Just as Ruby had been affronted by Elizabeth Ryland, I took an instant dislike to this Yvonne creature. And it wasn't due to the woman's stunning appearance. Well, not entirely. No, it wasn't her beautiful shell of smooth hair, trim clothes, and figure. It was that every facial feature conspired to create a perpetual slight smirk – not of pleasure, but of triumph and superiority. As if everyone amused her.

Yvonne responded to Elizabeth's eager greeting with two perfunctory pecks on each cheek. She sighed. "It's been ages, Elizabeth. I apologise for the brief outburst, but, well, this situation with Virginie...you must know how it is with these models. I'd be a rich woman if I wagered a franc for every one who's left us. They're perfectly exasperating at times."

Elizabeth slapped her navy gloves on Yvonne's shoulder. "Don't I ever. The little madams have such a way with them. They believe the world revolves around them."

Omar blew a long stream of smoke up at the ceiling.

"Speaking of which," Elizabeth continued, either unaware or uncaring about the manager's ironic gesture, "I must have this room—"

Joan of Arc returned, her skirts swishing through the archway. Her eyes locked on us, and her finger beckoned.

"You! Come with me. You will understand."

4

The appropriately named Hôtel D'Escalier's central feature was a gleaming marble spiral staircase winding upwards to the guest rooms, each floor with a distinct theme. When I had placed the reservation over the telephone, Omar described the first floor as Art Deco, or *style moderne,* and the second as Louis XIV.

Joan of Arc jerked to a halt on the first floor. Behind her, Ruby staggered backwards, her foot wobbling and slipping on the staircase.

Ruby suddenly doubled over.

"Ow!"

I rushed forward. "What happened?"

"I twisted my ankle. What a frightful bother." She grimaced and looked around. "I need to sit down somewhere."

"May I help?"

The amused, deeper voice did not belong to Joan of Arc.

A slim young man leaned over us, clad in shirtsleeves and brown pinstripe trousers, his hair closely cropped and parted to the side. A white beard descended from his small round nose dotted with brown freckles.

I blinked. The man couldn't be over twenty-five, and he had

a white beard. Then my eyes focused, and I realised it was shaving cream.

He crouched down and touched Ruby's ankle.

"Crikey! Don't touch it!" Ruby cried. "What are you doing?"

"I heard someone crying out, and I always respond to ladies in distress," he said in heavily accented French.

Then, realising we were all speaking English, he switched rapidly. "And broken bones are my speciality."

Joan of Arc crossed her arms and frowned, skirts still swinging. I was rather appalled that she hadn't yet apologised to Ruby.

"Oh, yes?" said Ruby in a biting tone. "Are you a doctor? One who goes around touching patients' wounds?"

"Yes. I'm training to be one. A doctor of archaeology. That's why I specialise in bones." He glanced at Ruby with a momentary smile and then studied her ankle.

"Might we move Ruby to somewhere more comfortable? Perhaps one of your rooms?" I asked. He was clearly developing a patch for Ruby, but Ruby was having none of it. For some reason, he had rubbed her up the wrong way.

"Give us a hand, Henriette, won't you?" he asked.

Despite my best efforts, I couldn't lift Ruby's top half. Admittedly, my small and soft frame did not help matters. "Ought we to call the front desk for help?"

The young man grunted. "No need for that."

Then the shaving cream slid over his mouth and fell onto Ruby's immaculate skirt.

Ruby groaned and gave me a pleading look. "I can stand up, but I can't walk. What if I walk with your help?"

I took one arm whilst the man took the other, and Henriette led the way. Together, we helped Ruby into the only room with an open door and lowered her onto a low, overstuffed armchair.

He peered at Ruby's ankle more closely, this time without touching it. "A minor twist. Time for ice."

He rose.

"I must say it doesn't feel minor," said Ruby.

Shrugging, he turned on his heel. "Glad to have helped." His speech had a peculiar clipped, almost staccato, pacing to it.

Then Ruby sighed. "But ice would be most welcome, thank you. And thank you for helping me."

His nodding reply was obscured by a white towel that hit his head, sailing from across the room.

Henriette yelled, "Clean your face before you leave, Maurice!"

Maurice dutifully wiped his face and toddled off in search of ice.

Henriette began pacing the room, weaving between square leather chairs. When we had been on a case in the past, Ruby also paced endlessly, but not like this. Henriette's restless pace was that of a tiger before feeding time at the zoo.

I settled onto a nearby footstool, guarding Ruby's ankle against any mishaps Henriette might have with the carpet.

"We must find one," Henriette murmured.

"Pardon?" Ruby looked up from her ankle, her eyes following the roving cat-like motion.

"A model. We need a model. Now!"

Ruby's eyes slewed towards me at a deliberately slow pace. I knew this look. It meant, 'let's humour them'.

"Can we help you with your problem?" I asked.

"Yvonne will fire me if we don't find a model. She said she'd sack me if I made one more mistake – even though this wasn't my mistake! Madame Lafitte is my auntie, but Yvonne might still sack me." She inhaled. "Maurice's girlfriend, Virginie, disappeared yesterday, and we haven't been able to find a replacement for her at the show this afternoon."

At the word 'girlfriend', I became miffed on Ruby's behalf. What business did the young man have making sheep's eyes at her if he had a girlfriend? And how had he managed to 'lose' this Virginie?

"I thought the show was tomorrow," said Ruby. "Why is it this afternoon? And why not postpone it?"

"We must have it now because the most important journalist for the show leaves Paris tomorrow. His name is Mr Reggie. And Maurice's silly girlfriend threw a tantrum – these models are so petulant."

Ruby and I both grinned at Henriette's own petulance.

"We had a pre-show planned for this afternoon, so everyone will adjust to the new schedule. Except that we cannot carry on without a replacement for Virginie." She snorted. "It's that stupid Maurice's fault."

"What's this? Taking my name in vain?" came the voice behind me.

Maurice loped into the room, now free of shaving cream and carrying a towel. "Ice, mademoiselle."

I surveyed him more closely now, approving of his affable smile and wide-set brown eyes. But I was still deeply sceptical of his intentions.

Ruby touched her ankle. "Thank you, but I think it's better now."

He handed her the ice in the towel. "Take it. You'll need it."

"No," she snapped, matching Maurice's shortness. "I'll soon be on my feet again."

"Not with that ankle, you won't," he retorted.

Ruby rarely snapped at anyone. Of course, she also avoided being dependent on anyone, which would account for her tetchiness. Since this had the potential to become a flaming row – particularly if Henriette joined in the fun – I intervened. "We were just chatting about the show this afternoon, and how they'll need another model."

Henriette perked up. "*Oui*, and we need her *now* because of Maurice's idiot girlfriend."

Maurice smoothed his hand over his curly, dark brown hair. "She's not a girlfriend. She's a friend. And she's not an idiot."

Henriette pointed at Ruby. "You would make a fine model, but you'll still be limping by this afternoon."

"I'll be fine." Ruby hoisted herself in her chair, and then collapsed back down into her seat. "Perhaps not."

Then she smiled. "What about Fina? She could do it in a pinch."

"Me?" I gulped. "I'm not a model, and I'm quite certain I wouldn't fit a model's clothes."

Henriette put her hands on her hips. "Stand up."

I did as I was told.

Henriette grabbed hold of my arms and spun me around like a slow-moving lighthouse.

Maurice's and Ruby's eyes wrinkled in amusement as I passed them.

"Splendid," said Maurice. Though he would say that. He was apparently responsible for Virginie's disappearance.

Henriette rubbed her hands together. "You will do. We have a few gowns designed for shorter women and women with your body. We are not afraid of curves in France like you English."

Ruby chuckled but stopped as soon as she saw Maurice do the same. "That's settled," she said. "Feens shall go to the ball, and she will have a special gown."

"Feens?" asked Maurice.

"It's short for Fina," Ruby replied curtly. "Is it customary for you to comment on people's names? My grandmother taught me it was rude to do so."

His eyes twinkled. "Where's your grandmother from?"

"St Kitts, if you must know."

"Mine's from Senegal, at least on my father's side."

"Fascinating," said Ruby sarcastically.

"And my grandmother is from Belgium," huffed Henriette.

"Steady on, Henriette." I was perturbed at her casual dismissal of what I found to be a rather touching exchange.

Her hair flew out again as she turned, narrowly missing my face. "You, Miss Fina, or Miss Feens. Will you do it?"

I fidgeted with the hem on my sleeve. "I'm not keen on being the centre of attention."

Henriette blew out her cheeks again and raised her eyes to the ceiling. "You like to dress up, do you not?"

I nodded.

"And you like helping your friend." She pointed to Ruby.

I nodded again.

Maurice held up his palms. "Virginie will thank you. Once she appears."

"*Bon*. It is settled, then." Henriette marched to the door. "I shall tell that spiteful Yvonne. I shall tell her the show is afoot, as your Sherlock Holmes says!"

5

I twirled around the dark gold-edged furniture and enormous feathered beds, wriggling my toes on the plush rugs lining the floor. "This suite is marvellous." I stopped only to snap up a chocolate from a nearby dish. "We've never had a room like this!"

Ruby grinned and snatched up a chocolate. "Omar said they had a last-minute cancellation – otherwise we would be in the garret."

"They wouldn't dare to move us, especially after your injury. And this chocolate is scrumptious, though it's neither Louis XIV nor Art Deco. It's simply delicious."

"Go on, have another." I handed her my dish. "The ones you ate were too plain – these will cure your ankle."

Ruby swiped a soft mound and popped it in her mouth. "Mmmm...I do feel better already, Doctor Aubrey-Havelock."

I flopped down onto the bed, surveying my friend reclining in a royal red chair. Her face was made up expertly, as always, but her lips were taut and pale.

"What's eating you?" I asked.

"The news you were about to share in the taxi. It's been

nagging me – perhaps that's why I collided with Henriette, though I don't know how I could have avoided it."

She shook her head. "I have this overwhelming sense of dread."

A corresponding sense of dread made me play for time. "But you're normally so optimistic. Not Pollyanna-ish, mind you, but positive."

An ambulance siren wailed past our open window. Birds chirped in the courtyard.

With her hands folded in her lap, Ruby looked at me expectantly.

I gritted my teeth. "The day we met in Lyon's, I had been perusing the shops."

"I remember, though you were rather vague about it."

"For good reason. You see, I'd spotted a delightful design that was very clearly your own, but without your label on it. The tangerine number."

Ruby's eyes widened, but she remained silent, her hands still folded.

"When I confronted the shopkeeper about it, she denied it vehemently. I didn't have time to see if the other gowns were also copies. The devil of it was the shop itself."

"What do you mean?"

Although we were alone, I lowered my voice. "It was Madame Lafitte's own shop!"

Ruby attempted to raise herself – no doubt to pace – but collapsed from the effort. Instead, she held a hand to her forehead, shielding her eyes. "I've heard of such things, but I thought it happened to established designers. My friend Nancy works at Poiret, and she said they'd had to fend off a few copyists. But again, one would expect it to happen at Poiret! It must be a mistake. Perhaps there was a mix-up."

I shook my head. Ruby was willing to give others the benefit of the doubt, though her keen sense of injustice saved her from being naïve. Unlike me. What was it the Americans said? I was a sucker. But not in this case – someone had intentionally pilfered Ruby's designs.

Ruby pressed on. "How would she even find my sketches? I share them with only a few people, and even then, it's rarely the finished product."

"I haven't a clue. But we must find out."

She stamped her non-injured foot. "We've been spies in service of justice in the past. Remember how complex our first case was? Discovering how my designs were stolen ought to be a piece of cake compared to that."

At the word 'cake', my eyes wandered back to the plate of chocolates.

"We must confront Madame Lafitte," said Ruby, more to herself than to me.

This idea was enough to distract me from my chocolate. Though I certainly had, well, flashes of anger, I always *intended* to avoid conflict. Ruby, however, kept her cool – but did enjoy the direct approach when the situation required it.

Then I realised Ruby ought to avoid confronting Madame Lafitte for another reason.

"Isn't this copying business actually a sign of your success with Madame Lafitte?" I asked. "Besides, why would she invite you to Paris if she wanted to merely copy your designs? That seems unnecessary or even counterproductive."

"You mean it speaks to her innocence?" She poked her forefinger in the air as if she were connecting points together. "You're quite right, Feens. Perhaps her partner, Yvonne, is responsible?"

She paused and smiled. "Eating chocolate and being nervous about the show seems to have prodded your little grey cells into action."

"Frankly, I'd rather just have the chocolate."

"Nonsense. Your debut on stage will be the talk of the city!"

Marvellous, I thought. I ought to have stayed in London.

Little did I know I'd soon have even better reasons to have stayed home.

6

A silk cape slapped me in the face, stinging my eyes.

The tall blonde model with angry, plucked eyebrows strode towards the full-length looking glass, smoothing her hair and puckering her lips, either unaware or unconcerned about her cape's behaviour.

Ruby interrupted my planned response. "There's Yvonne, coming towards us. I'd like to have a few words with her about this copying business."

Yvonne sauntered calmly amongst the thicket of models hurriedly dressing and undressing in the hotel's ballroom for the afternoon show.

She lifted her chin in my direction. "I'm Yvonne Jourdain. And I'll wager you must be our new model, Fina. Am I correct?"

"Quite correct." I moved to exchange air kisses. "And this is the famous Ruby Dove."

"Ah, the designer. Splendid." She glanced at Ruby, offering neither kisses nor a handshake.

Ruby stepped forward, sending Yvonne reeling backwards a few steps.

She recovered herself and moved forward two inches, her nose almost touching Ruby's.

In a low, warning voice, Ruby said, "I have a matter to discuss with you most urgently. About Madame Lafitte's designs."

They stood so close I feared Yvonne might bite off Ruby's nose.

"I'm terribly sorry, but you can see how busy I am at the moment." Yvonne waved a hand airily about the ballroom. "In fact, it would be better if you found your seat in the audience area."

Ruby made a fist, partially hidden by the folds of her frock. "When *will* you have time? It's most urgent."

Yvonne shrugged. "After the show."

She spun on her heel and pointed at Henriette. "Ah, there you are, Henriette. Fina, Henriette will take care of you." Then her eyes glided from my head to my toes. "She will find an appropriate gown for your...figure."

She glided away.

I snorted. Truth be told, I was less disgusted with Yvonne than with myself. This modelling business was decidedly the most idiotic thing I had agreed to in a long time. And the smells of perfume, thick cigarette smoke, and body odour didn't help matters, either. I shivered.

"Are you cold, Feens?" asked Ruby.

"Ah, no. Well, I suppose so." I looked down at myself, realising I was only wearing a slip.

"Here. Put this on until they're ready." She arranged a heavy woollen dressing-gown over my shoulders. My shivering stopped.

"I'm sorry about Yvonne – I'm certain we'll know more about your designs soon."

She grinned. Henriette was twisting me about as if I were a dress form.

"I'll leave you in the capable hands of Henriette." Heading towards the exit, Ruby called, "Perhaps I'll pick up bits of gossip amongst the audience for the show."

"Berthe!" Henriette bellowed over her shoulder. "Berthe's the head maid, and she also helps us with the show."

A young woman with an enormous bosom and tiny waist lumbered towards us. It looked as though she had just received this burden on her yesterday, and she still hadn't adjusted to it.

"Why aren't you wearing the brassiere I gave you, Berthe? You'll hurt your back with the load you're carrying," said Henriette.

I turned away, hoping to hide my rising shame.

"Mademoiselle is embarrassed!" Berthe's giggle shook her whole body.

"That's enough. Remember, Miss Fina is *Eeeng*lish," said Henriette, as if it were a disease. "She's a delicate flower, you understand."

Berthe wiped her eyes and presented me with a high-waisted emerald crepe gown. "This will look wonderful with mademoiselle's hair."

Perhaps I had judged Berthe too harshly.

"Thank you. I hope it will fit." Though on second thought, it might be better if it didn't fit. A glimmer of hope flashed on the horizon.

Henriette adjusted her crown of hair in the looking-glass and marched off through the flurry of gowns and haze of cigarette smoke.

Berthe hauled off my dressing-gown and pushed the emerald gown over my head. "Of course, of course it will fit. We had the measurements from Mademoiselle Jourdain."

"*Merde!*"

"What happened, Berthe? Why is it stuck?" I mumbled through the folds of material stuck around my head.

"The gown caught on my ring."

After a few moments, the gown slipped over my head, and I threaded my arms through the armholes. I noticed Berthe's oddly shaped silver ring, engraved with the letters B and S.

"Why don't you remove your ring when dressing?" I asked. "It would be a shame to lose it."

She poked her stubby finger in the air. "I must never take off this ring."

The sound of hands clapping brought the frenzied activity of the dressing room to a halt.

Yvonne stood on a stool, cool and efficient in a shimmering, silky grey-silver suit. "We are about to begin, girls."

She held up several numbered cards. "Remember your numbers. When I hold up yours, you go next. The numbers are not in order, so if you are number five, please do not think you will go after number four."

Though this seemed like a system designed to go horribly wrong, my clenched, nervous stomach made me too distracted to care.

Sensing my distress, Berthe placed a calming hand on my shoulder.

Yvonne's eyes scanned the room, halting momentarily on me. "Remember how we practised your walking. For those of you who are new and wearing long gowns, be especially careful. I don't have to tell you the consequences."

A man of about fifty in a rumpled brown suit provided a welcome distraction. He hurried towards Yvonne, tugging at his Mephisthophelean goatee. Spectacles sliding down his nose, he strode across the ballroom as if he were simply navigating around pedestrians on the streets of Paris.

"Good afternoon, ladies." He had a lightly clipped accent, possibly German or Dutch. "You're all looking most fine."

None of the models took notice, too busy with their final arrangements for the show.

The man whispered in Yvonne's ear and then exited as quickly as he had entered.

Yvonne tapped the stack of numbered cards against her cheek thoughtfully. Then she shook herself and clapped her hands.

"It's time, girls. Please queue up."

7

Yvonne held up a large, numbered card.

"Number thirteen!"

I sneaked into the queue of whippet-thin models behind the dreaded purple curtains. The gateway.

Gentle jazz floated in through the curtains, interrupted by spasms of applause.

Finally, it was my turn.

Pushing aside the curtains, I inhaled the perfumed air and stepped into the glare of the spotlight.

Slowly. Saunter, Fina. I repeated the words rhythmically in my head, mimicking the slowly undulating hips of the model in front of me. Finally, I settled for a slinking motion like a vamp in a film – all cigarette holders and lipstick.

"Move faster," Henriette hissed behind me. "And stop waving your hips."

I reached the end of the runway, stopping and smiling into the hot, glowing lights. With my blurred, hazy vision, my spirits lifted at the sight of Ruby smiling and bobbing her head in the front row. Next to her sat a rather striking man with a long, white face nearly matching his white mess jacket. He adjusted his striped bow tie and ran his fingers through his flaming red hair. Something about this gesture jogged my memory – I was quite certain I'd seen him before.

I turned back towards the curtains, the room blurring even more.

But I turned too slowly.

Henriette's cursing behind me followed a loud, excruciating '*crrrch*' of fabric tearing.

Craning my neck over my shoulder, I saw she'd trodden on the hem of my gown with her sharp-heeled shoes.

A few gasps came from the crowd, and then silence blanketed the room.

Somehow, I picked up my gown and marched off the stage as fast as my heels would allow me.

Behind the safety of the curtains, I fought back tears welling up like an unstoppable force. I fully expected to hear a stream of French invective, but all that met my eyes when I looked up was Yvonne Jourdain's smug countenance.

Blessedly, Berthe rushed towards me and began to remove my gown from behind. She clucked and fussed, but said nothing about the torn gown.

I peeked through the gap in the curtains to watch the proceedings, with a secret hope someone else would make a faux pas worse than my own.

Henriette had already changed into her next piece: a body-skimming sapphire velvet gown with ruching in all the right places.

Yvonne held up a numbered card and Henriette nodded.

"Leave it for a moment, please," I whispered to Berthe.

Now I could focus on the show properly. Well-dressed Parisians had packed the ballroom, despite the short notice about the change in time. Elizabeth Ryland sat next to Ruby in the front row, with the familiar bow-tied man close by. He chortled as he told Ruby what appeared to be an amusing anecdote. If her steely forward-gaze were any indication, Ruby wasn't having any of it.

The atmosphere positively crackled, though I knew not from what. Tension? Envy? Anger? A medium had once told me I had a gift for picking up on such things, but I had always dismissed it as harmless fun.

A bustling noise at the back made several heads turn. Maurice slinked in, looking slightly ashamed. He took up a spot against the back wall and began whispering to the man who'd spoken to Yvonne earlier.

Maurice swung a briefcase lightly in the air. Even after all eyes had turned back to the catwalk, Elizabeth eyed it with suspicion. I wondered why she was so intrigued by an empty briefcase.

My eyes slewed left to the hotel manager, Omar Abelli, whose suit fit him like the proverbial glove. I had admired his slow, languid drawl as master of ceremonies, his tone striking a relaxed insouciance evoked by Madame Lafitte's creations.

I scanned the crowd once more, hoping to spot Madame Lafitte. Ruby had described her as a woman of sixty, wearing drab clothing with a touch of the unexpected. All I could conjure was a woman in a potato sack with diamond earrings. But no such woman was in attendance, wearing a potato sack or otherwise.

Henriette stepped onto the runway with great confidence, which was particularly admirable since the frock she wore was a dreadful mistake. Just a few moments ago, I had spied her in a long, flattering sapphire velvet gown she must have exchanged for this late summer fluttery frock, paired with white laced Ghillie shoes. The frock itself was serviceable, but it was designed for an elfin body, not the statuesque proportions of Henriette.

She approached the end of the runway, smiled, bestowed the crowd with a few moments to admire her, and then turned on her heel.

Despite her smiles, something was dreadfully awry.

Her face contorted, lips and eyebrows scrunching together. She clutched her stomach, swaying perilously towards the right.

She jerked to the left, as if yanked by some unseen force.

Front-row observers gaped in surprise as Henriette Giroux toppled headlong into their laps.

8

Ruby grabbed Henriette's arm, holding the twisting, flopping body on Elizabeth's lap. Between the two of them, they managed to prevent the poor girl from slipping to the floor and hitting her head.

Nervous tittering erupted from onlookers gathered around Henriette. I leapt down from the stage, into the crowd of colourful hats, capes, and angular Schiaparelli-like creations of the fashionably dressed audience.

A muffled-sounding Omar Abelli said, "Doctor," without the requisite enthusiasm required by such an exclamation. Then, in a more confident voice, he called, "Dr Fischer?"

"*Ja, ja,* I come," said a distinctly Teutonic voice, rising behind the gawkers milling about. It was the man in the rumpled brown suit. "But I am not that sort of doctor, Monsieur Abelli. I'm an archaeologist."

Whilst Omar and the good doctor argued behind us, Ruby said, "Let's lay her on the floor and lift up her legs."

Elizabeth responded by jerking Henriette's legs onto the floor.

Poor Henriette would certainly have impressive bruises in the morning.

Ruby had a more difficult job as she tried to move Henriette's head from a chair onto the floor. Her hands clutched at the mass of hair, but her fingers kept slipping.

Still clutching his briefcase, Maurice appeared at Ruby's side. "Let me help. I'll take one shoulder. Fina can take the other. Ruby shouldn't carry anyone in her state."

"Reggie!" Ruby called to the red-headed young man in the bow tie. "Give me your jacket for a pillow."

"I say, my jacket? Perhaps someone else will volunteer?" he whined in a nasal, high-pitched voice.

"Give me your blasted jacket, you silly man," said Ruby.

"Do it," affirmed Maurice.

This Reggie character finally complied, stuffing his white mess jacket under Henriette's head.

Reggie. Yes, I definitely knew a Reggie, but from where?

"*Bitte*, please. You all must leave the patient to me." Dr Fischer adjusted his rimless spectacles and stroked his chin, much in the way I pictured him surveying an archaeological dig.

Omar assisted, waving us away with firm, outstretched arms, as if he were moving a recalcitrant herd of sheep. Despite his vigorous movements, his cigarette remained firmly attached to his lip.

Moving like Omar's herd of sheep, we all shuffled towards the entrance. As if we needed further assurance, Maurice said, "Dr Fischer will see to it."

"But he's just an archaeologist," Ruby shot back.

"But he's also an expert on the human body. Haven't you heard of Dr Fischer?"

"No, I haven't."

"Surely university students must know about archaeology."

Ruby clicked her tongue in obvious irritation. "Chemistry's

my line, Maurice. All that rubbish about digging up graves of ancestors. In my opinion, those sacred sites ought to be left undisturbed."

As I fancied this conversation was moving nowhere rapidly, I used my favourite diversion: the blunt approach.

"You don't think she'll die, will she?" I asked

"Why would you say that?" he asked.

"Oh, I—"

"Unfortunately, Fina and I have witnessed several deaths. It's an entirely plausible question," said Ruby defensively.

Maurice rubbed his chin. "Witnessed? Who are you? Some sort of sleuths?"

Elizabeth Ryland bounded up with her terrier-like energy. "What a terrible tragedy. Why isn't someone taking her to the hospital? You can be sure someone would do that in the States." Her monologue continued, unabated.

Elizabeth's list of America's greatest achievements was interrupted by the precise clap of Yvonne Jourdain. Then she pointed her finger at Omar, as if she were aiming a pistol.

"Ladies and gentlemen," intoned Omar. "We apologise for the disruption, but a model has had an accident and we therefore must conclude this afternoon's showing of Madame Lafitte's new line. Thank you."

He ushered our crowd into the cold lobby and then hastened to the reception desk.

"Where's Madame Lafitte?" asked Elizabeth. "I saw her at the start of the show, but then she vanished."

"Madame Lafitte always makes an appearance and then retreats to her workshop," said Yvonne.

"But I must buy two gowns. When can I do that?" Elizabeth moved closer to Yvonne. I was surprised she didn't withdraw a cheque from her bag, ready to hand over.

With obvious distaste for this gauche woman, Yvonne

twisted her mouth to one side. "Given this unfortunate incident this afternoon, I'm afraid Madame is not selling at the moment."

"What do you mean?" The large buttons on Elizabeth's coat quivered. "I came all the way from New York to see this show and to buy whatever was needed to take back with me."

Ignoring Elizabeth's dogged determination, Yvonne clapped her hands again. "Henriette has fallen ill, but Dr Fischer believes it's simply a *maux d'estomac* – an upset stomach, yes? Maurice and Dr Fischer have taken her to her room, where she is resting."

"I say, don't the French have real doctors?" asked Reggie.

Yvonne gave an exasperated sigh. "It is simply a mild case of an upset stomach, so we need not invite an outside doctor. Besides, a few journalists have already congregated outside the hotel. The vultures are in search of a scandal where there is none."

Reggie's previously vacant eyes gleamed with malicious pleasure.

"I'm Reggie Barrington-Loftus, journalist at your service."

I relished Yvonne's bulging eyes and halting gasp. "But I thought Simon Nash was reporting from London. Are you taking his place?"

He bowed. "Reggie the Hedgie, at your service, madam."

"Are you Mr Hedgie or Mr Barrington-Loftus?" she asked.

It was the first time I'd seen Yvonne lose her composure.

Reggie scratched his thick red hair. "Hedgie is an old school name, I'm afraid. I believe Old Snorty first used it after I was kicked in the gut by a mule. I rolled up into a little ball."

Yvonne held a hand to her. "Pardon?"

"In a ball. Like a hedgehog – those little blighters that trundle along with spines on their backs. But Snorty claims Badger-Buffington used it to mean someone who 'hedges', probably because I'm frightfully rotten at making up my mind."

Yvonne simply stared at him.

Omar's sleek head appeared in the doorway, breaking the awkward silence. "Mademoiselle Jourdain? Monsieur Colombe from Le Bon Marché is on the telephone. He requests to speak with you urgently."

"Tell him I am engaged," Yvonne said shortly. "Where is Maurice? I must speak with him this instant." She turned on her heel and stalked away.

With narrowed eyes, Elizabeth watched her go.

"Who *is* this Reggie character?" Ruby whispered to me.

"You two looked tolerably chummy from my viewpoint on stage," I said.

"I was being polite. He's rather a drip, though he did tell me a compelling story of what he called an 'injustice' he experienced as a boy. Some entertaining school mishap involving treacle."

"Barrington-Loftus, Barrington..." I murmured to myself. "Now I remember! His family came down to my aunt's in Devon one spring. Young Reggie showed up for an evening and then toddled off to the local pub."

"How old were you?"

"Hmm...perhaps ten, and he must have been seventeen or eighteen." I paused. "But how can he be a journalist? I'm quite certain he's never had to work a day in his life."

9

Yvonne's piercing voice interrupted my reminiscences.

"Madame Lafitte has an important announcement to make at supper tonight. We shall meet promptly at Maxim's restaurant at eight o'clock. You're all most welcome." Her voice was anything but welcoming.

"Where's this Maxim's?" I asked Ruby. "And what do they serve there?"

"It's famous! I've always wanted to try their *escargots*."

I wrinkled my nose. I loved food, but snails were not food. My father had urged me to taste them once on a summer holiday in France. They'd tasted like rubber, even though the butter did help. No matter, I'd find something delicious with butter in any French restaurant.

Ruby glanced at her watch. "I'm positively shattered. You must be, too, after your ordeal."

"You mean my shameful one-woman parade, followed by a near tumble into the crowd? Good Lord, if Henriette hadn't toppled over, I'd be the talk of the town."

"Oh pish, Feens. Don't exaggerate – you'll only make yourself ill." She tapped her teeth. "That reminds me. You've probably not had lunch, have you?"

"I wasn't keen on eating anything after Yvonne made clucking noises about my figure."

"She can go boil her head, that one," growled Ruby. "And I'll tell her as much at Maxim's tonight."

The hotel lobby had nearly emptied. Ruby glanced around the room and then at her ankle. "I'd better soak my ankle in Epsom salts before dinner. Would you ask Omar to have sandwiches sent up? I'll take my time with the stairs."

"Of course. Would you like me to help you?"

"If I move slowly enough, I should be able to hoist myself up that glorious marble monstrosity. And Feens?"

"Yes?"

"Don't forget the sandwiches. I don't want to be responsible for you if you don't eat soon."

"Well, I am a bit peckish. Are you certain you don't need me to help you?"

But Ruby had already begun to hobble down the corridor.

As I made my way towards the registration desk, the unmistakable yap of Elizabeth met my ears. The yaps emanated from a small telephone room near the library.

"What? No, I haven't told her yet. And I won't until this evening."

Pause.

"Sweetie, listen to me. She's not selling. Understand. Nothing. *Nada*. But I've got to get the goods somehow." Pause. "Yes, I've got to go. Bye."

Elizabeth's rapid footsteps approached, so I dashed into the lobby. I wondered what she'd do to 'get the goods'. I needed to tell Ruby about the call, as she would undoubtedly have a flash of insight about it – as with most things. Though her perfection was sometimes tiresome, I was honoured to be in her small circle of friends. Besides, I was close enough to her to see the tiny cracks in her perfect façade, making her all the more endearing.

Omar eyed me speculatively as I entered, his leaning elbow and omnipresent cigarette giving him the air of never having left his post.

"Monsieur Abelli—"

He exhaled a smoke ring. "I'd much prefer Omar, Miss Aubrey-Havelock."

"Omar, then." My cheeks flamed like some cloistered Victorian woman who'd never spoken to an unrelated man. "Would you have a plate of sandwiches and a footbath with Epsom salts sent up?"

"Right away." He scribbled on a notepad, one that also held a lengthy shopping list. It was surely more than any one person could eat, especially since Omar's diet seemed to consist of only cigarettes. The sting of disappointment hardened my jaw – he must have a wife, though I saw no ring on his finger.

He stubbed out his cigarette. "Anything else?"

"Is something the matter?"

He rubbed one eye. "It's nothing – just the usual worries of a hotel. Madame Lafitte insists on economy but the bills make that impossible. Dr Fischer makes too many telephone calls, Yvonne takes too many deep baths, and Henriette is constantly pinching the sweets we leave out for guests. Is it any wonder so many hotels in Paris are closing?"

"The threat of war must make it all even worse."

"War? Which one? It seems all around us, yet we are safe here. At least for now. But one can die any day, mademoiselle."

I had nothing to say to this realistic yet rather morbid statement, so I decided to change the subject. As Omar had been speaking, my mind had wandered to the image of Henriette wearing that ill-suited frock. Perhaps he would know something about it.

"What you say is very true." I gave an appropriate pause. "Talking of injuries, it's fortunate Henriette didn't injure herself seriously this afternoon. Did you see her before she fell?"

He lifted his eyebrows and puffed out his cheeks, as if this were a puzzling and rather tiresome exercise. "Like you, I watched her grimace and keel over."

"How did you know I was standing there?"

"I could see backstage from my position – it's vital in case anything goes amiss with the announcements."

"Was Henriette's summer frock just such a problem? It seemed better suited to another model. Was there an error in the programme?"

He arched one eyebrow.

"How very astute of you, mademoiselle. Yes, there was indeed a – how do you call it in English? A cock-up, yes. Yvonne said one of the models wore the wrong gown, so Henriette wore that unsuitable frock down the aisle. I don't know how it happened."

He sucked in his breath, as if this incident were an assault against all good taste and judgement.

"Did anyone else wear the long velvet gown? I didn't see another model wearing it."

"You're quite right. A pity, that. It was a gorgeous gown."

I gave him a slow nod and strolled towards the stairs, lost in thought. Shaking my head, I decided a plate of sandwiches might solve this puzzle.

"Pssst."

I scanned the lobby. Muffled street noises floated through the front door, and an imposing grandfather clock ticked pleasantly in the corner. But I detected no other movement or sound.

"Pssst...over here. Red!"

Only one person called me 'Red' after my tendency to flame scarlet at a moment's notice. And my hair colour, of course.

I spun around, but Omar had vanished into the backroom. I listened again and heard the rustle of leaves. A large potted plant stood in a small alcove near the staircase. The leaves quivered, and I spied a stocky figure crouched behind the plant.

I'd recognise that figure anywhere.

"Pixley Hayford! What are you doing here?"

"Shh! Fina. Hush." Pixley's round bald head moved left and then right. "I'm on a secret mission."

"Of course you are. What else would I expect from an intrepid journalist?" I would have hugged him, but he was stuck behind the potted plant. There were very few people whom I would embrace upon meeting, but my friend and accomplice Pixley Hayford headlined that list. He had accompanied Ruby and me on many adventures, and I was relieved to see him after our various Paris mishaps.

Pixley adjusted his round, black-framed spectacles, which complemented rather than fought with his round face and soft brown eyes.

"What are *you* doing here?" he asked.

"Isn't it obvious? There's a fashion show, and Ruby was invited to display her designs." I'd leave the details about them being stolen until later.

"Spiffing. I did spot you on the runway, but I was puzzled by you being a model – not that you're not handsome and all that rot, but..."

I held up a forestalling hand. "No need, no need. I'll explain. And you certainly have some explaining to do yourself. Why don't you come to our room instead of hiding behind this plant?"

"Oh, mademoiselle," he said in his best exaggerated French

accent, "though we are in the city of romance, what will the neighbours say?"

He broke into a fit of giggles.

"Most amusing, Pix."

10

"Where's Ruby?" I asked, poking my head into our bathroom suite.

Ruby's neat toiletries stood in an orderly fashion next to my messy array of silver tubes and tins.

"She's left a note," said Pixley from the bedroom.

I trotted from the bathroom and absently scooped up a cheese sandwich.

Brie. Not my favourite, but it would do. "Where has she hobbled off to?"

"Hobble?" Pixley put a finger to his lips. "Now that you mention it, I did notice a limp. What happened?"

"First read the note," I said between mouthfuls.

Pixley plopped down onto my bed and leaned back against the headboard.

I chuckled. "Make yourself at home."

Pixley was an innocent when it came to women, or at least to young women. Perhaps that's why I enjoyed his company – our relationship was delightfully uncomplicated.

"Don't mind if I do." Pixley popped a sandwich into his

mouth and swallowed it in one gulp. "Now, Ruby says: *Dear Feens, I just had to leave the hotel. Don't fret about me — I'll be at Maxim's tonight.*"

"Ow!" I cried, as a sharp pain stung my foot.

A white cat with icy-blue eyes sat at my feet, staring at the plate of sandwiches. The beastie had nibbled on my ankle!

"That's Attila, the hotel cat," said Pixley. "I fancy you'll forgive the minx now, despite her assault on your ankle."

Attila fluttered her tail against my leg in a half-hearted apology. I had to admit she was adorable. I pulled off a bit of sandwich and flung it across the room in Pixley's direction. The cat scampered after it.

Pixley moved his legs to the side. He wasn't overly fond of cats, though he tolerated them under some circumstances — much like Ruby did. However, Attila was not one of those circumstances.

"I cannot fathom your affinity for the beasts, but I'm glad you have a full belly now." He slapped his thighs. "So do we wait for Ruby, or do we follow?"

I looked at the clock. "It's only four o'clock now and we meet at eight. I'd like to follow her, but—"

I stopped myself, reviewing the day's events like a newsreel in my mind.

"What is it?" asked Pixley.

"I know where she's gone. But I'm not certain how to get there."

AFTER A BRIEF CONFERENCE WITH OMAR, we slipped out of the hotel's front door. The green iron edifice of the nearby metro station glowed in the dimming light. Though it was springtime, I turned my collar up against the sharp wind, hurrying into the shelter of the underground.

"This mysterious act is more in Ruby's line than yours." Pixley pressed his hand down over his brown trilby. "Why won't you tell me where we're going?"

Down the steps, the musty air greeted us as a comforting rather than alien smell. As a train left the platform, a gush of air gently lifted my hat.

I pulled my hat down over my ears. "Our stop is Clichy, if you must know."

A Clichy train chugged towards us.

"What's in Clichy?"

"You are most persistent, aren't you?"

The metro doors opened, and we stepped inside a half-empty carriage. "Rather than pester me, I have a few questions for you. For instance, you still haven't told me why you've graced us with your presence."

Pixley grasped a nearby pole as the train lurched out of the station. "Oh, very well. My editor sent me on a mission to dig up – pun intended – more about this Leo Fischer character. Dr Fischer, that is. He's a German archaeologist heading several controversial projects, though I personally find them quite sensible. Instead of digging up things, he wants to return artefacts from Berlin museums to the countries from where they were taken. Including old bones."

"But why the secrecy, like we were on one of our old missions? You were hiding behind a potted plant, for goodness' sake!"

"Good question. It seems the chap has a few old-fashioned skeletons in his cupboard. Ha! Another pun. Get it? Bones? Skeletons?"

I gave him a playful punch on the arm.

"So that's why I'm here. To dig up these jolly old skeletons on behalf of my editor and a benefactor."

"Ah…" I said. "A benefactor. Pray, continue."

"Not much to tell, I'm afraid. Let's just say he's a wealthy Egyptian gentleman familiar with my reports on so-called colonial ventures and adventures. This Egyptian gentleman wants to know whether he should give money to Dr Fischer. He believes that politicians will be persuaded by the righteousness of his cause if a European makes the case on his behalf."

"And this gentleman must be certain Dr Fischer is as clean as an apple," I said, using one of my grandmother's favourite Irish idioms. "But then why did you say you were working on a story for your editor?"

"My editor never met an opportunity he didn't like, though he's a tight-fisted chap. Once I told him I'd interview Dr Fischer, he insisted on me writing a story, though he wouldn't fund my ticket to Paris. Blooming cheeky, it is."

"I'm still baffled by all the secrecy."

Pixley rubbed his eye. "I couldn't simply toddle around like a lost tourist, so I used your show to wangle my entrance. Then I had a jolly poke around the hotel to get the lay of the land. And now that you're here, I have a properly convincing cover story."

"I'm puzzled by why Dr Fischer was at the hotel in the first place, especially his swanning into our dressing rooms before the show!"

Pixley chuckled. "The old devil. I learnt he's married to Madame Lafitte—"

"No—" I gasped. "I thought she was old! I mean, he's old – must be in his fifties, but she must be in her sixties."

He held up a hand. "No more interruptions of the great and wondrous Hayford, please. Yes, Dr Fischer is married to Madame Lafitte, and yes, she is about ten years his senior. They married five years ago, and rumour has it he married her for money. His archaeological adventures simply gobble up money."

The metro slowed to a halt, and I jerked my head up. It was Clichy. "Quickly, Pix. We've arrived at our secret destination."

11

A square grey monstrosity loomed before us, adorned with a simple carved wooden sign reading 'Lafitte' across the top.

"See?" I pointed at the sign. "Can you guess now, oh wondrous Hayford?"

Pixley pushed his trilby back on his bald head. "But why? And why the urgency for Ruby to visit, especially in her condition?"

As we ascended the stairs of the gloomy front area, I told him about the copied designs, and how Ruby must have come here to confront Madame Lafitte herself.

Whirring, thumping, and chatter echoed down the corridor. Madame Lafitte's workshop door opened onto acres of sewing machines along one wall, and a vast expanse of tables against another.

Groups of women huddled over tables, some talking above the mechanical din, whilst others focused intently on the task at hand. Unlike the darkened vestibule where we'd entered, this room was bright and airy. I was pleasantly surprised by these working conditions – other such places I had visited in London were abysmal. Places where I'd imagined myself linking arms with the seamstresses and whisking them away.

A flash of tangerine caught my eye, and I halted in front of the young woman stitching the silk skirt. I eyed the pattern over her shoulder, straining to see if it were one of Ruby's creations. With a mixture of relief and frustration, I saw it was a full-length gown, and certainly not Ruby's style.

Pixley squeezed my arm. "Come, Red. Let's see if Ruby is already in Madame Lafitte's inner sanctum."

I'd envisioned the legendary Madame Lafitte working in an efficient, well-lit office, with helpers all around her. But the small, dim room was nothing of the sort. Large windows glowed from the streetlight, weakly illuminating a white-haired round woman. She hunched over what appeared to be a child's doll, albeit one that was standing and naked.

Ruby was nowhere to be seen.

Madame Lafitte set down her pencil and peered at us through gold pince-nez perched atop a long thin nose. A brown shawl covered her equally brown voluminous shift. Her only concession to fashion was a pair of scarlet red slippers peeking out from her sack-like outfit.

Pixley and I exchanged glances but remained silent.

"Just a moment," she said in French. She had a lovely, fluting, almost sing-song voice. Deftly fitting a stiff red piece of fabric around the doll's midsection, she stitched the ends together and stuck her needle into the bun atop her own head.

Pixley whispered, "Blimey, why's the room so dark? How can she see?"

"Ruby said she only works in natural light, though that streetlight is hardly natural," I murmured.

Madame Lafitte finished her task and gave us a little clap. "Now, to what do I owe this joyful interruption?" she said, again in French. I couldn't tell whether her tone was sarcastic.

"We're terribly sorry to interrupt, but we're searching for our friend, Ruby Dove. The designer you invited to the show this afternoon," I said. "We thought she might have come here to—"

"—see your delightful designs," said Pixley.

Madame Lafitte slid off her short stool with surprising ease. She removed her pince-nez and squinted at us. "Ah yes, Ruby Dove's designs. Subtle grace. That's what I like: an emphasis on natural curves and colours that flatter rather than shout."

Then she kicked up one leg, exposing her un-stockinged white calf. "Except for little unexpected touches of colour here and there, like my slippers."

Pixley leaned towards her slippers. "Delightful."

"Yes, they are, aren't they?" She gazed up at us, making me feel like a giant hovering over her. "But who are you?"

"I'm Ruby's assistant, Fina Aubrey-Havelock, and this is Pixley Hayford." I put in hurriedly, "A friend of ours." Pixley gave a familiar sigh of relief at not being exposed as a journalist.

"Well, it's lovely to meet you, but I'm afraid I haven't yet met Miss Dove. I had hoped to meet her at the show this afternoon, but our paths didn't cross."

Pixley gave Madame Lafitte a little bow. "We'll be on our way, then. Apologies again for the interruption."

He looked at his watch. "I say, it's almost 7:30. We'd better find a taxi."

"I expect we'll see you at Maxim's soon," I said to Madame Lafitte.

"Maxim's?" Madame Lafitte raised her eyebrows. "Oh, yes. Sometimes I become so engrossed that time simply flits out the window. I forget whether it's a Monday or a Sunday!"

Pixley turned on his heel, but I remained, rooted to the spot.

Madame Lafitte cocked her head. "Anything the matter, dear?"

I gulped. Then the words simply tumbled forth. "Something

is the matter. Someone has stolen Ruby's designs and is selling them under your name."

She blinked rapidly. "Dear me, how frightful. I've heard of such things, of course, but I considered them scurrilous rumours. And I've certainly never heard any such rumours connected to House of Lafitte."

Staring forlornly at her doll, she continued. "You see, I leave my business to Yvonne, so I may focus on designing. I must work hard because...you never know when it all might come crashing down one day, do you?"

Her forehead wrinkled in apparent distress.

"Just so." Pixley touched my elbow. "Fina, we shouldn't upset Madame Lafitte before the celebratory dinner. I'm sure she'll have a chat with Yvonne about this little design matter later."

"I won't shatter like a looking-glass, young man, and I'm certain Yvonne will have an answer to this dreadful mix-up." With a catch in her throat, she said, "I don't know where I'd be without dear Yvonne."

"Did you call me, Mathilde?"

A figure stepped forward from the shadows, with that unmistakable saunter.

Crossing her arms, Yvonne Jourdain leaned against the door-frame. Her top lip was raised in that cursed smirk, telling me she had heard everything.

12

The gilded grandfather clock chimed eight o'clock, just as Pixley and I found our chairs at the end of a long, white linen-covered table. Warm candles glowed on each tabletop, creating tiny reflective dots in the Art Nouveau mirrored panels lining the walls of Maxim's. Stained glass lamps hung from the ceiling, casting cool blue and warm green shadows on the waitstaff as they moved seamlessly around the tables.

As we were set off from the main area in an alcove near the bar, the only noise was the background rhythm of drink-shakers mixed with indistinct murmurs from the two bartenders.

"That Yvonne is frightfully clever, isn't she? She avoided your questions like a politician during an interview." Pixley hung his trilby on a nearby hatstand. "Thank heavens that taxi ride with the two of them is over. Not even your humble servant, the garrulous Pixley, could cut through that tension."

"It was all a bit thick," I agreed. Yvonne had whisked us all away from the workshop in a waiting taxi. Although I was grateful, Yvonne had whispered strict orders that we must not upset Mathilde.

"No matter," I continued. "Yvonne will have to answer once Ruby appears."

All the seats were occupied, save the one next to Pixley and two next to Dr Fischer. The one by Pixley had presumably been saved for Ruby.

Elizabeth Ryland nudged me. "Where's your friend? Despite her mild-mannered appearance, Mathilde Lafitte is very serious about punctuality."

"We're not certain where Ruby is. I—"

Pixley interrupted me by whipping his cloth napkin with a snapping noise. Elizabeth scowled at him. Despite her apparent antipathy, I admired Elizabeth's boxy jacket in orchid, fitted like a suit of armour. I wondered idly what she might be protecting.

She elbowed Dr Fischer, sitting to her right. "Say, where can I get bratwurst in Paris? I once had some in New York, and it was fantastic."

Dr Fischer sniffed. "I'm a vegetarian, madam."

"Too bad. Though I suppose that means you're not tempted to eat French snails then, are you? They taste like rubber."

"Fortunately, it is the only French dish that tastes like rubber. I only wish they were more flexible with their attitudes towards the Germans. And vegetarians."

"They're so rude sometimes, aren't they?" said Elizabeth, scarcely *sotto voce*.

"*Ja!* They always turn up their nose when I ask for soup without broth from *fleisch*."

"Unbelievable."

I whispered to Pixley, "Why was Elizabeth scowling at you? Ruby didn't take to her, either."

"Oh, I had a little kerfuffle with her before the show. She told me I couldn't enter, because – well, I'll give you three guesses why. She even had the nerve to give that young chap Maurice the evil eye."

"Ah." I sipped my mineral water. "I see." I was all too familiar with the colour prejudice that Pixley and Ruby faced nearly everywhere they went. Undoubtedly the same went for Maurice.

"I don't believe we've met." A nearly translucent hand stretched out in Pixley's direction. "Reggie Barrington-Loftus at your service."

Pixley jumped back a little in his chair, unaccustomed to such a forward greeting. "Pleased to meet you. I'm Pixley Hayford, a friend of Ruby and Fina's. Here on holiday with them."

Reggie had changed into a loud green sports jacket. I spotted dark smudges on the sleeves, which looked like dirt or soot.

"I say, what do you do when you're not on holiday?" asked Reggie.

Pixley let out a little puff of air, almost as if it were an apology. "I'm a journalist, but I promise you this isn't a busman's holiday."

"Nothing to apologise for, my good chap. I'm one as well. At least, that's what I am at the moment."

"What do you mean, 'at the moment'?" asked Pixley.

"Well, my friend Simon Nash at the *Daily Roar* had a spot of bother with the missus – not an uncommon occurrence – and he said I could take over, since I fancied a bit of travel myself."

Pixley leaned to the side as the waiter poured his wine.

"You know Nashie?"

"For aeons," said Reggie. "His father was our chauffeur, so I've known him since we were in short trousers. Then we met again in London, as one does, and became bosom friends."

Pixley rubbed his chin.

The loping gait of Maurice into the restaurant broke the awkward pause. Behind him trailed a tiny waif-like creature, like a sprite from a fairy tale. She wore a pale pink gossamer frock, and her almost white-blonde hair was arranged into a tidy bird's nest with a few daisies scattered about.

Everyone at the table stared at them.

Elizabeth said in an attempted whisper, "Madame Lafitte does not approve of late arrivals." She was fundamentally incapable of whispering anything, so the statement hung over the table like a bad smell.

Pixley raised his voice a little in conversation with Reggie, helping to smooth over the social gaffe.

"Who's the girl?" Reggie asked Pixley. "Stunning. An absolute corker."

Pixley raised his shoulders and twisted his lips.

Maurice and the sprite had settled next to Dr Fischer, but our table was soon distracted by another appearance. The distinct, purposeful march of Ruby's heels clicked through the archway. By the sound of it, her ankle had healed.

Ruby nodded casually at those at the table, looking her usual confident self. However, a few strands of her hair had escaped her styling – a most unusual occurrence.

She slid into her chair silently, as if one of our Oxford tutors was just about to start a lecture.

And a lecture it was.

Yvonne rose from her seat. "Thank you all for your patience, despite our late start." She sent a quick, icy glare towards Ruby, Maurice, and the sprite.

Ruby jutted her chin in response, and Maurice leaned back in his chair, though I couldn't tell whether it was to avoid Yvonne's glare or to demonstrate he didn't care. The sprite simply stared at her nails.

I glanced at the clock, calculating that the poor devils had arrived no more than ten minutes late. My preconceived notions about the French being more relaxed about time were vanishing rapidly.

Madame Lafitte sprang up quicker than a rocketing pheasant. "I'm grateful to you all for gathering at such short notice. My husband, Dr Fischer, says that my darling sweet niece, Henriette, is recovering at the hotel."

She patted Dr Fischer's hand.

"Thank you to him and to Maurice Neuville, who assisted him most ably." She bowed in Maurice's direction, who had an appropriately sombre countenance, though he gave Ruby a half-wink.

I regarded myself as somewhat of an expert on winks, and this one was cautiously optimistic, rather than the full wink of the chronic cad.

In response, Ruby shifted in her seat and stared intently at a nearby radiator. I tried to catch her eye, but she focused studiously on her new best friend, an inanimate heating device.

"And thank you to Ruby Dove for her design inspiration, and to Fina Aubrey-Havelock for stepping in at the last moment."

Pixley slapped his hands together in wild applause, followed by an enthusiastic eruption from Reggie and Maurice.

"I'd also like to thank, ah, our new journalist friend..." She looked at Yvonne, who mouthed Reggie's last name. "Thank you, Mr Harrington-Eustace."

Reggie raised his glass, not bothering to correct Madame Lafitte's mangling of his name. "Good show. I'll write a perfectly smashing piece for you."

"Finally, I'd like to thank Yvonne Jourdain, without whom I'd be utterly at sea."

Reggie leaned over and muttered, "It's true, but I've heard rumours it's like being at sea with a shark circling your boat."

As if to emphasise the point, he slid a scrap of paper towards me. I suppressed a giggle at the credible doodle of a smirking shark staring back at me.

Apparently aware that no one wanted to applaud for Yvonne,

Madame Lafitte hurried on. "Please, everyone, enjoy your dinner. Afterwards, I shall make my announcements."

She returned to her seat and began speaking in rapid French to Yvonne. Unlike the wildly gesticulating Madame Lafitte, Yvonne kept her hands firmly under the table.

Waiters brought the first course, a simple but fragrant consommé. The sweet, earthy smell reminded me I hadn't eaten in at least two hours – but first things first. I had to discover why Ruby had disappeared.

But Elizabeth's voice ricocheted across the table, leaving no opening for my questions. "Reggie, are you really going to write a bang-up piece on the new designs?"

He put down his spoon. "Indubitably, dearest Elizabeth."

"You two have met before?" asked Pixley.

"Ah, Elizabeth and I 'go way back'," he said, expertly copying Elizabeth's twang. "Do you remember that night in Berlin?"

"Sounds rather scandalous," said Pixley.

Reggie winked at Pixley. "It was tame – at least by Berlin standards."

"Don't listen to him," said Elizabeth. "He's making a joke at my expense."

She took an angry swig of water. She was the only guest at the table forgoing alcohol. To be fair, Elizabeth was a woman who scarcely needed alcohol to release any of her inhibitions.

She leaned over her soup, eyeing Ruby speculatively. "Enough of that. Are you going to confront Madame Lafitte, Miss Dove? Or Yvonne? And why were you late? You look like the kind of young lady who is always on time."

Eyes goggling, Ruby glanced up from her soup. "Pardon. I must have misheard you. Did you say 'confront'? And as for my tardiness, you're quite right that I avoid making a habit of it."

I could tell she was playing for time, so I looked at Elizabeth.

"How long have you been a buyer? Do you travel to other countries besides France to find new pieces?"

Elizabeth waved a dismissive hand. "I've been travelling since you were a toddler, no doubt, and I go wherever pieces pop up."

She levelled a steady gaze at Ruby. "Now, back to my question. You know very well what I'm getting at."

Ruby thoughtfully turned over her fork a few times. "I hesitate to say when I shall do it. I'm keen to avoid embarrassing Madame Lafitte by speaking to Yvonne in her presence."

"I say, this sounds like a scoop," said Reggie. "Tell me more, Miss Dove."

Maurice scooted his chair closer to Reggie. "This sounds intriguing."

As Ruby froze, my own mind went blank. This story would reach Yvonne soon. What if she became so enraged she threw us out of the hotel? Naturally, I ought to have considered that before I opened my mouth at Madame Lafitte's workshop.

Always ready to rescue a friend, Pixley said, "By the way, Maurice, I don't believe you've introduced us to your charming friend."

"I've also been wondering about our new companion," said Reggie. "Spill the beans."

"I'm Virginie," squeaked the sprite in English.

Maurice ran a finger around his collar. "Ahem. Yes. I found Virginie. She wasn't lost."

"Sounds like she's a precious object of yours," I said.

"Maury is the precious one, aren't you, *mon chéri*?" burbled Virginie.

Maurice sipped his wine and carefully replaced the glass on the table. Though he had the good grace to forgo the lovey-dovey talk, I was rather affronted on behalf of Virginie.

I whispered as much to Pixley, and he held a hand over his

mouth to stop a laugh. Spurred on by his infectious muffled snorting, I, too, succumbed to the giggles. I wasn't as successful at hiding it as Pixley, however.

The only way out was to leave. I was certain I would burst into a belly laugh if I didn't leave the table, post haste, so I excused myself and dashed towards the toilet.

Behind me, Pixley muttered, "No, we weren't laughing at you, Miss Ryland. I assure you…" but the rest of the conversation was drowned out by a scuffle near the toilet.

Rather than peering around the corner, my eyes fixed on a gilt-edged looking glass hanging opposite. What I took for a scuffle was actually an embrace. Dr Fischer's arms loosely encircled Yvonne's waist, whilst she gripped his shoulders.

I looked away in case they might spot me staring into the glass.

"We already discussed it before your little event today. Soon, *mein Mäuschen*, soon."

"But not soon enough, Leo."

"Maurice will take care of it. You know he will."

"Selkies and kelpies," I said to myself. Dr Fischer and Yvonne. For one mad moment, my mind turned towards extorting Yvonne. Not because I wanted the money – though a few extra quid wouldn't go amiss – but because she was such a thoroughly dreadful woman.

When I looked up, Dr Fischer had disappeared, and once again, Yvonne Jourdain stared back at me from the looking glass, with her cold, fish-like eyes.

13

I picked at my *Poulet Basquaise*, still disquieted by what I'd just witnessed, not to mention Ruby's vanishing act and Henriette's tumble. And despite Reggie's good-natured bonhomie, I sensed something lurked underneath it. The atmosphere was generally convivial – and became only more so as the wine continued to flow – but even the sight of the mouth-watering food failed to distract me.

Pixley enjoyed himself immensely, ignoring the lingering coldness between him and Elizabeth. His face was as happy as a cuckoo's in the nest of its neighbour. He even wandered from his seat to engage the distracted Dr Fischer in conversation, undoubtedly to butter him up for a longer interview.

Ruby ate single strands of pasta from her bacon and gruyère dish. Then she set down her fork. "This is hopeless. I must speak to Yvonne. Should I take her aside?"

I raised my eyebrows. "You're already wielding that fork like a weapon, so you'd better wait." And since Yvonne and Dr Fischer's romance might be important somehow, I added, "I'll tell you more later," and gave her a knowing wink.

Her watery smile told me she was unconvinced.

Perhaps a distraction was in order. "When are you going to tell me where you went this afternoon?"

"I'll tell you later. I promise. It's not important now."

At the other end of the table, Madame Lafitte cleared her throat. It must be time for her announcement.

The dishes had been cleared, and small cups of after-dinner coffee were handed around, lightening the atmosphere considerably. Madame Lafitte's bid for everyone's attention, however, made everyone sit up a little straighter.

She leaned over the table, adjusting her long strand of pearls on her otherwise uninspiring navy outfit. It was so peculiar that the woman didn't wear her own creations. I fancied that made her a true eccentric.

"It's been a most lovely dinner, hasn't it? I'll now make my announcements, as promised." She licked her lips and beamed, clearly enjoying the suspense. "As you may be aware, I come from a poor family in the countryside. I was always told that a woman ought to stay home, and though I excelled at sewing, my skill was considered merely a pleasant quality of a good wife. I ran away to Paris – scandalously, at the time – where I worked in trying conditions as a seamstress. I vowed that if I ever had my own house of couture, I should never treat my employees in such a dismal manner."

Reggie raised a glass and Pixley said, "Hear, hear."

I had never seen Pixley one over the eight, but he was decidedly tiddly. And I suspected Reggie was much the same, though there was something a little squiffy about his affect in general.

Madame Lafitte smiled indulgently. "Now, the years have dimmed my eyesight, and threading a needle or sketching a design is not as easy as it once was. Therefore, I'm afraid and delighted to announce my retirement."

Gasps echoed around the room.

Only Dr Fischer nodded, a tiny grin lighting up his impassive face. Then he pinched his lip in studied concentration, as if to cover the grin.

Reggie knocked over his unsurprisingly empty wineglass, but maintained a cheerful face. Everyone else shifted uncomfortably in their seats, except for Yvonne, who remained nonchalant. Clearly, she was the only one who had already heard this news, besides her apparent lover, Dr Fischer, of course.

Madame Lafitte tugged on her pearls. "I'm joyfully anticipating growing vegetable marrows in the country and drinking fine wine into my twilight years. Perhaps I'll even take up knitting. I never enjoyed the country as a child, and I'm most determined to do so before I die."

"But you're not old!" cried Elizabeth. "You're only sixty!"

Ignoring Elizabeth's outburst of enthusiasm and the gaffe about her age, Mathilde tilted her head towards Dr Fischer. "My dear husband has agreed to move to the country, though we will keep a flat in Paris so he can carry on his important work."

"*Ja, ja, mein Leibchen.*" He turned to the crowd. "You are all invited to our new country home, and I will naturally see you if we have any soirees in town. In fact, Professor Boscoe Fitzwilliam, the famous antiquities scholar, will be giving a talk tomorrow at our soiree at my flat in the Latin Quarter. You're all invited."

Madame Lafitte brushed a wisp of white hair from her forehead. "Yes, Leo. You shall have your parties, whilst I shall enjoy my knitting and wine in the country."

She turned back to us. "Now, what does this mean for all of you? I see the little cogs in your pretty heads whirling around, so I'll save you the distress of guessing. Tomorrow, I'll sign the papers giving Yvonne Jourdain full control of the House of Lafitte, and all its assets. She will decide whether to continue our support of various causes and investments. This includes whether to keep on the staff at our hotel, and at House of Lafitte."

Murmurs of protest arose from the table.

The click of her tongue was enough to make everyone silent. "The French Commercial Guild has also decided to restrict our designs to France, and to stop selling abroad, due to competition and counterfeit concerns. If you are a foreign buyer," she said, vaguely flopping her pearls in Elizabeth's direction, "this may present several difficulties. Yvonne will decide whether we withdraw from the commercial guild."

Reggie dared to speak. "I'm certain we all support your delightful adventures in the country, but what will happen to the heart and soul of the company? Madame Lafitte's delicious designs?"

Mathilde Lafitte gave him a wry, wistful smile. "I was saving the best news for last. Though Yvonne will retain full control over creative decisions, we obviously need a talent who will move my line in new directions. I also wanted someone who worked hard and fought her way to becoming a designer."

She paused, her eyes roaming around the table. "And there is no one better for that role than the talented Miss Ruby Dove. That is why I am delighted to offer her the post of lead designer."

14

"Feens! Wake up!"

I rubbed my eyes. "Bother. What time is it? Why did you wake me, Ruby?"

Blinking at the now-empty armchair, I remembered the blurry figure of Pixley had sat in the armchair all night, snoring placidly with his arms crossed and his short legs up on a footstool. He had been fully dressed in day wear, save a blue nightcap perched on his bald pate.

"Didn't you hear the scream?" Ruby pushed her arms into her silk dressing-gown and cinched it around her waist. She traded her nightcap for a grey scarf. "I don't know where Pixley's gone."

"Scream? Where's Pixley?"

"Meet me downstairs as soon as you can."

She rushed out of the room.

I stared at the ceiling, trying to rouse my addled brain – no mean feat at six o'clock in the morning.

A shriek echoed from somewhere downstairs, finally jolting me into action.

Running barefoot, I flew down the corridor and the stairs. A small crowd milled about on the first-floor landing in various stages of undress. Omar Abelli was fully dressed in his perfectly tailored suit, though the sheen of sweat across his forehead showed he'd been up all night. Elizabeth Ryland hugged herself in a tight-fitting red quilted dressing-gown, whilst Madame Lafitte shivered in her serviceable grey flannel. In striped pyjamas and a green nightcap pulled over his red hair, Reggie spoke softly to Maurice, clad only in black trousers and a thin black top.

"What's happened?" I asked, finally catching up with Ruby.

Maurice looked at us.

He raised his hand and let it hover over Ruby's arm, ready to comfort her. Clearly thinking better of it, he let his hand drop. "It's Yvonne Jourdain. She's dead."

Images of Yvonne shrieking at Ruby and Pixley whilst chasing them down the staircase with a knife flashed through my mind. This was the nightmare I'd had last night. I'd stood at the top of the stairs, watching the drama unfold. Pixley had taken the knife from Yvonne and then stabbed her with it, again and again.

I shuddered and then shook myself. It was all just a dream, Fina. Just a dream.

Ruby's voice brought me back to reality.

"Did she die in her sleep?

"Of natural causes?" I put in, realising the inanity of the question even as I asked it. Yvonne Jourdain was in her mid-thirties and the picture of physical health. Though one might say her personality was far from healthy.

Maurice shrugged at our questions. "Your friend Pixley is inside."

Ruby and I weaved through the crowd to the open bedroom door. Omar stood inside the room, speaking softly to Pixley and Berthe.

Pixley wobbled towards us as if his stocky legs were as spindly as those of a new-born foal. "Thank heavens you're here. You'll never believe what happened. I entered this room and Berthe was standing over the bed, and she screamed, and..."

"Pix, Pix, take a deep breath." Ruby squeezed his arms. "Calm yourself and tell us what happened."

I spotted a jug of water and filled a glass. As I handed it to Pixley, Ruby suddenly jerked it away. "Better not drink anything until we understand what's happened."

Pixley nodded and then promptly fell into a nearby chair. He drew out a tiny silver flask, unscrewed the lid, and threw his head back. "Thanks for the offer of water, Red. Brandy will do just fine."

He sighed and waved us closer, out of earshot of Omar and Berthe. "I woke up and toddled – or rather, wobbled – downstairs to find a spot of breakfast. On my way downstairs, I thought I'd have a poke around Dr Fischer's room."

"You what?" hissed Ruby. Omar glanced at us and frowned. Ruby waved at him as if we were simply discussing the weather. He returned to his quiet conversation with Berthe.

"I thought I'd have a little peek," said Pixley. "No harm in that. Besides, it's all for a good cause and Dr Fischer's own benefit. Well, the door wasn't open, but it was unlocked. I opened it and noticed Berthe standing over Yvonne Jourdain, who lay on the bed – right there."

He pointed at the bed without looking at it. "Berthe had a breakfast tray in her hands. When she saw me, she screamed."

"If Yvonne Jourdain was dead, why did she scream when you arrived, but not when she found the body?" asked Ruby.

Pixley sighed. "Must have been delayed shock. She was frozen in place, looking quite horrified."

"What did Yvonne die of?" I asked.

"Haven't a clue. She was the picture of perfect health. There are no obvious signs of foul play, but it seems doubtful she died of natural causes."

"Especially since she's in Dr Fischer's room," said Ruby. "Where is he, by the way?"

"I surmised he'd be on a vigorous walk this morning, which is why I ventured to enter his room in the first place," Pixley said. "I assume he must still be out."

"Why does Dr Fischer have his own room?" I asked. "Shouldn't he be sharing with Madame Lafitte?"

"I don't think they have *that* sort of marriage," said Ruby.

"I'll say," I murmured, recalling his embrace of Yvonne the night before.

A commotion erupted in the doorway. Dr Fischer's rimless spectacles peered over Omar's arm. Omar held his arm straight, barring Dr Fischer and everyone else from the room.

Dr Fischer threw up his hands. "Why are they in *my* room?"

Madame Lafitte tugged on his hand. "Come, dear. Let's go."

Reggie's head popped up over Dr Fischer's shoulder. "I say, the good doctor has a point."

"Please, everyone, I will explain after the police arrive." Omar nudged Reggie away from the door. "I'm acting on instructions from Madame Lafitte. Miss Dove and Miss Aubrey-Havelock are here to help Mr Hayford with a case of delayed shock, and Berthe was already in the room."

Pixley did his best to appear shocked in response to Omar's clear stage direction, raising his eyebrows and leaning back in his chair.

"Why is Omar protecting us?" whispered Ruby to Pixley.

"I told him we were detectives," said Pixley

"You fathead. What on earth did you do that for?" asked Ruby.

"Well, it's almost true – we've successfully solved murders in the past. And you were our super sleuth, Ruby."

"But we don't know if this *is* a murder." Ruby smoothed her hair and skirt, clearly trying to regain control of her nerves. "And if it were murder, you'd be a prime suspect."

Pixley poked a finger at his chest. "Me? Why not Berthe?"

"Berthe, too. The point is, we always avoid the police for good reason, remember?" she said, not unkindly.

My heart sank as the distinctive wail of sirens outside became louder. We had snooped in the past on behalf of what a friend at Oxford called 'colonial exploitation'. And I was almost positive the French police had records about at least one of us. But Ruby and I had made a pact: we'd resolved not to focus on these campaigns until we had taken our degrees at Oxford and made a go of the fashion business. We'd had too many warnings from tutors about our unexplained absences, and we certainly wished to avoid being sent down.

The sirens halted abruptly, just at their loudest point.

"Look lively, you two." Ruby sprang into action, suddenly unable to suppress her sleuthing instinct. "The police will be swarming around Yvonne in a matter of minutes. Let's peek at the body before they arrive."

15

Berthe gripped the sides of her chair, as if she were prepared to descend sixty feet on some fiendish carnival ride.

"I know nothing...nothing, I tell you."

"Calm yourself, Berthe," said Ruby, in a low, authoritative voice. "We aren't here to interrogate you. We simply wish to look at the bed."

The body of Yvonne Jourdain lay on top of the four-poster bed in the centre of Dr Fischer's room. Her arms were folded neatly on her chest, her face was made up subtly as it had been the night before, and not a blonde hair on her head was out of place. Mercifully, her eyes were closed.

I pointed at the long sapphire velvet gown Yvonne was wearing. "That's the gown Henriette was supposed to have worn at the show yesterday, but never did for some reason," I whispered.

Ruby's head moved to and fro slowly, apparently taking in my comment whilst still staring at the body.

Yvonne's skin was smooth and unmarred, except for a long bruise on her left arm.

We leaned closer.

"See?" Ruby nodded towards Yvonne's ear.

There were red markings on her earlobes.

"See what?" Pixley had his back to us.

"Turn around," said Ruby.

"I can't. I'll be sick if I do. Besides, I'm already queasy from my night of debauchery with dear old Reggie. That chap can certainly hold a drink or two."

"I'll narrate, then," said Ruby. "Yvonne wore a russet-coloured suit at dinner, and now she's wearing this sapphire velvet number. There's a long bruise on her left arm, and her gold earring has red marks around it, as if the skin is irritated."

She walked around to the other side of the bed. "Same red marks here, but no obvious bruises."

"A lover's nibble followed by a lover's quarrel?" asked Pixley.

"You *would* think so, Pixley Hayford," said Ruby.

"Well, it's logical, especially if there isn't anything else out of place," said Pixley.

"That's just it," I said. "Everything is out of place! Why is she in this gown, and why is she in Dr Fischer's room?"

"As I said, Dr Fischer had a nibble. Perhaps I'll interview him about it," said Pixley.

Ruby tapped her teeth.

"What is it? You never tap your teeth without good reason," I said.

"You told me that Yvonne and Dr Fischer were in a rather compromising position at Maxim's last night."

"Well, well," said Pixley. "Seems I was right. A lovers' quarrel?"

"Even if Dr Fischer did kill her," I said, "surely he wouldn't leave the body here."

"Maybe it's one of those deuced double-bluffs I'm always reading about in detective novels. You know, some clever-clogs implicates himself to throw the bumbling detective off the scent," said Pixley.

"This isn't a detective novel, Pix," said Ruby. "And despite her behaviour, Yvonne didn't deserve to die."

"It may not be a detective novel, but we certainly have a detective on our hands," murmured Pixley. "Brace yourself – the Lily Law have arrived."

A bevvy of uniformed men swarmed into the room, moving in unison towards the bed.

We all moved into a corner, away from the oncoming stampede.

"*Arrêt!*"

Every man in uniform froze on the spot.

A comfortably built man, balding but with wisps of white hair, ambled in with his hands behind his back. His navy suit was suitably conservative for his role, but I noticed the pink skin of his ankles peeking out when he walked. Perhaps he had been in a hurry this morning and hadn't time to put on socks.

He twiddled his thumbs behind his back, whilst padding softly to the window.

Not a single officer moved.

Without warning, he spun on his heel and held up his hands.

"Please leave, everyone. Except Monsieur Coste."

The uniformed officers streamed from the room as briskly as they had streamed into it.

Our little trio, plus Berthe, turned to leave as well.

"Ah-ah. Not you."

He crooked a finger at us. We all stood in place, transfixed by his commanding presence.

A tall young man with an insolent bow-like mouth, a pointy nose, and a luxuriant moustache whispered into the older man's ear.

"Yes, yes, Albert. I know." The older man gave us a little bow. "I'm sorry to keep you waiting," he said in French. "But you are English, I'm informed."

Berthe rose a hand. "*Je suis française.*"

As he puckered his lips and surveyed Berthe, I detected the tiniest of smiles around the corner of his mouth. "Quite," he said.

"We speak enough French to comprehend, Monsieur," said Pixley hastily.

Ignoring Pixley's offer to continue in French, he said in English, "Thank you, young man. I'm Inspector Edouard Toussaint, and this is my able assistant, Monsieur Albert Coste."

The sergeant – or whatever the French police equivalent to sergeant was – clicked his heels together.

"No need for that, Albert." Toussaint waved a hand. "Now, you must be Miss Fina Aubrey-Havelock, Miss Ruby Dove, and Mr Pixley Hayford." He bobbed his head at each of us in turn.

"And this must be Berthe Dumont."

Berthe crossed her arms and said nothing.

Toussaint drew his face an inch away from Berthe's. "Tell me, what brought you here this morning?"

She stepped back and sniffed. "I was doing my duty, Inspector. Bringing breakfast for Dr Fischer."

Toussaint held out a hand and motioned around the room. "I understand he was not here. So why did you enter?"

"Dr Fischer was a habit-like man. He always breakfasted at 7:14 when he returned from his walk."

"What did you do when he hadn't returned by 7:14?"

"I knocked on the door and didn't hear anything – not even snoring. So, I turned the knob and peeked. I didn't hear a peep and the door opens so as you can't see the bed directly. I thought I'd put his breakfast on the desk. Then I sensed something amiss. Just like I did last night. I knew Madame Lafitte would retire, and I was right, wasn't I? My auntie tells me I have a sixth sense."

"Do you, now?" Toussaint said with a grave face.

Albert scribbled in his notebook.

Berthe's button nose tilted upwards. "I do at that, and it told me that something wasn't right in that room. I looked at the bed and saw Mademoiselle Jourdain there, just as she is now."

"Why didn't you scream when you spotted her?" asked Pixley. The journalist in Pixley couldn't be suppressed, even under these circumstances.

Toussaint regarded Pixley like an indulgent father entertaining his offspring's endless questions.

"Because I've seen plenty of bodies before," said Berthe.

Albert's eyebrows rose. "Where?"

"My father is an undertaker. Seen plenty of bodies laid out like Mademoiselle was on the bed. Her makeup and hair done up like that. Mind you, I was in shock, but I wasn't scared."

"Then why did you scream when I entered the room?" asked Pixley.

"Well, that was different, wasn't it? You surprised me because I was watching the body. I thought you might be the murderer, too."

"Why do you say 'murderer'?" asked Ruby tentatively.

"I dunno. None of it seemed natural. Especially since she was in Dr Fischer's bed – not in the way you'd expect, either, if she were, well…"

"If there were a bit of hanky-panky, as the English say?" Toussaint gave Berthe a playful nudge.

Albert worked his jaw but kept writing.

Berthe giggled. "I've seen that plenty of times, sir – by accident, of course. But that wasn't what happened here."

"Thank you, Berthe. That's all for now."

Toussaint turned to us.

Berthe stayed put, her arms crossed again over her ample bosom.

"You may leave, Miss Dumont. Thank you."

She stomped off, and the inspector turned his unnerving gaze on us.

"Now, Omar Abelli says the three of you are friends," said Toussaint.

"Yes, we're all staying together," I said.

"Are you, now?" Toussaint bounced on the balls of his feet, his hands still behind his back. "Just what sort of *friends* are you?"

"Inspector, if you're implying—" I said.

"What Miss Aubrey-Havelock means is we're all good friends from London," Ruby said. "Nothing more. Mr Hayford is here on business but slept in our chair last night. The hotel was completely full."

Two plain-clothes men rushed into the room, one holding a camera.

Toussaint jabbed his finger at the bed. "Gaudin and Blaise, you can start taking photos of the body, but I'll take a look before they take it away."

He turned back to us. "I have several questions for you, but those can keep."

"It's all so ghastly," said Ruby. "May we leave the hotel – simply for a stroll? Perhaps after a spot of tea?"

Toussaint gave Ruby a watery smile. "Yes, though I wouldn't stroll too vigorously with your ankle, mademoiselle. You need to be in tip-top shape if you are to take up the prestigious position you've been offered at Maison Lafitte."

Even without the brain-boosting benefit of my morning tea, the proverbial fog began to lift.

My stomach clenched. The inspector was implying that Miss Ruby Dove had a motive. A motive to ensure Yvonne Jourdain would never grace the halls of House of Lafitte again.

16

"May I join you?"

Henriette's pleading face stared down at us. Her cheeks were sunken, and her long, silken hair had dulled. Even her polite request to join our breakfast table seemed uncharacteristic – the Henriette of yesterday wouldn't have thought twice about asking permission.

"Please, do join us." Ruby patted the empty chair next to her. "I expect Fina is still in shock about Yvonne."

"Ah yes, the shock. Miss Fina, your hair looks like it had an electric shock, too." She chortled. "I've seen it before." Apparently, her rather bad humour had already returned.

I ran one hand over my fringe, though I suspected it had little effect.

"Hardly the time for such flippant comments," said Ruby in the tone of a Victorian governess.

Henriette slid her plate of a solitary few inches of baguette, butter, and jam onto the table. She eyed Pixley's full English breakfast – a new hotel speciality – and scowled.

"How can you eat so much in the morning?" she asked.

Pixley smiled and stabbed a sausage.

I also tucked into my plate, piled high with bread, cheese, jam, and butter. Chewing thoughtfully, I sat back and took in the high ceilings and French windows onto a small terrace. A white curtain fluttered in the breeze. Even the small tables, piled high with continental and English breakfast delicacies, were spaced in an orderly yet delightfully nonchalant way.

Ruby stirred her tea rhythmically. "Are you feeling better after yesterday, Henriette?"

She bit into a crusty piece of bread, sending crumbs flying onto the table. "Much better. It was something I ate for lunch – perhaps a bad oyster."

"A bad oyster?" I echoed. Surely Henriette's budget didn't run to oysters at lunch. "Sounds like quite the lavish lunch."

"Oh yes, I could never have afforded it myself – even famous models make very little money. Miss Elizabeth and Mr Reggie invited me, though I knew they would interrogate me about my aunt, the show, and Yvonne. But I let them. A free lunch is a free lunch. And I dream of becoming a professional model one day in New York."

"Would you like to become a mannequin in a shop?" I asked.

"Pah. They are not models – they are furniture!"

"Yes, of course. You would make a splendid model," I said doubtfully, as Henriette's recalcitrant character wouldn't carry her as far as the train station, let alone New York. On the other hand, she seemed to bend others to her will.

Henriette frowned at her coffee. "Miss Elizabeth and Mr Reggie insisted I order the oysters."

"Did they eat the oysters as well?" asked Ruby.

Henriette tapped her finger against her nose. "I thought of that. We all ate the same meal – we were sharing it with some champagne. I didn't eat or drink too much as I knew I needed to be prepared for the show, and it would never do to have a full stomach."

She sighed. "Fortunately, none of that matters now. Yvonne is dead, and so she cannot run the business into the mud. Or is it the ground?"

Pixley dabbed the corners of his mouth. "What makes you say that? She seemed most efficient."

Henriette banged her fist on the table, sending crockery rattling. "Yvonne was efficient, yes, but it was at the expense of all the people around her. She'd do anything to please my auntie, and my aunt believed all her lies."

"Why did your aunt trust her so much?" asked Ruby.

"Auntie only trusts a few people and treats them like princesses and princes. And she just wanted to make beautiful gowns, not run a business."

"I can sympathise with that," sighed Ruby.

"Ah yes, you would. I heard Auntie wants you to be the new designer, but I doubt you could fill her shoes," said Henriette.

"I believe Ruby's feet are at least two sizes larger than Madame Lafitte's," quipped Pixley.

Henriette's eyes narrowed at Ruby. "But Yvonne would have found a way to get rid of you. She would never have let you design Auntie's clothes."

"Why not?" I asked.

"Because she must have someone she can control. Someone she can manipulate, yes?"

"She wouldn't have manipulated me," squeaked a voice from behind me.

Ruby turned. "We haven't been formally introduced. I'm Ruby Dove. Do you prefer Virginie or Mademoiselle Corbin?"

"I'm Virginie."

Virginie's dusty-rose silk pyjama suit complemented her

bright reddish-pink lipstick. She also wore a fabulously large emerald ring set in gold, one that could scarcely be bought on a model's salary. At least according to what Henriette had just told us.

With one lithesome movement, she slipped into the chair next to me and folded one leg underneath herself.

Pixley put down his fork. "We were just discussing the tragedy this morning. Were you in the crowd outside Dr Fischer's room?"

Ruby put a hand on Pixley's shoulder. "You'll have to forgive Pixley – he's a journalist, so he's rather direct sometimes."

"A journalist!" Virginie's high-pitched voice rose two octaves higher. "Are you a fashion journalist? Which magazine?"

"Well, I'm more of a newspaper man myself, but I have dabbled in the fashion pages. As you can see, I dote on menswear." Pixley rubbed his beloved red jumper, a special gift from a certain Ukrainian designer.

Ruby shot Pixley a withering look.

"As a journalist," he continued, "I must have your opinion on what happened to the unfortunate Mademoiselle Jourdain. Care to speculate?"

"Speculate?" Virginie asked, as if she were a spelling bee contestant.

"He means tell us who murdered her," said Henriette.

"Murder?"

"Why do you say murder, Henriette?" asked Ruby nonchalantly.

"Berthe said it was murder," said Henriette. "She found Yvonne's body, didn't she? Or was it you, Mr Pixley?"

"I was the second unfortunate soul on the scene, after Berthe. I had come down to speak to Dr Fischer, but alas, he was on his morning walk." He sipped his tea, gazing at Virginie and Henriette. "If it was murder, who did it?"

Virginie held her teacup to her lips and hummed an unrecognisable tune.

She seemed perfectly batty. What did Maurice see in her?

Henriette blew out her cheeks. "Yvonne had many enemies, so it is difficult to say."

"That may be so, but the timing is curious," said Pixley. "It happened right after Madame Lafitte's retirement announcement. Who stood to lose something if Yvonne took over?"

"Maurice lives at the hotel without paying rent, so that may have ended. She might have also found a way to stop funding Dr Fischer's flat in the Latin Quarter."

"What else?" asked Pixley.

Henriette opened her mouth and then closed it.

"Go on." Pixley hitched his chair closer. "It's just between us."

"Sometimes I hear whispers. Whispers about the accounts, and maybe some underhanded – or is it overhanded – deals."

"Do you know anything else about the deals?" asked Ruby. "Or the accounts?"

She shook her head and crossed her arms. "But there's the hotel staff, who might have lost their positions – or what's left of them. Omar and Berthe, I mean. A few weeks ago, Yvonne sacked six hotel workers without notice." She paused. "And even us models might have been threatened. Though Auntie wouldn't have allowed Yvonne to fire me."

"Models?" Virginie goggled. "She would have kept me as a model. Everyone says I'm the best, especially dearest Maury."

Ruby's teacup clattered in its saucer.

"Virginie lives in a fantasy," said Henriette. "Yvonne wouldn't have hesitated to fire you, especially after you vanished yesterday."

This was my chance. "Why did you disappear yesterday?"

Virginie returned to humming and staring at the flowers on her teacup.

"I do not know where she was yesterday, but I'm sure she was going to meet a lover after the dinner at Maxim's," said Henriette with malicious glee. "She was dressed for such a night. A woman knows these things."

Virginie sipped her tea, her pinkie held high in Henriette's direction. She might as well have treated her to a two-fingered salute.

"A sophisticated woman of the world such as yourself must understand these things," said Pixley. "But returning to our earlier subject, why would Yvonne sack the staff?"

"She liked control, that one," said Henriette. "The staff were not loyal to her, so she wouldn't trust them. She would want to... how do you say? Start fresh."

Ruby shifted in her seat. "What happened between the time you fell ill and the time Berthe and Pixley discovered Yvonne's body?"

"I was ill all day and all night," said Henriette. "I did walk around once, perhaps at one or two in the morning, when I saw Mr Pixley and Mr Reggie come in, singing. That is all."

Elizabeth Ryland brushed past with a toast rack and a cup of coffee. She turned and put a hand on Henriette's shoulder. "So glad you're feeling better, my dear, after the performance you gave."

She turned and marched away.

"Peculiar woman." Henriette mumbled more to her plate than to her breakfast companions.

"Decidedly." I tried to refocus our conversation. "And did you see anything this morning?"

"No, but I heard a commotion in the corridor. That is all."

Ruby persisted. "Something was curious about the body.

Yvonne was wearing a sapphire velvet gown with a deep plunging line in the back. Does that sound familiar to you?"

"That velvet gown I ought to have worn at the show yester-day?" Henriette's eyebrows rose. "Yvonne changed her mind at the last minute, so I wore that silly frock instead."

17

A toddler pushed her sailboat onto the green, placid pond and clapped her hands. Her tiny reddish hands recalled the puzzling redness of Yvonne's ears. Perhaps a peculiar poison had caused it? But I'd have to save my thoughts for later – after we'd finished answering Inspector Toussaint's questions.

The inspector held up welcoming hands at the blue sky on this glorious morning, a stark contrast to the one we'd left behind at the hotel. We were winding around a lush green pathway near the hotel, into a nearby park. In contrast to English landscaping ideas, the park's straight pathways led to angular crossroads, bisected by a reflecting pool. The hedges, grass and trees were contained and tidy. Red and white tulips burst from their round beds, defying their confinement by falling into the grass surrounding them. Whilst I appreciated the orderly effect, I preferred a more unruly version of nature.

"Thank you for agreeing to chat in the park," said the inspector. "Can't stand being cooped up with all those officers."

Albert trailed after him, head buried in his notebook.

Toussaint looked sideways at the two of us. "It's a pity your friend Mr Hayford couldn't join us."

"I left a note for him," I said. "I expect he popped out to the chemist for a little tummy fizz. He was fairly sozzled last night."

Ruby shot a glance at me, clearly worried I'd said too much. Pixley had vanished shortly after breakfast. He must have been following his journalist's nose somewhere – I just hoped it wasn't into trouble.

Toussaint scratched his neck. "Yes, yes. No matter, we'll locate him later, won't we, Albert?"

Albert clicked his heels together.

"This isn't the military, Albert. A simple 'yes, sir' will do."

Albert's feet moved an inch but then stayed put. "Yes, sir."

"As for the two of you, I gather you're both guests of Madame Lafitte, but I must know if you have any connection to Mademoiselle Jourdain."

"Yvonne made the arrangements for Fina and me once we arrived, and she also approved Fina to become a model for the show," said Ruby.

"But it was Henriette's idea," I added.

"This Henriette Giroux is everywhere already," said Toussaint. "What's your impression of her?"

We passed a merry-go-round filled with children shrieking from joy and terror on their animal steeds. One little girl slapped the side of her painted pony, urging it forward, whilst a little boy gripped the neck of his seal for dear life. Parents encircled the ride, some shouting encouragement, whilst others looked on, simply amused by the spectacle.

As Ruby paused amidst the din, I spoke. "Henriette is a force of nature. She has very definite ideas about right and wrong, which probably made it hard for her to get on with Yvonne."

"Though not enough to harm Yvonne," put in Ruby. "If that's what you're suggesting."

"Interesting," said Toussaint. "The Mademoiselle Giroux I saw this morning seemed to lack this 'force', as you call it. Yes, most interesting..." He trailed off, staring at a snail crossing their path. "Anything else?"

"Henriette was supposed to wear the gown Yvonne was wearing – or rather, her corpse was wearing – at the show yesterday," said Ruby. "Yvonne made a last-minute change in the programme."

"Henriette looked stunning in that velvet gown, so it's peculiar that Yvonne told her to wear an ill-fitting, ill-suited frock," I said.

"Hmmm...so you believe Mademoiselle Giroux killed Mademoiselle Jourdain because she made her wear this frock rather than the velvet gown?"

Ruby said quickly, "Not necessarily, Inspector. We're simply telling you what we know."

"Please, do go on, Miss Dove. You were about to say something more?"

"Ah yes, well," she said, in an uncharacteristic tangle of interjections.

I couldn't help myself. "The thing is, Inspector – Yvonne pinched some of Ruby's designs."

A flock of pigeons in front of us took flight, offering Ruby ample time to glare at me.

Behind us, Albert's pencil scribbled furiously.

"You see," continued Ruby. "Fina spotted one of my designs in a London shop featuring Madame Lafitte's creations. Though I did not discover this until yesterday, I intended to confront Yvonne, and possibly Madame Lafitte."

"Though it sounds as if you did not," he said.

"Well, I did speak to Yvonne before the show, but she said she was too busy to discuss it."

"Why did you confront Mademoiselle Jourdain rather than Madame Lafitte? Surely Madame Lafitte was responsible."

"Yvonne was the one responsible for the business, and she was going to run the business after Madame Lafitte's retirement," I said.

Toussaint halted. "Pardon. Did you say *retirement*?"

"Madame Lafitte announced last night that she planned to retire, and Yvonne would assume all aspects of the business," said Ruby.

"But who would create the designs?" Albert's voice came up sharply behind me.

"Excellent question, Albert," said Toussaint.

Ruby smoothed her skirt. "Madame Lafitte invited me to become the designer."

"Well, well, Miss Dove." The inspector bounced on the balls of his feet. "Looks as if you're very *entwined* with this business."

"Sounds like a motive for murder to me, sir," said Albert.

Ruby shot back, "I'm not sure how it's a motive. Even if I clashed with Yvonne, I'd still need her expertise to run the business. I haven't a clue about that."

The inspector pointed to a long park bench, tucked behind a statue of a mischievous Pan, prancing on his cloven hooves.

"Let's sit for a moment, shall we?"

Ruby and I sat next to Toussaint. Albert stood behind us, as if he were guarding us against a potential attack. Perhaps from the pigeons.

Then I spied something peculiar.

The inspector was unlacing his shoes and pulling them off. "That's much better. Though I have nothing but contempt for German politics, I must say their view of the natural body is very attractive. Wouldn't you say so, Miss Dove and Miss Aubrey-Havelock?"

Though Ruby had more definite ideas about decorum, even I found this behaviour, well, at the very least, surprising. But if the inspector's ideas of bodily freedom were adopted, I feared a mass fainting fit from the unleashing of foot odour upon the population.

Ruby sat up a little straighter. "Look here, Inspector, if we might focus on the matter at hand, Fina and I would be most appreciative. It's been a tiring few days for us."

Toussaint surveyed Ruby. I had the distinct impression she had just passed some unknown test. He grunted, as if he were laughing to himself. "But of course. As you can tell from my questions, I suspect foul play was involved in Mademoiselle Jourdain's death. Tell me about your movements yesterday, after the show."

"I intended to speak to Yvonne or Madame Lafitte after the show about the designs." Ruby played with the catch on her bag. "Unfortunately, Henriette had this mishap—"

"Yes, Monsieur Abelli told me. Most unfortunate."

"In the chaos that followed, I couldn't speak to Yvonne or Madame Lafitte, particularly as Madame Lafitte had slipped out early from the show."

I put in, "She's apparently a recluse, so she leaves her own shows early."

"Before arriving in Paris," Ruby said, "I had already marked Madame Lafitte's offices on my old Paris map, so simply took a taxi to the House of Lafitte workshop to speak to her."

"And? Did you – speak to her, that is?"

I held my breath.

Ruby rubbed her nose. "No, Inspector. I lost the courage as soon as I arrived. As I couldn't find a taxi, I spent at least thirty minutes deciphering how to travel to Maxim's via the metro. In fact, I had to abandon a few metro lines because of my dreadful sense of direction. That's why I was late to the dinner."

I gazed at Ruby.

She appeared perfectly natural from the outside, and indeed, the inspector seemed convinced by this explanation.

But he didn't know what I knew.

Whenever Miss Ruby Dove rubbed her nose, it meant she was lying.

18

Attila purred happily on my lap, both of us taking in the afternoon sun on our tiny balcony. As long as I didn't scratch Attila's belly, we remained friends.

"But why did you lie to Inspector Toussaint?" I asked.

"I was simply playing for time," said Ruby. She applied a new lipstick she had bought before our departure to Paris. It was a slightly brighter red than her usual subdued tones. Nothing too splashy for Ruby Dove.

She puckered her lips in the looking glass.

"There. Now I'm ready for anything."

"You still haven't told me *what* you lied about," I said. "It's clear you weren't telling the whole truth about your visit to House of Lafitte. And I suspect the inspector wasn't entirely convinced, either."

"Pish." She waved her favourite blue handkerchief, the one her grandmother in St Kitts had given her. Sometimes, I thought Ruby was closer to her grandmother than her parents. But perhaps it was just that her grandmother had a way with words.

"He probably doesn't believe anything I told him," she said. "We'll discover the miscreant before he does, anyway."

I sighed and tapped my foot.

Her eyes fixed on my tapping foot. "You're quite right, Feens. It's cheeky to hide anything from you. The story I told was completely truthful, save one omission."

"Which was?"

"I spied Maurice leaving the Lafitte workshop."

"And?"

"Yvonne said Maurice went with Dr Fischer to Henriette's room after her fall. That means either she or Maurice was lying."

"Perhaps Maurice wanted a private word with Madame Lafitte?"

"About what?"

I frowned. "The whereabouts of Virginie?"

"Even if we leave aside who was lying and why, there's the issue of the briefcase."

"Briefcase?" I shook my head. "Sorry I sound like a parrot, but I'm not following."

"I watched Maurice enter the building. I held back because I wasn't keen to meet him on the stairs."

I stroked Attila and smiled inwardly, wondering how Ruby really felt about Maurice.

"The point is that he had a large briefcase when he went in, but when he came out, it was bulging. So much so that bits of paper were sticking out. And his eyes were darting about in a most suspicious manner."

"So you followed him."

"I tried. I hailed a taxi and told the driver to follow."

"Thrilling!"

"It was, for a few minutes. Then I completely lost sight of him."

"I didn't notice any briefcase when he entered Maxim's."

"Nor did I. He must have left it somewhere. And as for me,

my driver became rather lost, which is why I was late to the dinner."

"Only ten minutes."

"Enough to raise Yvonne and Madame Lafitte's hackles." She chuckled. "Speaking of taxis and arrivals, did you notice who returned to the hotel with us last night, after the dinner? I know we all split up in taxis, but I couldn't quite picture if everyone had actually returned."

"Is it important?"

"Haven't a clue, but I wanted to ask you whilst your memory is fresh. It's so much stronger than mine!"

Attila's blue eyes bore into me, as expectant as Ruby's. I squeezed my eyes shut, picturing the scene. "Yes, I remember we stayed behind in the lobby since Pixley and Reggie rode together in another taxi. When they arrived, it was the final taxi. Though they ultimately left the hotel to paint Paris red, or some such nonsense."

I furrowed my brow. "I still don't see why that matters if Yvonne was alive at that point."

"I'm not certain why it matters, either. Yet."

Attila hopped off my lap and dived underneath my bed. Scuffling ensued as one white paw stretched out from underneath the counterpane hanging over the side.

"A creature must be under the bed," I joked.

Ruby stiffened and gaped at the bed. "You don't think it's a…"

To my utter astonishment, a small round brown animal scurried across the floor, making for the exit as fast as its tiny legs would carry it.

Ruby leapt onto a footstool and used it to climb atop a tallboy in the corner.

"Feens! It's, it's a—!"

"Such a cute baby hedgehog!" I dashed after it, with Attila

not far behind. In a flash, I scooped up the wobbling blob with the hem of my dress and popped it into my pocket.

"It's a rodent, Feens!"

"No, no, it's an *Erinaceidae*, which is part of the family *Eulipotyphla*. They're more like shrews than rodents. My father and I used to play with them in our garden."

"I don't care which blasted family they belong to. Just remove the creature now!"

Though I rarely like to apply the word 'hysterical' to any female, much less the cool and collected Miss Ruby Dove, I'm afraid the word described her behaviour at this moment quite well. Whilst I knew she didn't care for hedgehogs, I had no idea her fear would drive her to stand on furniture.

"I'll just pop her downstairs and see what Omar fancies we should do."

But just as I reached the door, the knob began to turn slowly, seemingly of its own accord.

I twisted the knob and flung open the door.

Pixley stood in the doorway, a sheepish grin on his face. "Hullo, hullo. I wasn't certain if the door was locked, and I don't have a key. Sorry if I startled you."

"Why didn't you simply knock?" Ruby was still perched on the tallboy.

"Ah, well. I was trying to avoid that frightful sergeant."

"Indeed. The police are looking for you," I said.

"They can wait. Let me show you something."

"We've had a little excitement, so you'll need to wait a moment." I pointed to my bulging pocket. "We found a hedgehog, or rather, Attila found a baby hedgehog in our room."

"Get rid of it, Feens!"

"This place is becoming a regular zoo." Pixley squinted over my shoulder. "I say, Ruby, what are you doing on that tallboy?"

She crossed her arms. "I don't like hedgehogs."

"I'm not an acolyte of the little blighters, but it would take more than a spiny ball to convince me to climb that tallboy."

"It's not rational, Pix," I whispered. "Don't tease her."

"Her otherwise perfect personality makes it irresistible."

"Can't you see she's terrified? Distract her whilst I figure out where to take the beastie."

"What are you two whispering about?" Even in a state of terror, Ruby's curiosity couldn't be suppressed.

"Nothing!" I called over my shoulder. "Just discussing your friend."

I leaned over again. "How did the beastie enter the hotel and climb to the second floor? And where ought I to take her now?"

"Ah, I have information on both points," said Pixley. "As to the first, a little bird told me that Maurice keeps hedgehogs in his room. Berthe refuses to clean his room as a result."

"Well, that should put a damper on any budding romance between him and Ruby."

"Are you two discussing me?" called Ruby again.

"No, I was just saying that anyone who would let in a hedgehog must be a complete booby," I said, trying to find a word rhyming with 'Ruby'.

Returning my gaze to Pixley, I whispered, "So we know how the hedgehog found the second floor since Maurice's room is just along the corridor. What was the second point you wanted to make?"

"I found something of related interest."

"You're just as mysterious as Ruby when she's almost discovered a murderer," I sighed. "Will you come along with me to Maurice's room?"

He bowed. "But of course."

Then he called over my shoulder, "We'll be back in a jiffy, dear Ruby. You can leave your pedestal now."

"You're not amusing, Pixley Hayford," Ruby shot back.

He chuckled. "Back on top form, aren't you?"

We closed the door and padded along the thick rug until we reached Maurice's room. The door was slightly ajar.

I tapped on the door. "No wonder the sweeties escape."

No reply was forthcoming, so Pixley pushed open the door with a finger. Despite Berthe's lack of attention to Maurice's room, his quarters were just as orderly and simple as his personal appearance.

Quickly, I advanced towards a glass tank and wire cage near the window. A large hedgehog drank from a dish, sending ripples across the water, whilst another, smaller one appeared to be napping in a suntrap. I lifted the lid, carefully extracted the ball of spines from my pocket, and lowered her into the tank. I backed away, letting her regain her bearings.

"Look at this, Red." Pixley held up a scrap of paper with dates, numbers, and franc signs.

27 juillet – Printemps – F 452 – livraison retardée

4 août – Boutique Jean-Michel – F 139

5 août – Bon Marché – F 571 - livraison retardée

There were many more lines, all similar. "What's it mean?" I asked.

"Not a clue, but I'm drawn to anything with franc signs."

"Let's show it to Ruby."

We tiptoed back to our room with the paper but sans hedge-hog, much to Ruby's relief.

Once she'd climbed down from her perch, she surveyed the note. "I'm not certain of its significance, either. '*Retardée*' means some sort of delay. And those numbers must be dates and sums of money – quite substantial ones, at that. But I'm sure all will become clear. Now, I believe you said Pixley had something to show us?"

Ruby and I slipped on our shoes and followed Pixley as he strode to the end of the corridor – away from the spiral staircase – towards a portrait of a plump, rosy-faced man with brown curls and a rifle in his hand. Not to my taste, but I supposed it must have been some royal personage. The painting itself wasn't particularly skilful, at least to my untrained eye.

Pixley bent down under the frame and ran his forefinger along a seam in the green wallpaper.

Another seam ran from underneath the painting to the floor. Pixley held up a triumphant finger and slid the painting to the side, revealing how the seams formed a rectangle. He pressed a little round circle where the painting had been, and a door popped open!

We filed in silently behind him and shut the door.

"Blast it. Where's the cord to the light?" he whispered.

"Don't you have a lighter?" I hissed.

"Half a moment. I'll search my bag," said Ruby.

"You have a lighter, Ruby?" I asked, disbelieving her words.

"I left mine somewhere," said Pixley.

"I think you left it with me," she grumbled. A blessed flicker of light soon followed. "Here," she added. "You take it, Pix."

"Just as well," he said. "I found the cord, but the light has gone out. I suppose we'll need to make the best of it. Follow me down these stairs. Be careful – they're slippy."

"Why are we here if you've already been? Can't we leave?" I whined.

The light flickered towards me as Pixley turned around.

"Careful with the lighter! It's awfully close to my hair," I said.

"Where's your spirit of adventure, Red? You're not usually so cross."

Ruby put her hand on my back. "Here, Feens. Take this."

She placed a hard, round object in my hands.

"What am I supposed to do with this?"

"Put it in your mouth. Trust me," she said.

I popped it in and ran my tongue over it. Chocolate. "Thanks – just what I needed. I'll follow you, Pix."

"You're a good egg, Red," he said in an alarming mixture of affectionate slang. "At least when you've eaten. Now, let's get to the bottom of these stairs."

"How did you find this place, you marvel?" asked Ruby.

"Simple, my dear Watson. I draw your attention to the literature supplied in your room, detailing the history of this hotel. It says the back staircase was installed well before the grand spiral staircase that gives this hotel its name. To make it even more enchanting, it's also said to be haunted."

"Delightful," I said. "A murder isn't enough. We must have a ghostie, too."

"The hotel encourages guests to use these rather rickety stairs?" asked Ruby.

"Not quite. They suggest that guests should enjoy the puzzle of opening the door to the stairway. After popping open the door, they should return to their rooms to avoid injury."

"And the ghost, I assume."

"Just so, Watson number two," Pixley said. "The ghost – Clotilde Féret – haunts this hotel because her lover died under mysterious circumstances in 1754. On these very stairs."

"Good Lord." I shivered. "So the hotel already has one unsolved murder."

"Don't scare Feens," said Ruby. "I should have known Pixley would have already learnt the history and layout of the hotel."

"Part of the service, madam." He chuckled. "In any case, I located the staircase on the first floor and climbed up. But I did not see how far down it went, hence our return."

Brushing past cobwebs, we descended into the gloom.

Wooden crates lined the floor, and a laundry bin attached to a pulley system sat in the centre of the room. It looked as though Berthe hadn't attended to the laundry lately, as the bin was overflowing with towels, staff uniforms, and bed linen.

"Isn't Yvonne's room on the ground floor? Along with the rest of the staff?" I asked.

"You read my mind," said Ruby.

"Now you mention it, that's important because you cannot enter the corridor of those ground-floor rooms without walking past the registration desk. Omar said there's someone there at all times," said Pixley.

"Surely Omar isn't stationed there all the time. When does the man sleep?" I asked.

"Precisely," said Ruby. "We ought to investigate further." She halted abruptly on the stairs, almost re-creating the collision she'd experienced the day before, except with me in the role of the injured party. "Listen! Do you hear that?"

"What?" whispered Pixley.

I leaned over the railing, towards the wall that separated us from the hotel's rooms. A scraping noise was followed by someone humming. Oddly enough, it was the same tune Ruby had been humming yesterday: *Puttin' on the Ritz*.

"Feens can hear them," hissed Ruby. "She has sensitive ears."

"That's not all that's sensitive," murmured Pixley.

I held up a warning hand and leaned even further over the rail, just so my ear skimmed the grimy wall.

We can't talk now, mon chéri.

Those squeaks were unmistakable. Virginie.

Why the devil not? It's as decent a place as any, and my room is the last along the corridor. We'll keep our voices low.

Though I didn't recognise the voice, the language unmistakably belonged to Reggie Barrington-Loftus.

I'd still feel better if we weren't in the hotel. There are spies every-

where! Let's meet at our usual spot in two hours. Where fashion sits. The weather will be fine.

The door to the room banged shut. I strained my ears, but only footsteps were audible. Then I heard running water, probably from the bath.

I straightened up and recounted my findings.

Ruby tapped her teeth. "Most intriguing."

"So he likes his bread buttered on both sides," murmured Pixley.

I scratched my head. "What do you mean?"

"It means, dear girl, that he is singularly attractive to many *different* kinds of people, including yours truly."

"You fancy Reggie?" I squeaked. "He's such an idi—"

Ruby held up a hand. "Friends, this endearingly romantic conversation must wait. I know where they'll meet."

"Well, then, what are we waiting for?" asked Pixley. "Let's toddle off to wherever you think they're headed."

Ruby slid her hand down the bannister, moving forward. "In a moment. First, however, I think we have enough time to search Yvonne's room. I just hope the police are still busy upstairs."

19

I pressed my fingertips against the door, easing it inwards until it gave a satisfying click.

Pixley flicked on a switch in Yvonne's room, illuminating a chaotic mess of open cupboards, makeup-strewn tabletops, and an unmade bed. Even the paintings of the French countryside hung askew on the pale pink wall.

"Whew," said Pixley. "Did the Rozzers do this?"

Ruby scanned the room. "I overheard Toussaint berating Albert about something. Perhaps the uniformed men became a little overenthusiastic about their job."

She rolled up her shirtsleeves. "Right. You two have a look around here whilst I poke around her bathroom."

"What are we searching for?" asked Pixley.

"You're both keen observers, so I'm certain you'll find something."

Ruby slipped through the green door to the bathroom, leaving us to our task.

"Right." I blew a little puff of air against my fringe, realising it was time for a trim. "I'll search her clothes, and you search her desk."

"Aye, aye, Captain Red. Say, I quite like that. Captain Red."

"And Ruby would be?"

"Commander Dove. And I'll be First Mate Hayford."

"Onward, matey." I rifled through the frivolous nonsense of Yvonne's underwear drawer. Did all French women wear such frilly underclothes? They were pretty but looked singularly uncomfortable. And chilly.

Focus, Fina, focus. But what did I hope to find? Surely not anything like a secret panel. Perhaps something was out of place?

Then, as I drew back the umpteenth pair of pink lace cami-knickers, I spotted a tiny leatherbound notebook. I untied the string around it and flipped through the pages of scribbled numbers with dates. It was perfect gibberish.

"I found something, Pix."

"Love poems, I hope." He rubbed his hands together. "All I've found are frightfully insipid letters to a few friends or relatives, mostly of the 'I'm keeping well, how are you' variety."

Ruby popped her head round the door. "I'm finished in here. Her bathroom looks just like ours – a toilet, bathtub, and sink. What have you two found?"

I held out the tiny notebook in my hand.

Just as Ruby reached out to take it, heavy footsteps sounded in the corridor.

The door to Yvonne's room swung open, and Inspector Toussaint lumbered in, hands behind his back.

He jerked one hand forward, outstretched. "I'll take that if you don't mind, Miss Aubrey-Havelock."

He slowly scanned the notebook, wetting a finger each time he flipped another page.

Pixley edged towards the door.

With his head still bent, Toussaint said, "It's a pleasure to see you, Mr Hayford. You've been an elusive character this morning. We've been looking all over for you, haven't we, Albert?"

Albert had padded in, his moustache freshly coated with pomade.

Pixley wiped his smooth head with a handkerchief. "Apologies for my absence, gentlemen. I had fully expected to see you, but as a journalist, one must follow one's nose."

Toussaint swiftly spun on his heel, thrusting the notebook behind his back. "And where did your nose lead you, Mr Hayford?"

Pixley gave Ruby and I a sidelong glance.

The inspector held up a hand and waved at Ruby and me. "You two may leave the room – for now. We're still awaiting the post-mortem results, so I expect you to return to the hotel tonight. Under no circumstances are you to leave Paris."

"Poor Pix," said Ruby. "He dislikes the police even more than I do."

I couldn't say I enjoyed their company, either. Inspector Toussaint was intriguing, though, especially since Pixley had told me earlier about the rather strict turn the police had taken in Paris. French politics was rather chaotic at the moment, so I supposed I shouldn't be surprised.

As usual, Ruby seemed to be reading my mind. "Inspector Toussaint seems to have more imagination than most police I've met."

Then she shuddered. "But I dread the day someone like Albert becomes an inspector."

We wound our way around the maze of corridors on the ground floor. A small door opened, and a large maid ambled out, her face obscured by the tower of blankets she carried.

Her gait was unmistakable, however.

"May I help you with those blankets, Berthe?" I asked.

"*Merde!*"

The blankets tumbled to the floor. "Mademoiselle, you gave me such a fright!" Berthe held a hand over her heart." What are you doing here?"

Ruby folded the blankets into neat rectangles and handed them back to Berthe. "Apologies, Berthe. We're all a bit jumpy after what happened. Fina and I were simply, well, sleuthing a bit."

Berthe pulled at her ridiculous lace maid's cap. "Miss Dove, I do not approve of such sleuthing. It is dangerous, you understand?"

Ruby gave her a light-hearted cluck in return. "Surely not, especially as Yvonne probably died in her sleep. Just one of those unfortunate, inexplicable accidents of nature or life."

"Then why are you sleuthing, as you say?"

"Well, if you must know, we want to discover who stole my designs, so we were searching for clues in Mademoiselle Jourdain's room."

It was a rather thin pretext, but Berthe seemed to buy it. "Ah, yes, I heard whispers about that around the hotel – the walls have ears."

"Do you mean the ghost?" I asked.

"Speaking of walls having ears, do you ever use the back stairs?" asked Ruby. "The secret back stairs?"

Berthe shrugged. "Yes, from time to time, but not often. It is too dusty, and I sneeze."

"Then what do you use it for?" I asked.

"If we have a very famous person in the hotel, we have them use those stairs to avoid being seen." She elbowed Ruby playfully. "We even had the Zorro character and Don Juan in the hotel last year."

I blinked.

"You mean Douglas Fairbanks – the actor?" asked Ruby.

"Yes, yes! Mr Fairbanks. So charming, but a little on the old side, I think."

"Thrilling," Ruby said with girlish enthusiasm. "But even if they use the stairs, they still must leave by the front door, surely."

Berthe nodded. "It is the only exit from the hotel, as the renovations many years ago blocked the old rear door. No, the only way in or out is to climb from a window and down a drainpipe."

"Could someone climb down a drainpipe?"

"Perhaps. But not so recently. The drains have been under repair for over three months." Berthe snorted. "By a lazy good-for-nothing."

"So why would a famous person use the stairs?" I asked. "They still will be recognised if they use the front door."

"No, no, no, mademoiselle." She wagged a finger at me. "They wait in the doorway by Omar's desk until he tells them no one is about. Then they slip out of the hotel."

"Is someone at the desk at all hours?" asked Ruby.

"Omar is, or one of the staff."

"I thought you were the only two left," I said.

"Yes, it is horrible, that. Yvonne sacked the others a few weeks ago, so I must do everything now. Though it is easier for me than it was for the others. I am better."

"Did Madame Lafitte approve of Yvonne sacking everyone?" asked Ruby.

Berthe leaned against the wall. "I do not know. Perhaps. But perhaps not."

"So when does Omar sleep?" I asked.

"Sometimes I am at the desk, and sometimes Yvonne is there. I must do everything! We have a cook who makes breakfast for us, but she comes from outside and only speaks French. She cannot help guests. She is stupid."

Berthe's eyes narrowed. "Why are you so interested in these comings and goings? They have nothing to do with mademoiselle's designs."

Whilst I struggled with an answer, Ruby simply redirected. "I have a rather peculiar mind. May I ask you one more question?"

Berthe handed me her stack of blankets. "My arms are tired – please hold them."

Though I couldn't see Berthe or Ruby now, I could still hear them. "Yes, ask me your last question, Miss Dove."

"Did you notice anything out of the ordinary last night? Perhaps downstairs or near your room?"

"No. I was asleep when the guests returned from the dinner, so I did not see or hear."

"What about when you woke up this morning? Before you... entered Dr Fischer's room?"

"No." Berthe paused. "Yes, maybe. The lights – the electric – to our rooms had gone out."

"But wouldn't Omar have noticed? He was at the front desk."

Berthe sniffed. "No, because the – how do you say? The little box with the electric. It is only for the rooms here. Not anywhere else."

"So Yvonne's room would have been dark," said Ruby. "That *is* intriguing."

20

I blinked in the weak sunlight outside the hotel. "I'll wager you won't tell me why the electrical cut is significant, nor where we're going now. And won't Pixley be upset that we've disappeared?"

"Dearest Feens, you are so patient with me." Ruby opened the door to a taxi.

I must have looked perplexed by this rather wanton use of our meagre funds.

"I have plenty of money left from the cheque Yvonne sent me, and we simply haven't the time to take the metro," she said.

So we entered the warm taxi, and Ruby handed the driver a folded note. The car lurched into afternoon traffic.

Ruby snapped her handbag shut and nestled into the seat. "To answer your question about Pixley, I wouldn't be surprised if he pries more information out of Toussaint than the other way around."

"True, though Inspector Toussaint seems as clever as any policeman we've encountered before."

"Yes, *and* I hope it will prove to our benefit." She frowned. "Tell me about that notebook the good inspector confiscated."

I closed my eyes, conjuring the first page in my mind. "Do you have a pen and paper? I'll draw it for you."

Ruby rummaged in her capacious handbag and pulled out what appeared to be a silver cigarette case at first, but was actually a case for a notepad and a tiny pen. Quintessential Ruby Dove.

I scribbled, glancing up from time to time to avoid becoming queasy. Fortunately, we were now sailing along a long, straight boulevard. The tip of the Eiffel Tower loomed once again between the gables atop the white apartment buildings that lined the road. I found it remarkable how it managed to be peeking over your shoulder, no matter where you were in Paris.

"Here." I held out the paper.

11/5 – 32F
13/5 – 30F
15/5 – 33F
20/5 – 28F

"Impressive," said Ruby. "How did you remember all that? Especially the numbers – they would have been only a blur to me."

"I don't actually remember them," I said. "It's like my mind photographs them and files away the image. I couldn't have remembered the individual numbers without putting them all together in a picture."

"I daresay that's similar to this case. There are many little details that haven't produced a photograph of any kind yet. Early days, I suppose."

The taxi circled around an enormous column-like monument, coming to a halt in front of an impressive façade of stone archways and tall windows sparkling even on this suddenly cloudy day.

The driver waved an expansive hand.

"The Ritz."

Ruby paid whilst I stood with my mouth slightly open, staring at the surrounding splendour. The puzzle pieces finally fell into place – I should have realised Virginie's mention of 'where fashion sits' referred to the song about the Ritz. A commissionaire beckoned me, and I gladly followed with Ruby in tow.

As we stepped into the foyer, Ruby hooked her arm in mine and propelled me forward.

"We must try to make it look as if we belong here, as much as possible. Let's march past the desk with purpose."

Heeding her advice, I whispered to her as if I were in intense conversation. The wiry man at the registration desk gave us the slightest of nods.

Ruby's plan had worked so far, at least.

"Where are we going?" I tripped along on the balls of my feet, acutely conscious of the clack of our heeled shoes on the marble floor.

Ruby walked swiftly to a side corridor, though even a side corridor in the Ritz was a sight to behold. Plush rugs lined the floor, and elaborate chrome sconces gleamed in every alcove.

She leaned against the wall and exhaled. "I felt certain they'd stop us – or rather, stop me. But it's simply amazing how walking with purpose works in these smart places."

"I expect they'd rather avoid unnecessary fuss."

A small woman in a floaty, flowered tea dress scuttled past us, grasping a straw hat in her hand.

"We'd better get a move on," I said. "I fancy our loitering will look suspicious."

"That's it!" Ruby snapped her fingers. "Did you notice that woman's gown and hat? There must be a garden somewhere. That's why Reggie and Virginie mentioned the weather."

I sighed with relief. "I'm delighted we can avoid the dining room. That maître d' was so stiff that I fancied he'd throw us out on our ears."

"Did you see where the woman with the hat came from?"

"Around the corner."

I looked both ways and then marched towards a podium with another Cerberus guarding a main door, flanked by sets of French windows on either side. This one was younger and less imposing than the first, but his rigid posture and upturned nose indicated we had little hope of entering.

I also hoped that Ruby had a few more francs than I did in my purse. Tea at the Ritz must run to a few quid. The stylish clothes and hairstyles of those sunning themselves at small tables dotted around the open courtyard confirmed my fears.

"How about you distract him, and I'll sneak past?" Ruby suggested.

"Good Lord. Me? Distract someone?"

"Well, I certainly will distract him, but it will probably lead to a scene rather than to a diversion." She paused. "I've got it! Tell him you wish to surprise your great-aunt Agatha on her birthday, but you're not certain when she'll arrive. Then he'll let you wait in the garden without ordering."

I bit my lip and sighed. "Sounds implausibly plausible enough. I'll do it!"

"That's the spirit. I'll hide and will follow after he allows you in."

"But what will you do once you're in the garden?"

"Hide behind a bush? I spied several through the glass."

I raised my eyebrows. "Will it work?"

"If not, we can always tell our grandchildren about how we were summarily ejected from the garden of the Ritz."

Despite this rather dubious motive, Ruby's sudden enthusiasm was infectious.

I tentatively stepped forward.

"Confidence, Feens."

I threw back my shoulders, held my head high, and marched to the desk. The smell of early gardenias wafted through the door, along with sounds of lazy bees buzzing and even more languid chatter floating from beyond.

The young man smoothed his moustache. "May I help you, mademoiselle?"

I lifted my chin. "Yes, I'm looking for my great-aunt. Agatha. That's her name."

"Agatha." He arched one eyebrow. "And her last name?"

"Uh. It's, well, Havelock. Havelock-Aubrey."

Though it was accidental, I thought the reversing of my last name was a rather clever touch.

I turned my head, seeking Ruby.

The sight that met my eyes meant I no longer needed an excuse – Aunt Agatha or otherwise – to enter the garden of the Ritz Hotel.

21

A crowd of young women in stunning tea gowns and hats streamed in from all directions, like elegant locusts descending on a field.

The moustached young man calmly opened the French doors onto the courtyard, allowing the women to flood through.

Someone grabbed me from behind and propelled me deep into the crowd, through the French windows and onto the terrace. As the women gradually dispersed, I was pulled again to the side of the garden, near a statue of Dido and a pink rose bush. A small fountain burbled merrily away, replete with chirping songbirds shaking themselves from their dip in the bath.

"Pssst. Feens – move behind the statue."

Ruby popped her head out near Dido's feet. I scurried on the other side of Dido and crouched down.

"What the devil is going on?" I asked.

"Look – it's a fashion show!"

She was right. Those tea gowns were stunning for a reason: they were the latest designs. The women gathered along the rear hedge, forming two parallel queues. They floated down the pathway as a woman with a booming voice and an imposing bosom narrated the latest creations. Many of the French words for various fabrics were unfamiliar to me, but there was definitely something familiar about the show.

"Did you notice the green chiffon frock with the white hat?" I whispered.

"It's mine!" Ruby squeaked. She unbent herself and began to march towards the main pathway.

I weaved my arm between Dido's legs and caught her arm just in time. "Wait! Remember why we're here?"

"To solve two mysteries! One is the murder, and the other is who stole my designs!" Her voice was now a growl rather than a squeak. I had never seen her so agitated.

Then came another squeak.

It was Virginie Corbin, naturally. "I told you, I'm not going through with it. Do you understand, Reggie? I'm finished. We're finished."

Still grasping Ruby's arm, I piloted her to a table tucked behind the hedge and the Dido statue. And, as a waiter just happened to be trotting by, I covertly ordered a plate of petits-fours. After all, a girl must keep up her strength.

"I say, keep your voice down," came Reggie's voice.

"Don't tell me how to behave. In fact, I'm through following your orders. See where it's landed me? The police will suspect us, and I'm certainly not going to the guillotine for a cheap, toffee-nosed gambler like you."

Virginie had an impressive grasp of English insults.

From this vantage point, we could see Reggie now, grinning at the girls on parade. "You haven't much choice in the matter, my girl," he said out of the corner of his mouth. "You're just as much in the soup as I am, and I'm certainly not going to let some little jumped-up, half-witted gold-digger haul me off to the blasted station, either."

"Half-witted? Jumped-up?"

"Keep your voice down, you nitwit," said Reggie.

"Yes, it's better to keep calm in these situations." Elizabeth Ryland jerked back a chair and scooted in next to Reggie and Virginie.

She plopped her handbag on the table and snapped at a passing waiter. "I'd like tonic water with lemon. And ice. Plenty of ice."

"Madam." The waiter barely paused before gliding away.

Elizabeth removed her gloves, finger by finger, levelling a calm gaze first at Reggie and then at Virginie.

When she'd finished removing her gloves, she slapped them on the table. "Now, you two, explain what exactly is going on. I'm a very busy woman, and I don't suffer fools gladly, let me tell you. In New York, we don't put up with these kinds of shenanigans."

"Virginie says she's finished with our little scheme. Her rather excitable imagination thinks we're going the gallows," said Reggie.

"That's not what I said. You're as stupid as your feet, Reggie. I said I wasn't prepared to go to the guillotine for *you*."

Elizabeth lit a cigarette and exhaled a long stream of smoke. "No one is going to the guillotine, gallows, or electric chair under my watch. In fact, no one is going to be questioned by the police – at least not about our activities."

"I say, but give a chap a moment—"

Elizabeth held up a warning hand. "Button it, Lord High-and-Mighty. In your world, titles talk. In my world, money walks. You can hurry back to the safety of your stately manor in England, but it will only get you so far when it comes to those pesky debts of yours."

She turned to Virginie. "As for you, sweetie, girls like you are a dime a dozen. No, make that a penny a dozen. You're not so precious that you can start making demands. Do I make myself clear, you two?"

She stood up, took the tonic water and lemon the waiter had set on their table, downed it in one gulp, and slammed it down.

"We were just leaving, *garçon*. Mr Barrington-Loftus will pay on our way out."

As Reggie and Virginie trailed behind Elizabeth, I spied Henriette striding past them in a pretty tea dress, turning and flouncing on the gravel path with the other models.

She had a ghost of a smile on her face.

Whether it was genuine or malicious was perfectly unclear.

I puckered my lips and gazed into our bathroom's looking glass.

"Are you almost ready, Red?" called Pixley from the other room. "You've been aeons, and Dr Fischer's expecting us at eight for his soiree."

"If we're late, it's because you couldn't stop chatting with your new best friend, Inspector Toussaint," I said.

I looked longingly at our grand standalone bathtub, with its gleaming pipes and roomy white basin. After the trials of the past two days, I longed to luxuriate and linger in that bathtub. Perhaps Ruby would solve this case this evening and I could do just that.

"Feens?"

Leaving my fantasy behind, I closed the bathroom door behind me and dropped a little curtsey with my green skirt. "What do you think of Ruby's new frock? I'm the first to wear it."

Pixley crossed his legs on the footstool. "Well, your togs are marvellous, as long as you remove that cat hair, Red."

He turned to Ruby. "That wine colour looks particularly fabulous, but I'm still rather foggy on why you're wearing these new creations to Dr Fischer's tonight."

"Ruby thinks someone may recognise one of the gowns as one of Madame Lafitte's, not realising they're actually Ruby Dove originals."

"And then what?" asked Pixley.

"And then we probe them about it further," said Ruby. "Maybe they'll reveal something more about what we overheard in the Ritz garden this afternoon."

"So you're convinced Elizabeth, Reggie, and Virginie are responsible? Do you think they have anything to do with the murder?"

I shuddered. "I don't think so – they used the words 'guillotine' and 'gallows' too casually."

"I agree with that," said Ruby, "though perhaps only one of them is the murderer." She rubbed her eye. "Talking of other news, I forgot to tell you that I telephoned one of the hotel maids whom Yvonne had sacked."

"How did you manage that?" I asked.

"I enlisted Omar's help. When I asked her about her typical duties, they sounded like those Berthe had. I also asked if she'd noticed anything peculiar going on – besides being sacked – but she was just as baffled as we are."

"I say, do you think Yvonne was losing her marbles?" asked Pixley.

Ruby gave him a rather doubtful look. "Yvonne struck me as both ruthless and intelligent, and not unstable. Erratic, perhaps, but quite sane."

He shrugged and slapped his thighs. "Since you've both finished dressing, I can now tell you what I learned from Inspector Toussaint."

Ruby and I laughed.

Pixley's forehead wrinkled. "I say, what's so funny?"

"Even though Toussaint was interviewing you, you managed to squeeze more out of him," I said.

He put a hand to his chest and bowed. "But of course, dear lady." Then he became business-like. "First, the pathologist says Yvonne died of heart failure."

"My foot! She was the picture of perfect health," I said. "Even if that were the case, why was she in that velvet gown in Dr Fischer's room?"

"And what about the red marks around her ears?" asked Ruby.

Pixley held up his hands. "I'm only the messenger! The police found pills in her room to calm irregular heartbeats and confirmed that others knew of her condition. She'd often speak of it."

Ruby raised one eyebrow. "Therefore, she died of heart failure?"

"Toussaint agreed the whole setup was suspicious, but police bigwigs are pressuring him to wrap up the case."

"So the official explanation would be that she simply had a heart attack on Dr Fischer's bed?" I asked.

"Something like that," said Pixley. "The story would be that Yvonne and Dr Fischer planned to toddle off to a swanky night-club, hence her equally swanky gown. Before they left, she had a heart attack and collapsed on the bed. He panicked and moved her so it looked like she was sleeping on top of the bed. He then walked the streets of Paris until early morning, ruminating on his little problem. Then he returned to complete bedlam."

"But Berthe said Dr Fischer rang the bell for an early breakfast. How does he explain that?" asked Ruby.

Pixley rubbed his chin. "Good question. Toussaint didn't mention it, but I assume either Berthe was mistaken, or Dr Fischer absent-mindedly pulled the bell for breakfast."

"The latter option seems ludicrous," I said.

Pixley held up a finger. "I just remembered something else.

Toussaint said there were bruises on her left leg and a slight bump on her left temple."

"Did those occur before or after death?" I asked.

"The pathologist was uncertain."

I turned to Ruby. "Where does that leave us?"

"That washes out the suffocation theory I'd been considering because the pathologist would have detected it."

"How about an old favourite?" said Pixley. "Some unknown poison?"

"It's possible," said Ruby, "but I fancy the pathologist would have found some abnormality along those lines. Unless the pathologist was in a hurry."

"Which is also possible," said Pixley.

"What if someone surprised her?" I suggested. "What if she actually had a heart condition and died from it?"

"Perhaps. As you know, however, I belong to the sceptical school of thought." Ruby began to pace around a small rectangular rug. "My father is a great sceptic. The war did that to him."

"You don't mention him very often," I said.

Ruby ran a finger along the mantelpiece. "He'd always tell me to 'follow the swallow', meaning that people always return home, in a metaphorical sense. They return to their little habits and routines. And they also return to petty grudges or feelings of being wronged."

She rubbed her arm, as if she'd caught a chill.

Then she stared at the electric clock on a nearby table.

Suddenly, she lunged at the clock, picked it up, and, to my utter astonishment, kissed it.

"You little beauty!"

Pixley and I exchanged worried glances.

"Ah, Ruby, dear," said Pixley quietly. "I know the strain of the past few days—"

"Dash it, Pixley," said Ruby. "No need to speak to me like I'm a doddering fool."

She shook the clock until its little bell clanged. "Don't you see? This explains how she died!"

∿

THE DOOR to Yvonne's bathroom creaked open. Ruby switched on the light, but to no avail. The overhead light didn't even flicker, leaving the room in darkness.

"Aha!" cried Ruby. "I knew the bathroom light wouldn't work."

"What are you on about, dear one?" asked Pixley. "Enlighten us, please?"

"Most amusing, Pix." I fumbled around my bag, finally locating a torch I'd put in it after our adventure on the back stairs. "Do you want my torch, Ruby?"

I heard a scraping noise, like a chair being moved.

"Thank you, Feens. Could you shine the torch on the ceiling?"

Ruby's head appeared in the torchlight as she stood on the chair. "That's right. I'll just remove the lightbulb."

"Wait!" cried Pixley.

Ruby wobbled on her chair. Quickly, Pixley hugged her legs, preventing her from falling over.

"You frightened me! What is it, Pix?"

I heard the click of a switch and Pixley letting out a sigh. "I wanted to be certain the light was off so you didn't shock yourself."

"Thank goodness," she said. "I was a little carried away with my experiment."

Something white fluttered to the floor. I picked it up and held it to the light. "It's a scrap of linen. Is it important?"

Ruby was too intent on reinserting the lightbulb to answer. "There. Could you flick the switch again?"

The light came on, and Ruby grinned from her perch. "Perfect."

She dusted her hands together and climbed down from the chair. "Now that I've solved that problem, it's time for an experiment."

"Uh oh," said Pixley. "This sounds ominous."

"Rubbish," said Ruby brightly. She slipped off her shoes and stepped into the bathtub. She crouched down and then sprung up, lifting one foot over the side.

I wondered whether Ruby's hedgehog encounter had turned her brain.

Pixley crossed his arms. "Care to tell us about your little acrobatic routine?"

"You'll both agree that when you bathe, you step into the bathtub and then lower yourself down...correct?" As she said the words, she lowered herself into the basin.

We nodded.

"Now, let's assume I'm about to lower myself into a piping hot bath. Then I'm shocked."

"By your own nakedness?" Pixley chuckled.

Ruby lifted her eyebrows. "Be serious for a moment."

"Sorry. Yes, you're shocked – by electricity?" he asked.

"Precisely. What happens if you're jolted as you get into the bathtub?"

"You fall over." I waved my hands. "You fall over to the left."

Ruby pointed at her left leg. "If I fall over the edge of the bathtub to the left, I'll end up with a bruise on my leg here, and—"

"—a thumping great bruise on the side of your head," put in Pixley.

"You mean?" I gasped. "That's why she has those bruises?"

Ruby suddenly put a finger to her lips.

I held my breath, listening to the rustling noise behind us.

Someone was in Yvonne's room.

Pixley lifted each of his legs in an exaggerated motion, sneaking up on the bathroom door. Then he pushed it open with both hands.

"Hullo," he said. "What are you doing here?"

An open-mouthed Henriette gaped at us. She stood irresolute, her eyes moving towards Ruby in the bathtub.

Henriette turned on her heel and fled the room, slamming the door behind her.

"Well," I said. "That *is* peculiar."

Pixley turned back to Ruby. "What does Holmes have to say about that interruption?"

But Ruby was now leaning over pipes jutting from the floor near the bathtub tap. "Henriette is a prime suspect, though we can discuss that later. I don't want to lose my train of thought."

She straightened up and smiled. "Are you game for an adventure?"

Without waiting for our undoubtedly tenuous answer, she turned on the tap.

Pixley peered over the lip of the bathtub. "I say, you aren't going to drown us in there, are you?"

My mind was running along the same lines. "Are you sure you're feeling quite well?"

"Never better, Feens." She rolled up her sleeves and pointed at an electrical outlet where a small bedside lamp had been plugged in, sitting atop a stool. "See that outlet? What do you notice about it?"

I peered closer. "It has some black marks around it."

Pixley scratched his head. "Scorch marks?"

"That's my diagnosis," said Ruby. "I've plugged in the lamp next to it. I must say it's a rarity to have outlets in a bathroom, even for the continent."

"Maybe Yvonne had them installed," I said. "Omar said Yvonne enjoyed her deep baths."

She began searching her handbag, finally pulling up a ball of yarn. "I hope Madame Lafitte won't mind that I borrowed her yarn."

Pixley and I looked at each other again.

Unwinding the yarn, Ruby said, "You two think I'm barmy, but just humour me."

"Right-o," said Pixley.

"Here." Ruby handed him one end of the yarn. "See how one of the pipes from the floor to the bathtub is bent? Our murderer did that, so it creates a gap. That's where you can thread in this yarn."

Pixley's head disappeared as he leaned over. "Aye, aye. I've threaded the yarn into the pipe. Now what?"

"Look at this, Feens." Ruby turned on the tap.

I peered into the filling bathtub. The red yarn had snaked through the hole where excess water drained.

Ruby pointed at the hole. "When you normally fill the bathtub, this little hole prevents you from overfilling it, right?"

Pixley rose from his knees and joined us. "Deuced helpful, too. It's hard to know how much water you'll need."

"Since Yvonne liked deep baths," said Ruby, "one would presume she'd let the bathtub water rise as high as possible, which means it would hit this hole and then begin to drain, right?"

"Correct." I watched the water slowly rising in the bathtub.

Ruby stepped over to the lamp she'd plugged in on a stool near the bathtub. "Stand back, you two."

She held the lamp in her hand and moved towards the bathtub.

"Ruby? What are you doing?" There was definite alarm in Pixley's voice this time.

I stepped forward. "Just tell us what you're—"

Before I could finish, Ruby tossed the lamp into the water.

A sizzling, crackling noise came from the outlet.

And everything went dark.

"WHILST I APPRECIATE YOUR IMAGINATION, Miss Dove, I'm tempted to charge you with tampering with evidence from a crime scene," growled Inspector Toussaint. He rubbed one eye and sat on the edge of the bathtub.

Ruby's eyes glowed in the restored light of the bathroom. "If I'd asked permission beforehand, would you have let me throw a lamp into the water?"

"Well, no," he admitted. Then he wagged a finger at her. "It still doesn't excuse such behaviour."

I cleared my throat. "Inspector, my friend has just demonstrated how Yvonne Jourdain was likely electrocuted in her bathtub. Shouldn't you be praising her?"

"As the inspector says," Albert said, "you were tampering with valuable evidence."

Apparently, Albert's parroting of his own words was enough to change the inspector's mind. "You win, Miss Dove. Tell us precisely how this fiendish contraption worked."

"The red marks around Yvonne's earrings first gave me the idea, as did all the discussions of 'shock' around her death. If I hadn't been studying electrochemistry last term, none of this might have occurred to me. The scorch marks on the outlet – and the electrical outage on the night of her death – seemed to confirm the possibility."

"A recent lightning-strike case we had did show how an electrical shock can produce erratic patterns on the skin." Toussaint shook his head. "Though it's very difficult to identify if the person received the shock via water."

"Quite right," said Ruby. "I couldn't be certain, however, until I figured out *how* the murderer did it, and whether they needed to be present to commit the murder."

Pixley let out a low whistle. "You mean they didn't need to be here whilst Yvonne was bathing?"

I held up the scrap of linen that had fallen to the floor during Ruby's first lightbulb experiment. "Does this have anything to do with it?"

Ruby nodded. "First, the murderer had to ensure the overhead light wouldn't work, so they put this scrap of linen underneath the lightbulb, guaranteeing it wouldn't switch on."

"Why?" asked Toussaint.

"So Yvonne would be forced to turn on the lamp next to the bathtub instead."

"Because it was the source of the electrical current," said Toussaint.

Ruby moved towards the front of the bathtub, where the pipe had been bent. "Then our murderer needs to make sure there is an exposed wire that will touch the bathtub water. So what do they do?"

I scratched my head. "They cut a flex from another electrical fixture? Perhaps the lamp in their own room?" My mind raced. "They snip the flex from their own lamp, and then they have an exposed wire at one end and plug at the other."

"Hey presto!" said Pixley. "Then the murderer snakes it in

through the bent pipe leading into the bathtub, just as I did with the yarn. Then they plug it into the outlet."

Ruby smiled. "Imagine the scene. Yvonne enters the bathroom and tries to switch on the overhead light. It doesn't work, so she turns on the small lamp instead. Everything is normal so far. Then she fills the bathtub."

"Then she gets in." Toussaint stared at the water. "And the water rises to the overspill hole. Once it rises and hits that hole, the excess water goes down that hole – as it ought to – but it also hits the live wire!"

"Yes, the water is electrified now, and it shocks her," said Ruby quietly. "Either enough to kill her by electrocution, or at least enough to induce a heart attack. Then she falls over onto the floor, bruising her leg and hitting her head."

A soft silence blanketed the room as we all stared at the floor. Even though I'd never liked Yvonne, my fist tightened as I pictured her final indignity.

Albert's voice cracked, breaking our contemplation. "How would the murderer know that Mademoiselle Jourdain would take a bath after dinner at Maxim's? What if she had taken it before? Or not at all?"

Ruby bit her lip. "Our murderer is a risk-taker. On the other hand, once the device was set up, all the murderer had to do was wait."

"How would the murderer get into her room?" I asked. "What if Yvonne locked it?"

"I can answer that," said Toussaint. "The hotel keys are kept in a deplorable state – anyone can take them if they simply distract Omar."

I stared at the lamp, my mind whirring. "I'm still puzzled by the flex on the lamp. Wouldn't Yvonne notice another flex plugged in next to this lamp – the live wire? Or the fact that the flex would be visibly trailing from one of the pipes?"

"An excellent question, Miss Aubrey-Havelock." Toussaint turned to Ruby and smiled. "What say you, Inspector Dove?"

I had to admit the inspector was growing on me.

"Two possibilities spring to mind. First, we must consider the psychological angle. As long as everything is in its usual place, Yvonne wouldn't necessarily pay attention to the additional flex. After all, she expects to see a lamp in its usual spot, and there it is. She's not looking for anything out of the ordinary."

"And the second possibility?" asked Pixley.

Ruby handed Toussaint the lamp flex from our little experiment.

"By Jove," he said. "It's sticky."

"Whilst Yvonne is elsewhere," said Ruby, "our murderer slips into the bathroom, and then sticks cellulose tape or spirit gum to bind together the cut flex and the functioning lamp flex."

I nodded. "They snake the live wire flex into the bathtub pipes, plug it in, and affix the live wire flex to the functioning flex. That way, if Yvonne happens to look at it, it will just look like one flex since they're stuck together."

"Ingenious," breathed Pixley.

Inspector Toussaint rose to his feet. "Now we just need to identify the author of this ingenious scheme. Any ideas on that score, Miss Dove?"

Ruby rubbed her nose.

"Not at the moment, Inspector."

Pixley looked at his watch. "We must dash, Inspector. We're already late to Dr Fischer's soiree."

The door to the fashionably shabby garret creaked open.

"Ruby!" Maurice half-exclaimed and half-whispered. "And Fina and Pixley. Professor Fitzwilliam is just finishing his lecture. Now that you've arrived, the festivities may commence!"

The floorboards groaned in Dr Fischer's delightfully decrepit flat in the Latin Quarter, the one Madame Lafitte had mentioned at dinner last night. It seemed doubtful, however, that she would have condoned such a party in the wake of Yvonne's death.

Holding a finger to his lips, Maurice led us into a small room near the entrance. A pleasant voice perorating on African civilisations floated in through the other room. Maurice removed Ruby's jacket and carefully hung it on a peg. He then took mine and Pixley's and tossed them haphazardly onto the sofa.

I gently squeezed Maurice's arm as we walked towards the murmur of voices. "Why did Dr Fischer insist on the soiree?"

Maurice grimaced. "He said Yvonne would have wanted it."

"Had she ever attended before?" I whispered.

"No, she was too busy. But she did show up at the end sometimes. When guests were leaving."

The growl of a saxophone and the rumble of drums erupted from another room.

We caught up with Pixley. "Who comes to these soirees?" I asked him.

"I've heard they're absolutely ripping. Artists and intellectuals of all sorts practically beg to be invited to Dr Fischer's dos. Not quite as scandalous as some of those petting parties you heard about a decade ago, but still quite fun."

Before I could ask what a 'petting party' might be, the music swelled, and a tinkling piano solo broke into the steady hum of a jazz song. Pixley and I skipped into the room, following Maurice and Ruby into a gyrating, hopping, and whooping crowd.

I removed my shoes, like everyone else, and moved next to Pixley, who was all thumbs and elbows as he danced. The saxophone, drums, and piano grew louder and louder, until I expected someone would call the police.

Pixley handed me a lovely sweet red drink, and we moved towards the edge of the crowd. Maurice and Ruby danced near one another but not *with* one another. In contrast to Maurice's clipped speech, he was a smooth and fluid dancer.

In the corner, sipping a red drink like mine, Dr Fischer tapped his foot and beamed indulgently on the crowd. Next to him, the dapper little man in a bow tie who'd been giving the speech earlier leaned against a bookcase. This must be Professor Fitzwilliam.

The professor gestured with his wineglass at the dancing crowd. "Which one is your assistant, Leo?"

"Maurice is dancing with the lovely woman in dark red. He is a most able assistant, though sometimes I think I give him too much."

"Too much money?" asked Professor Fitzwilliam.

"No, no." Dr Fischer chuckled. "Too much work. The other

day, I walked in on him with stacks of papers everywhere, and I thought the poor man might faint."

"Who is that woman watching him with keen eyes?"

Dr Fischer adjusted his spectacles. "Virginie Corbin." He gulped his wine. "Just a model with my wife's business."

Virginie left off staring at Maurice and began prancing about with an assortment of men, briskly moving from one to another as if it were a traditional village dance.

I spotted Elizabeth in an alcove, talking excitedly to a small, balding man who was rapidly draining his tumbler of whisky. "I'll admit the French know how to make a baguette, but let me tell you, sir, there's nothing like a New York bagel. Yes, yes. Boiled to perfection, and soft and chewy as salt-water taffy on the Shore. New Jersey Shore, that is. You should try one when you're in the States..."

Her monologue continued with nary a breath in between sentences. The man swigged from his tumbler as if it were a shot glass.

Then the music ground to a halt, ending with a sour honk from the saxophone.

Henriette was the last dancer to stop twirling around, arms outstretched and hair flying.

Madame Lafitte entered, this time in a navy shift and pink slippers.

The saxophonist raised his eyebrows at Dr Fischer. "Please, everyone, carry on," said the doctor.

Across the room, Ruby cocked her head towards the entrance, where Dr Fischer and Madame Lafitte were exiting together. Finally understanding her meaning, I sprinted across the dance floor, nearly colliding with Madame Lafitte. I had grabbed a door handle just in time, stopping me from sliding into her.

Ignoring me, she and Dr Fischer strode swiftly from the room.

As the music became louder, I realised I couldn't eavesdrop from my position. Mounds of shoes lined one wall, and I couldn't hide behind them, so I settled on the bulging coat stand. I slipped behind a frightfully ratty fur coat. Recalling Ruby's point about how people only see what they expect to see, I surmised I'd look like a stuffed animal mounted on the wall.

Madame Lafitte's sing-song voice ranged the full chromatic scale. "Leo, darling, you must understand how this looks. I'm not one for putting on appearances, except where clothing is concerned. But even this is simply too gauche for words. Yvonne is laying on a cold slab in the morgue whilst your guests dance the night away?"

"I know, *meine süße*. We had already arranged the soiree, and Professor Fitzwilliam travelled from the Caribbean just to present his newest ideas to the salon. I couldn't very well cancel because your assistant—"

"Yvonne was my partner, Leo."

He sighed. "Partner, then. I couldn't cancel simply because she died of a heart attack. It is very sad and tragic, yes, but life must go on."

"Perhaps she didn't die of a heart attack."

Dr Fischer's voice rose. "Didn't die of a heart attack? Well, what, then? An incurable disease?"

I longed to tell them our discovery about Yvonne's ill-fated bath, but I thought I'd better keep quiet.

"You ought to know – she was in your room." Madame Lafitte paused. "Dear heart, I've ignored your little dalliances over the years, as I believe wives must make allowances. But to carry on in front of everyone in the hotel! And with Yvonne! Yes, we live our separate lives, but this is beginning to reflect poorly on the House of Lafitte's reputation. Not to mention your own."

Dr Fischer moved towards Madame Lafitte, circling his arms around her waist. He growled something in her ear, and Madame Lafitte giggled in response, saying, "my little goat" in French.

But then she straightened and adjusted her pince-nez. "This is a matter most grave, darling. Even if Yvonne meant nothing to you, the police are demanding answers. They're not satisfied with your story."

Someone nudged me, but I pretended not to notice.

The nudging continued, and a voice sounded in my ear, uncomfortably close. "Pardon, but are you a bear from the zoo?"

I soon found myself gazing into the dilated pupils of Reggie Barrington-Loftus.

"If you don't stop right this moment," Madame Lafitte barked at her husband, "then I shall be forced to take other measures."

Reggie put his hands over his ears. "I say, she's too loud. I expect it's too loud for bears in the zoo like you."

He was petting the fur coat wrapped around me.

Where were Ruby and Pixley?

Reggie held the fur coat taut, so I was pinned against the wall, my mouth muffled by the disgusting fur.

"I'm not a bear, but I lost at poker." Reggie continued in a high falsetto, "*Reggie, you're nothing but a gormless whiffle waffle.*" Perhaps he was mimicking one of his teachers or a schoolmate.

It seemed pointless to engage, but I had nothing to occupy me until I was rescued. "How much did you lose at poker, Reggie?"

"Are you the bear?" he asked.

Rather warming to my role now, I growled in my best baritone, which was still probably an alto, "Yes, I'm the bear. Bears like poker. You like poker, don't you, Reggie?"

"Poker is fun. Except when you lose. Reggie doesn't like to lose. He loses a lot of money."

This situation was deteriorating rapidly. Reggie was referring to himself in the third person and was rubbing the fur sleeve of the coat against his cheek. "You're a nice bear, aren't you?"

I spotted Pixley's bald pate behind Reggie. "There's an even better bear behind you, Reginald, my boy."

Reggie swung round, arms outstretched. Fortunately, Pixley was a few inches shorter than Reggie, so his arms landed in the air, or rather, landed Reggie on the floor. He toppled over, flat on his face.

Now free from my fur suit, I hurried forward. "Is he hurt?"

Ruby bent over him and grimaced, a halting snore filling the room.

Madame Lafitte scurried towards Reggie. Hands on hips, she shook her head. "A most disagreeable sight." Sighing, she lifted and tugged his hand. "*Allons-y,* let's take a taxi back to the hotel. We'll go together."

Reggie's eyes remained fastened shut.

"That's right, Reggie." Pixley cradled his head. "Off to Bedfordshire with you."

He remained inert.

Madame Lafitte's patience snapped.

She slapped Reggie's cheek. Hard.

I gasped. Not because her gesture was necessarily unwarranted, but because Madame Lafitte seemed such a gentle creature.

Her sudden violence had the desired effect. Reggie's eyes popped open, and he stumbled to his feet.

As the pair headed to the door, Pixley held up a hand to his mouth. "Madame Lafitte is most surprising, *n'est-ce pas?*"

25

Pixley peered up at the street numbers. "It must be around here somewhere. What was the address again?"

"Henriette said it was 67 Rue Pigalle," said Ruby. "The entrance is hidden because there are more fascist elements in Paris by the day. The club is trying to be discreet."

"So discreet we cannot find it," I grumbled.

After we'd left the scene with Madame Lafitte and Reggie, Dr Fischer announced the party was at an end. Professor Boscoe Fitzwilliam, however, told us he planned to find a local watering hole since it was his last night in Paris. Henriette suggested the Barrelhouse, one of the most fashionable yet open nightclubs in Paris. By 'open', she meant that our crowd would be most welcome. No colour line at a club run by a Miss Mabel Barrelhead, known lovingly as Miss Barrel.

"Grumble, grumble, Red," said Pixley.

"You weren't the one pinned against a wall with a fur coat and a drug-addled poker player talking to you as if you were a fuzzy animal in the zoo."

Pixley clicked his tongue. "Reggie's perfectly harmless."

"Harmless?" I strove to control myself. "The man is a

scoundrel. Remember, we have evidence of that from the Ritz today."

"My dears." Ruby held up a gloved hand, made ghostly by the swirling, rising fog. "We're hopelessly lost. Perhaps we should have taken the metro to Pigalle." She squinted at a street sign. "Instead, we're on Rue Joseph de Maistre."

"Never fear." Pixley held up a folded map. "In less than two shakes of a donkey's tail, we'll be at Chez Barrelhouse."

He unfolded the map and held it up to his nose.

"Hmmm…" He murmured a list of French street names. "If we – no, no, that's not right."

He turned the map. Lights from a lonely car glowed and flickered as it passed.

"The fog's rising, Pix," I said.

Ruby switched on her pocket torch. "Here, Pix. Use this."

"Thank you." He juggled the map and the torch. "Let's continue down this way. We should be there shortly."

I doubted it very much, but Ruby and I marched forward. The fog had begun to approach Old Blighty standards, muffling our footsteps on this empty boulevard. Pixley trailed behind, still in a one-way conversation with the map.

"What are those little houses up ahead?" I pointed at small stone structures disembodied by the fog.

"Good Lord," breathed Ruby. "It's the entrance to Montmartre Cemetery. Those must be family crypts or mausoleums."

"Selkies and kelpies! Where are you leading us, Pix?" I shivered and looked over my shoulder.

"Pix? Pix? Where are you?" I called.

Ruby put a hand on my arm. "Wait. Let's listen."

We halted by a melancholy angel atop a tombstone, looking heavenward. No chance he'd be able to see heaven through this fog.

"I don't hear anything," I whispered.

"Shh! I think I hear something."

She was right. Footsteps tapped in our direction.

"Boo!"

My heart stopped.

Pixley held the torch under his face and broke into a fit of giggles. "You should see your faces!"

"What would your mother say about your behaviour, Pixley Hayford?" I asked.

"My mother loves pranks, actually."

"Well, we do not." Though Ruby put on a brave face, her shoulders had risen almost to ear level. "Give us the map and the torch."

He handed them over. "If we just keep to this boulevard, we'll soon be there."

Before long, we rounded a corner with glowing lights and more sounds of footsteps. The fog was still obscuring everything else.

"Now that we're on the right track," said Pixley, "let's see if we can solve this murder. What say you, intrepid sidekicks?"

"Let's review, shall we?" said Ruby.

"Ah, the Poirot touch," said Pixley. "Order and method, *mon ami.*"

"I wouldn't say no to a bit of order and method, as it happens," said Ruby. "Dr Fischer remains the most obvious candidate, even though we know now that Yvonne was killed in her bathtub."

Pixley paused under a dim streetlamp and peered at the map again. "What I cannot fathom about the Dr Fischer set-up is what an absolute corker like Yvonne saw in him."

His comments rang true. Dr Fischer was a middle-aged man with odd facial hair, a paunch, and a personality that could scarcely be described as charming. Of course, he was intelligent, worldly, and his research seemed intriguing. But it still didn't add up to a Casanova.

"I caught a glimpse of what it might be," said Ruby.

Pixley leaned forward. "Do tell!"

"Wait!" I cried as a blue street sign materialised out of the fog. "There's Rue Pigalle. Turn right!"

Ruby smiled. "Thank goodness for Feens – otherwise we'd probably end up at the Paris catacombs."

We turned onto a meandering side street and Ruby continued. "Dr Fischer has a remarkable knack of listening and asking questions. He asked me about Oxford, inquiring about chemistry and my plans after taking a degree. And though I asked about his archaeological projects, he was having none of it. He made me feel I was the centre of his world – at least whilst I was in his orbit."

"And you didn't feel it was an act?" asked Pixley.

"He was genuine. However, I fancy if he thinks someone isn't worth his precious time, he wouldn't be so attentive. Very calculating, our Dr Fischer. That's why I don't buy the jealous rage theory," said Ruby.

"Yvonne might have threatened to tell Madame Lafitte about their affair," I said.

"Though from what you overheard at the soiree tonight, it seems she already knew," said Ruby.

"He could have thought she didn't know," put in Pixley.

"True. Dr Fischer's other motive involves his research," said Ruby. "Yvonne might have threatened to cut off his funding."

We joined the queue outside the Barrelhouse. The entrance might be discreet, but the high-spirited crowd outside was smoking, laughing, and even singing.

"What about Madame Lafitte herself?" I grew excited. "I've got it. She kills Yvonne in what Pixley calls a jealous rage!"

"Oh yes, a cream passionel," said Pixley. "Mmmm..." Pixley

always discussed his favourite murder theory as if it were a delicious pudding. Pudding. My stomach rumbled.

"Or, Madame Lafitte could have been after two birds and one bally stone: kill Yvonne and frame her husband so he gets the chop."

"You have such a delicate way with words, Pix." Ruby smiled. "But why wouldn't she have simply sacked Yvonne? Even putting aside imagining her hauling Yvonne's body up the stairs to Dr Fischer's room."

"We've completely forgotten Henriette's peculiar behaviour. Why was she in Yvonne's room?"

"Would Henriette bump off Yvonne just to continue modelling for her aunt?" asked Pixley. "Even if Yvonne sacked Henriette, couldn't Madame Lafitte find her a modelling position elsewhere?"

"Henriette does have a temper," I said. "But this crime seems so premeditated."

"It would be most uncharacteristic of Henriette," said Ruby. "However, she still tops my list of suspects given her motive and opportunity. She also knows the hotel and most of the other suspects."

"What about darling Virginie?" asked Pixley.

"She is mixed up with Reggie and Elizabeth, but I don't see how it relates to Yvonne's murder. At least not yet," said Ruby.

"Besides," I said, "I'd put my money on Elizabeth as the killer. She has the brains and, my goodness, the energy."

"Elizabeth is a definite possibility," said Ruby.

"That's because you're so fond of her," said Pixley.

Ruby grinned. "Yvonne seemed to be unwilling to sell to her, and she also had a definite personal antagonism with Elizabeth."

"Aren't we leaving out Omar Abelli and Berthe Dumont?" asked Pixley.

"Quite right," said Ruby. "When Berthe screamed, do you think she was pretending?"

Pixley winced. "Her shriek was utterly convincing."

"If she were the murderer, why would she plan to be one of the first on the scene?" I asked.

"Perhaps as a double-bluff?" Pixley shook his head, even as he said it. "No, that scream was genuine."

"That leaves Omar," said Ruby.

I suddenly felt defensive. "If he killed Yvonne, then he and Berthe would most likely lose their jobs. Even if a new manager kept them on, they might be even worse off than they are now."

"How so?" asked Pixley. "They must be terribly overworked."

"At least they have some freedom now," said Ruby. "If someone new came along, that freedom might vanish."

She shook her head. "But they wouldn't murder someone over that. Jobs are certainly scarce, but those two seem most resourceful."

The muffled beat of jazz from inside the club grew closer. Thank goodness we were nearing the front of the queue.

Pixley stared at the pavement and clicked his tongue. "I hesitate to mention it, but what about Maurice?"

Ruby crossed her arms. "Why do you 'hesitate to mention it'?"

"Well, I, ah, thought you might be less inclined..." Pixley trailed off.

"I know you think I find him attractive, but I assure you I don't."

Pixley shot a glance at me. The words *the lady doth protest...* floated across my mind. Ruby Dove had a highly selective taste in men, mostly men who were unavailable in some way, like her old flame, Ian Clavering, who always popped in and out of her life. Maurice fit the bill on that score, so I assumed she must be in denial.

"The case against Maurice hinges on this daft briefcase," I said. "And his bizarre relationship with Virginie. As Elizabeth would say, she's two-timing him."

Ruby stared at her feet. "What *was* in that briefcase?"

"Women's underclothes?" Pixley suggested.

"Your mind is like a sink, Pixley Hayford," said Ruby.

"I couldn't help it. It's so easy to provoke you two, especially dearest Red."

"I'll tell you one thing," I said. "If I don't eat soon, you won't believe how provoked I can be."

26

We descended the dingy stairs of the Barrelhouse, lit by a single, flickering lightbulb. A winding corridor opened onto a fabulous vista of a sunken nightclub, just as I had imagined it. Fashionably dressed couples whispered in corners, whilst larger parties burst into raucous cackles. Clouds of smoke drifted over tables where earnest young students and world-weary women discussed politics, life, and lost loves.

Ruby pointed to plush banquette seating lining one wall. Henriette waved two muscular arms at us.

"Marvellous choice, Henriette." Pixley unbuttoned his jacket. "Do you come here often?"

Henriette saluted us with a short-stemmed, wide-mouthed glass, half full of green liquid. "No, I've never been here. Someone at the hotel recommended it, especially the absinthe." She smacked her lips.

"I thought absinthe was illegal," said Pixley.

"It's exquisite," said Henriette. "A delightful anise flavour."

I blanched at the thought of anise, recalling a frightful tonic my mother used to coax down my throat when I was a child.

"Well, I prefer cognac, or, on the other extreme, a delight-fully frou-frou cocktail," said Pixley.

"I'll drink anything," said Ruby, "but I prefer simple affairs, like a gin and tonic. Or just a glass of fizz."

I couldn't see how this conversation was getting us anywhere. And as there was no obvious opening, I chose the direct approach. "What were you doing in Yvonne's room this evening?" I asked.

To my astonishment, it worked. "Yvonne had borrowed some things from me," said Henriette. "I was taking them back."

Before I could go further, she redirected the conversation. "Isn't that one of Madame's gowns? You look stupendous, Miss Ruby!"

Her enthusiasm was clearly the result of the absinthe, not a sudden change of personality. But she was lucid enough to recognise the copy of Ruby's design. There was certainly more to Henriette than met the eye.

"It is one of her creations." Ruby smoothed the gown across her hips. "Where did you see it before?"

Henriette puffed her cheeks and let out the air, dissolving into a giggle. "Perhaps they know." She gestured around the table, though everyone was studiously ignoring her.

Dr Fischer sat to Henriette's left, chatting amiably with Professor Fitzwilliam, who would tug on his striped bow tie whenever he became excited.

Elizabeth absently twisted her square tumbler on the table and tapped her feet to the music.

Maurice made desultory conversation with Virginie. She had an elbow on the table and was twirling her hair, looking decid-edly bored. I half expected to see Reggie as well, and then I remembered he was probably unconscious in bed at the hotel.

Other guests from the soiree sat at another table, discussing Ada 'Bricktop' Smith, Josephine Baker, Sigmund Freud, and the newest exhibition of one of the guests' paintings. A tiny lady in a slinky mauve dress yelped, "Fat Claude! Yoo-hoo! Over here!" in a loud American accent. A couple turned towards them and waved, one lady with a delightful pink feather in her hair and an ample woman in a well-tailored suit. They wandered into the shadows near the front of the stage.

Pixley rubbed his hands together. "The mood is perfect. I'll get started."

"Perfect for what?" I asked.

"To interview Dr Fischer for my story."

"Is there a story? I thought Dr Fischer's affairs cast a rather dim light on his character, given what you said about this Egyptian benefactor."

"Dashed if I know whether it's enough to sink his character reference. I'll report what I've found, and he can make up his mind. In the meantime, I can still write up his adventures for my editor. I need moolah to cover this busman's holiday."

"Moolah?" I asked.

"You know, spondulix, readies, cash. Good old money. The story must be scrumdifferous, so I'm going to the source."

"I despair of you sometimes, Pixley Hayford." Ruby laughed. "But I suppose that's why you're a writer."

A tall man in a loud yellow tie suddenly pushed past me.

"Pardon!" I said, expecting him to reciprocate.

The man glowered and said 'pardon' as a sneer rather than an apology. He leaned over the table and whispered into Virginie's ear. She chirruped back and hopped onto the floor. Soon, the two of them were dancing with the few other brave couples in front of the stage.

Maurice didn't miss a beat, even after this rather awkward display by Virginie. He held out his hand to Ruby. "Care to dance?"

Ruby pinched her lips in indecision.

"Go on," I said in a low voice. "Henriette's having a conversation with herself, or the absinthe, rather. Pix will talk to Fischer, and I'll find someone to talk to – perhaps Elizabeth, since I know how much you enjoy doing that. Maybe you'll even overhear Virginie saying something to her new dance partner."

The table's configuration changed. Only Henriette, Dr Fischer, and Elizabeth remained, but they completely ignored one another.

Pixley returned from the bar with two cognacs. He slid one across the table to Dr Fischer and sidled up to him on the smooth leather bench.

I had nothing to offer Elizabeth, except a smile. She returned the gesture, though instead of her usual broad grin, her lips were tight and narrow. And her glass was nearly empty.

"I'll hazard a glass of fizz," I said. "Would you like one?"

"Thanks. No alcohol for me. I'll just have another tonic with lots of lemon and ice."

"Right." I trotted over to the most approachable bartender, a loose-limbed, baby-faced young man.

"Mademoiselle." His eyes twinkled. "I believe you require champagne. Am I right?"

"Absolutely." I leaned over the bar, or rather hoisted myself up. "Would you do me a favour?"

He winked. "But of course. I always fall for auburn-haired women."

"Do you see the woman in the boxy suit?"

"Ah yes, the American who only drinks tonic, ice, and lemon. A shame."

"My thoughts, precisely. She's rather bored, so a touch of gin in her next tonic, ice, and lemon might not go amiss."

"I believe you're right."

"But not too much. Only a teensy bit."

"Enough to allow her to enjoy herself, but not to become a

spectacle for the enjoyment of others."

"Perfectly said." I placed a few coins on the counter. "Thank you."

He pushed the money back towards me. "As I said, I fall for auburn-haired women. The pleasure is all mine."

With what I considered my best winning smile, I collected the drinks and weaved through the crowd to our table. Pixley's head was bent at a listening angle, shifting only when the doctor banged his fist from time to time. He winked at me. The interview was going swimmingly.

"Here's your tonic with lots of lemon and ice." The glass slipped through my fingers, but Elizabeth caught it just before it toppled over.

"Thank you!" I said. "And I haven't even had much to drink yet."

"That's why I don't drink. I like to be in control at all times." Elizabeth took a long sip from her glass. "Tastes great. Did the bartender put something extra in it? Maybe lime?"

"Henriette said they make fantastic drinks here, and that must include those without alcohol." I sipped my champagne and slewed my eyes to the left, trying to watch Elizabeth's face.

The tight little grin had eased at the corners, and her eyes had brightened.

Perfect.

She took another sip and smacked her lips. "Tasty."

"Indeed." What should I ask her? If Ruby were here, she'd know what to say. Right now, Maurice was whispering into her ear whilst they were dancing. I sighed. I held out no hope of Ruby helping me, or of Pixley's excellent interviewing skills intervening on my behalf. I had to push on.

"Are you enjoying your time in Paris?" Though it was a tepid opening gambit, it was all I could muster under the circs, as Pixley would say.

"It's all gone to hell," said Elizabeth. "Yvonne, the designs, my clients. Nothing is going as planned."

"What had you planned?"

"For everything to go the opposite way. Madame Lafitte wasn't supposed to retire. Yvonne wasn't supposed to die, and Miss Ruby high-and-mighty Dove wasn't supposed to become the head designer, that's for sure."

"What do you mean by high-and-mighty?"

"Well, you know."

"I'm frightfully sorry, but I won't allow you to insult my friend. Her designs are fabulous. They're so fabulous, in fact, you apparently feel compelled to pinch them."

"*Moi*?" Ice clinked as Elizabeth swung her glass. "Sorry, sweetie, but I didn't steal them. I'm sure Yvonne did it. A real snake in the grass, that Yvonne."

She chuckled and then began to giggle. "That little floozy Virginie and nincompoop Reggie. They're snakes in the grass, too." As she leaned in, strong gin fumes wafted into my nose. That bartender must have made it at least a triple. Perhaps he was a snake in the grass, too.

Suddenly, Elizabeth slammed her glass on the table.

Pixley and Dr Fischer jumped.

I hadn't planned on Elizabeth becoming aggressively sozzled. My plan for light, happy tipsiness like Henriette's had gone awry, so I gave Pixley a pleading look.

Pixley cupped his hands and yelled across the table, "Henriette said a special act was coming on soon. Shall we all watch? I'll order another round of drinks."

Elizabeth began clapping. "Bring them on! And get me another drink, Pixford! *Grazie. Merci.*"

Pixley held up a two-fingered salute without glancing back. I was impressed. It was the only time I'd ever seen Pixley be deliberately rude.

From behind the curtained front stage, swinging opening chords rumbled across the club.

A swarm of dancers rose from their seats and streamed towards the musicians.

The curtains drew back on a piano player with a cigarette hanging from his mouth, staying perfectly still as his long, delicate fingers jumped about the keyboard.

Elizabeth pointed at the stage.

"Hey! Isn't that the hotel manager?"

It was indeed. Omar Abelli in the flesh, exactly as I had pictured him on our first day in Paris. Save for his fingers, his entire body remained passive and languid. Only his eyebrow twitched from time to time when he completed a challenging line. The dancers were entranced, swaying and twisting across the floor. The song soon came to a rousing close, and everyone clapped madly, some calling out for more.

Omar's only acknowledgement of the compliment was a tiny lift of his chin. The curtains closed again.

Pixley returned with the drinks. "Did you see that? It's Omar! What the deuce is he doing here? Seems like too much of a coincidence."

"It is peculiar, as you say, Mr Hayford," said Dr Fischer. "My wife will be most displeased when she discovers this."

"He's a damn good player." Elizabeth studied her fresh drink with a downcast look in her eye. "This isn't as delicious as my last one."

Ignoring her, Pixley leaned towards the doctor. "Why will Madame Lafitte be displeased?"

"Monsieur Abelli has strict instructions to be at the front desk at all times. Though I admit he is a superior piano player."

Any further chatter was forestalled by a loud crash and a bang. The curtain opened again, this time revealing a large band, with Omar as the leader at his piano.

A bass player plucked out the bouncy notes to a familiar song, though I couldn't quite place it.

A trumpet blared, mimicking the bass's opening lines.

The band began snapping their fingers, and a masked singer in a tight, shiny silver gown glided onto the stage.

"What-ta-do, What-ta-do, What-ta-do-ta-ta-do-do." She leaned over and jiggled and joggled her ample backside. Then she straightened, grabbing the microphone and waving at the trumpeter.

The trumpet resumed his solo, mimicking her opening lines.

She smiled and growled in a surprisingly silky voice, "It don't mean a thing if it ain't got that swing."

Pixley's jaw dropped as he held up a trembling finger. "That's – that's Berthe. The maid. From our hotel."

"No. It can't be," said Elizabeth.

"Most improbable," said Dr Fischer.

The singer pulled off her mask. I gasped. It *was* Berthe. She bobbed and weaved with the microphone in hand, the small silver ring I'd seen earlier glinting in the stage lights.

"Good Lord!" Pixley tapped his foot. "She's fantastic! Sounds just like Ivie Anderson with Duke Ellington. I can't wait to hear her again."

But it was not to be. The applause died, replaced by a piercing whistle. Soon the air was filled with the high-pitched, ear-shattering noise. Gasps became shrieks as the crowd realised what was happening.

"It's the fuzz," slurred Elizabeth. "Better move your keister, sweetie."

IN THE ENSUING CHAOS, chairs and tables were flung aside, bartenders hopped over the bar, and the band, including Omar and Berthe, rushed backstage. I was momentarily jealous of their backstage exit, though the sheer terror of the raid made me freeze in place, watching everyone else around me flee.

"Pssst – Red– come with me!" Pixley grabbed my arm and marched me behind the bar. We crouched down near the bottles of Cointreau and brandy.

"They're still going to find us here," I whispered.

"They probably wanted to frighten everyone," Pixley whispered back. "Maybe they'll go away."

"Where's Ruby?"

"She was near the stage, so I expect she followed the band."

The sound of breaking glass underfoot broke the eerie silence.

Pixley held his finger to his lips. We moved closer to the bar, as if it would somehow shield us from being discovered.

The footsteps turned towards the front of the club and slowly faded into the distance.

We poked our heads up over the bar. The place was a shambles, but at least there was no sign of the police. I surveyed the empty stage, where the microphone had fallen, and instruments perched precariously on chairs. During the chaos, the front stage curtain had been torn, revealing a backstage exit into a corridor. I dashed towards it, waving at Pixley to follow.

We stepped over broken glasses and discarded hats, scarves, and gloves, strewn about the exit. The lights had gone out, so I trod carefully, trying not to slip in the dark.

The passage was wide enough for Pixley to walk alongside me. We held onto each other, slipping on the broken drinks glasses that had been crushed underfoot in the mad dash to leave the club.

As we turned a corner, I trod on someone's heeled shoe and lost my balance. I reached out to lean on Pixley, but he had fallen behind. I tumbled over into the darkness, catching my hand on something sharp. I let out a yelp of pain.

"Pix! Help!"

"Here. Take my hand. Then I can help you up. Blast this confounded darkness."

I gave Pixley my unscathed hand, and he lifted me to my feet. I leaned on him, more for moral support than from any real need. After all, I hadn't injured my leg. But my hand hurt like the dickens.

"I'd better find a bandage soon." The sticky blood oozed down my arm.

"We'll get you out of here. It can't be long now," said Pixley.

The light from a torch suddenly lit our way.

Then another. And another.

"*Arrêt! Police!*"

Damn and blast it.

We halted and scanned our surroundings now that we could see the passageway. I tried not to look at my own sticky mess of a red arm. Instead, I stared straight ahead, also avoiding what must have been the disapproving faces of the police.

What met my gaze, however, was far more disquieting.

"Selkies and kelpies," breathed Pixley.

"Well, well, what have we here?" said the unmistakable voice of Inspector Toussaint.

But it was not Inspector Toussaint's voice that made me tremble.

It was Ruby Dove.

She stood over the prone form of Henriette Giroux, whose long hair partially covered her face, eyes agog and mouth open. Henriette's arms were outstretched, and her head lolled to one side. A dark red pool spread from her abdomen.

That was not all.

Miss Ruby Dove gripped a long dagger covered in blood.

27

A lazy fly buzzed against the windowpane in a fruitless attempt to escape the police station. I also longed to escape but was simply too exhausted to flee.

"Here, Feens. The constable brought us hot sweet tea."

I sipped the thin brown liquid. "Ow! I burned my tongue."

"This night has truly become a nightmare." Ruby's face was drawn, and her left eye twitched.

She buried her face in her hands. "I can't erase Henriette's face from my mind. That look of utter horror and shock."

"Your face was quite a picture itself." I paused. "Sorry – I didn't mean to make light of it."

Ruby gave me a wan smile. "You might as well. I expect we're in for an endless night."

The clock over the window was caked in dust, but I could just make out the time. Four o'clock. No point in telling Ruby it was morning. It scarcely mattered.

"How could I have been so wrong?" asked Ruby.

"You mean about Henriette?" I asked.

She nodded. "If I hadn't fixed on her and had instead found the real culprit, perhaps she wouldn't have been killed."

"Don't say that, Ruby. You cannot possibly blame yourself for this."

Heavy footsteps approached, and the door to the interview room opened. Everything in here was a dull yellow, from the rugs to the peeling wallpaper and the envelopes on the desk, yellowed with age and covered in dust.

"Mademoiselles." Albert had that crooked smirk on his bow-shaped mouth. I'd known Alberts before. He was the boy who always tattled on others in school. The one who would gleefully sell his sister to the devil if it meant a promotion.

"Inspector Toussaint has arrived." Albert waved as if he were introducing a royal personage.

"Miss Dove. Miss Aubrey-Havelock." Toussaint nodded at each of us in turn. His hands stayed firmly behind his back, even as he sat down in a chair across from us.

Albert took another chair and set it in the corner. I was grateful I wasn't sitting across from him.

"Where's Pixley?" asked Ruby.

"I wanted to speak to you two alone. After all, you both had blood on your hands."

"Fina has already explained the blood on her hands was her own."

"Quite so. We're sending it to the lab to check. In the meantime, however, I'm not ruling out that it may belong to the victim."

I bit my lip. Perhaps it was better I was here for Ruby, at least for moral support. The lab results would soon exonerate me, and I expected Ruby would also be free to leave soon.

Well, perhaps in a little while.

The inspector took out a silver case and removed a cigarette for himself. "Would you care for one?"

My response was a grimace.

"Yes, please, Inspector," said Ruby.

I stared at my friend. She never smoked, not even in the most stressful situations.

Nevertheless, Toussaint lit her cigarette. She took a long drag, leaned back in her chair, and blew a stream of smoke at the ceiling.

Her shoulders relaxed. Miraculously, she didn't even cough. "Most kind. Now I'm ready for your questions."

Inspector Toussaint spread out a sheaf of papers on the table. Then he propped his elbows on them as if they were merely cushioning. Without taking his eyes off us, he said, "Albert, tell us what we know thus far about Henriette Giroux."

Albert licked a finger, flipping the pages in his notebook. "The deceased was found at two o'clock this morning at the following address—"

"Yes, yes, Albert. Get to the good bit."

"The deceased had two stab wounds, one in the heart and a deeper one in her left abdomen. There are no other outward signs of trauma, except those consistent with a fall after being stabbed."

A tiny, twisty grin played across Albert's lips. "And the dagger found in Miss Dove's hands appears consistent with the knife wounds."

The sheets of paper crinkled under Toussaint's elbows. "What say you, Miss Dove?"

"I was fleeing the club, as was everyone else. Then I heard someone call my name."

"And you recognised the voice?"

"It sounded like Fina." She waved the cigarette between two fingers. "Naturally, I waited for her. When I realised she wasn't coming, I continued until I came upon Henriette lying in the passage, exactly as you all saw her. It was absolutely horrid."

Then she closed her eyes. "Henriette was still breathing, so I crouched down to comfort her."

"And where was the knife?"

"Next to her body, but I didn't notice it until after she died. I was too focused on her to see anything else. They were such quick little breaths." Ruby stared at the window, her eyes moist. "I tried to calm her, though I knew she would die. She said nothing, except one word."

Toussaint leaned forward.

28

"'Fake'."

"Fake?" Toussaint folded his arms behind his head and frowned. "That was all?"

"I'm perfectly certain. Just as certain that I heard Fina's voice – or someone parroting her."

"Someone *was* masquerading as me," I put in.

"Tell me what happened next, Miss Dove."

"Henriette stopped breathing, and I looked around frantically for someone to help. That's when I spotted the dagger."

"Why did you pick it up?"

"You must have seen this before, Inspector. A suspect does something inexplicably stupid, as I did."

He gave her a crooked smile. "You'll have to do better than that, Miss Dove."

She licked her lips. "Let me tell you a story. As a child, I returned home one day to an empty house. The rear door was open, which was unusual but not alarming. I entered, and as I was walking past a bookcase, I spotted a dead blackbird lying atop the bookcase. I reached out and brushed my fingers against it!"

In between cigarette puffs, she continued. "Now, there was an easy explanation for what occurred – my mother had not locked the door, so it blew open, and this poor creature flew inside and died on our bookcase. My physical reaction was spontaneous, much faster than my brain. I experienced the same phenomenon with the dagger. It was so disturbing and out of place that I picked it up before my mind realised what I was doing."

She paused. "I expect my reaction was similar to Berthe's – when she didn't scream at the sight of Yvonne's body. It was only Pixley's entrance that jolted her back to reality."

Toussaint folded his arms. "Let's assume your theory is correct. Miss Aubrey-Havelock claims the blood on her arm is from a cut. Can you think of any other reason she might have blood on her arm?"

"Inspector—" I began.

He held up a hand. "I'd prefer Miss Dove's explanation."

Ruby raised her shoulders and let them fall in an exaggerated shrug. "It's unfathomable. If you're implying that she ran ahead of me, killed Henriette, and then pretended she was behind me, it's simply impossible. There was only one way in and out backstage."

"Is that true, Albert?" asked Toussaint.

"Yes, sir, that's what you said when we planned the raid."

Ruby smiled. "I fancied you were responsible for the raid, Inspector."

"I must admit an affinity for undercover work. We had a man undercover at Dr Fischer's soiree, partially to eavesdrop on suspects, and partially because it was deuced odd to have a party after Mademoiselle Jourdain's death."

I pictured the guests at the soiree. "What did he look like?"

"A most unassuming, short, balding man. Likes whisky. That's why I chose him."

"Because he likes whisky?" I quipped. Before he could respond to my poorly timed joke, I hurried on. "Elizabeth Ryland was talking to him about bagels."

Toussaint grimaced. "He mentioned that. In any case, after the party, he rang headquarters from a nearby telephone box and told us you were all off to the club. That's when I decided on the raid."

"To stir the pot, as it were?" asked Ruby.

A rather wicked grin spread across his face.

"How did you find so many officers at the last minute?" I asked.

"A colleague had already been planning a raid, so we collaborated." He cleared his throat, as if he'd become too cosy with the two of us. "And that's as much as you need to know."

"Perhaps all three conspired to kill Henriette," piped up Albert. "These two plus the journalist."

"A not unintelligent proposition." Toussaint outstretched his hand, first to Ruby and then to me.

"Rubbish," I said. "Would we be stupid enough to be found with quite literal blood on our hands? We were framed."

"Are you saying this was premeditated?" asked Toussaint.

"It might have been, Inspector," said Ruby. "Insofar as the killer had to kill Henriette, but they didn't know exactly when the opportunity would arise."

Toussaint stuck out his tongue, curling it up and then zipping it back inside his mouth. "A most distasteful suggestion. You're claiming I gave the murderer their opportunity."

"I wouldn't feel too poorly about it. As you said, the raid might have happened without you. This was a desperate act and one completely different from the first murder."

"Are you suggesting we have two different murderers?"

"Not necessarily. Just someone who is either over- or under-confident in their abilities."

"Which means?"

"The killer became rather cocksure after murdering Yvonne. Alternatively, they might have been in a panic and attempted to hide their first crime by committing this murder."

"You believe the two murders are connected?"

"Don't you?"

The door opened a crack.

Toussaint turned around. "Yes, yes. What is it, Girard?"

"It's Mr Hayford, sir."

"Spit it out, man. We haven't all day."

"Yes, sir. Mr Hayford says he stabbed Henriette Giroux."

29

I swung my leg in the narrow, fetid corridor outside the interview room, almost hitting Ruby. She paced fifty steps and then spun around. The only clue to her thoughts were her acrobatic eyebrow jumps.

Albert's head popped around the doorframe, interrupting Ruby's pacing.

"Miss Dove?"

He handed her a brown envelope. "Mr Hayford asks you to wire this letter to his editor in London. He won't give us a written confession until you agree."

Ruby took the envelope. "Inspector Toussaint is too clever to let me send it. Why didn't he tell you to send it? After all, how would Pixley know who sent it?"

Albert grimaced. "Inspector Toussaint read the wire and said he couldn't see any harm in it."

I gulped. "Did Pixley say why he committed the murder?"

"Not yet. In the meantime, please remain near the station or at the hotel."

He slammed the door.

"What is Pixley playing at?" I sighed.

"Give him more credit, Feens. He always lands on his feet."

"You're right." I rubbed my sandpapered eyes. "I haven't slept or eaten, so I'm a bit short-tempered. Talking of which, I spotted a cafe on our way into the station. It might be open now."

"Trust you to notice a cafe after a night like that."

I SWALLOWED the last bite of my enormous omelette, whilst Ruby munched on a croissant and sipped black coffee. As I cradled my third coffee, I could sense my little grey cells were slowly waking from their slumber.

"*Garçon*," I called to our passing waiter.

He made a great show of scuffling his feet as he halted at our table, like a runaway train forced to stop.

"I'd like a strawberry millefeuille, please." I licked my lips, anticipating the layered cream and cake delicacy in the glass case.

The waiter's eyebrows disappeared into his shaggy blond hair. "One strawberry millefeuille." He sniffed and turned on his heel.

Dusting the croissant crumbs from her fingers, Ruby gave me a wry smile. "Shall we pay? Then we can leave once you finish your...dessert. The sooner we solve this murder, the sooner Pixley will be released."

I nodded and shook my handbag, hoping to see past the top layer of detritus. There was a receipt from Maxim's, my tin of tummy-calming mints, and...blast it. No coins, no coin purse. I stuck my hand in, straight towards the bottom.

Aha. Something cold brushed my fingers. It was round, cold, and hard.

I withdrew a smooth pebble with a folded note stuck to it, rather disgustingly attached via a masticated stick of chewing gum. Instinctively, I let it drop into my lap as if it were a hot potato.

"Ruby, I—"

But someone was approaching our table.

"I'm frightfully glad to see you." Maurice had wandered into the cafe, apparently with the same idea of refuelling after a long night. His face wore his usual amiable smile, but his eyes were red-rimmed, and his side parting was now a crooked zigzag.

"You look like you've been enjoying Inspector Toussaint's hospitality," I said. "Won't you join us? I've just started on my breakfast-dessert."

I plunged my fork into the moist millefeuille.

"Jolly kind." He unbuttoned his jacket and slid in next to me. "Coffee is what I need."

"No breakfast?" I asked.

"Or dessert?" Ruby chuckled.

"Just coffee."

Though I wanted to say, "you need to eat to keep your strength up," I kept my mouth shut. Ruby seemed to be holding her breath, so I let her make the next move.

She said nothing, but her eyes averted his gaze.

Maurice ran a finger around his collar.

Dash it. Someone had to turn this ship around.

"Tell us what you saw last night, Maurice," I said.

"I simply dashed out the door. After the chaos."

"The front door?" I asked.

He nodded.

"Did you see anyone else leave?" asked Ruby, suddenly coming to life.

"Miss Ryland. Dr Fischer. And Professor Fitzwilliam."

Ruby sipped her tea. "And then what happened?"

"The police were waiting outside. They drove us to the station."

"And?" Ruby's teacup clattered in its saucer, a sure sign of her exasperation with Maurice's staccato responses.

I stepped in. "Maurice, I'd like to ask you a rather impertinent question."

"I relish impertinence."

I rubbed the pebble in my hand, as if it were a talisman giving me courage. "Well, it's just...you have a short-ish way of speaking. As if you're cutting yourself off before you finish your thought. Is it nervousness, or do you usually speak this way?"

Ruby goggled at her plate, clearly too embarrassed to look up at me.

Maurice chuckled. "You're right."

He let out a great stream of air. "I had a dreadful stutter as a child. This wasn't helped by my mother and father speaking French at home, whilst I attended school in English. My mother is English by birth, but she insisted we all speak French at home. At first, I learnt to stop stuttering by making my sentences very short. This habit worsened when my chattering magpie of a French auntie came to live with us."

Ruby's eyes softened. "So you can speak in full sentences if you feel comfortable?"

"That's about the size of it," he said.

Maurice was clearly nervous around Ruby, but even my impetuous tongue forbore to point it out. At least he was calmer now.

"I have another impertinent question." I ploughed on. "You were seen exiting Madame Lafitte's workshop with a stuffed briefcase on the night of the murder. More importantly, you were looking rather shifty about it. Why?"

Maurice shrank back like a startled turtle. "Y–Yvonne asked me to bring the accounts back to the hotel. They were in a bit of a state."

Ruby's eyes turned as hard as ice. "You're involved in the accounts? I thought you were Dr Fischer's research assistant."

He laced his fingers together and set his hands on the table. "I am, but once Dr Fischer discovered I had also managed my family's greengrocery business in London, he asked me to help with Madame Lafitte's accounts. Or rather, Yvonne's handling of the accounts."

I pounced. "Was Yvonne fiddling the accounts?"

It fit the picture of Yvonne as utterly ruthless and selfish.

"No, no. Nothing like that. The business was growing, and Yvonne didn't want to pay anyone to help with the accounts. I was an easy solution."

So that was it! The note with the dates and sums we'd found in Maurice's room must refer to the accounts. Those shops and boutiques he had listed must have received deliveries of stock from the Lafitte warehouse. Or failed to receive them. I recalled how often the word 'delayed' had appeared.

"Do they pay you?" asked Ruby.

"In a matter of speaking. As Dr Fischer's research assistant, I receive room and board at the hotel, and a tiny stipend."

Just as I was considering another impertinent question, the impertinence herself waltzed into the cafe.

Virginie ignored the waitress and marched towards us. Or rather, skipped-marched.

She looked as pleased as punch. And as fresh as a blasted daisy.

Ruby turned her head and stiffened. Maurice did his shrinking act all over again.

I sighed. Love triangles were rather complex, and I, for one, was glad to be an observer rather than a participant. At least in this case.

"There you are, Maury!" Virginie punched his arm, a bit too hard to be playful. "You should be tucked up in bed. You know you cannot handle too much activity. Remember how the doctor said too much strain isn't good for you?"

Ruby's hand tightened into a fist under the table.

"I am rather all in," admitted Maurice.

"I expect we all are," said Ruby.

Then she smiled sweetly at Virginie. "*You* look rather well-rested. Did you escape police questioning?"

"Well, I did offer details to Albert, that nice sergeant. Such a darling sweetie."

"And what details did you offer him?" asked Ruby drily.

Virginie's eyes narrowed for just a moment. Then they popped open, making her face appear so innocent. "I cannot tell you! You're their prime suspect for poor Henriette's death, aren't you?"

Ruby remained silent, turning her fork over and over on the table.

"Oh, go on, Virginie," said Maurice. "You know it must have been some drug-crazed fiend who killed Henriette."

"Well..."

"Continue," I said. "Even if Ruby were the murderer, how would it harm anything to tell her your whereabouts?"

Virginie's eyes wandered aimlessly around the room. Was it the wandering of a vacant brain or someone playing for time? It was deuced difficult to tell.

She closed her eyes and lifted her face like a medium at a seance. "I was dancing with a gentleman when those horrid whistles sounded. Then I ran towards the musicians – I spied them streaming through a back curtain, so I followed. Everyone was screaming and running about. It was all so confusing. Then I saw Miss Ryland, so I followed her. I thought I'd never make it out alive!"

Ruby coughed.

"Did you see Henriette?" I asked.

Virginie put a finger up to her cheek and cocked her head. "I saw a woman with long, straggly hair, like Henriette's. She was staggering a bit, but I expect alcohol was responsible. She also clomps around like a horse."

She held her hands up to both sides of her face in mock horror. "Sorry. She *did* clomp around like a horse."

So much for speaking ill of the dead.

"Do you think she was injured?" asked Maurice. "Since she was staggering, I mean."

"No..." Virginie considered. "Henriette was stabbed, wasn't she? Wouldn't I have seen a dagger sticking from her side?"

30

"Good Lord." I blinked in the mauve sunrise outside the cafe. "That woman is insufferable."

"Indeed." Ruby rubbed her eyes. "And her relationship with Maurice is baffling."

I suddenly recalled the pebble and the note. "Wait. Just before Maurice joined us, I found something peculiar in my bag."

"Dear Feens, something peculiar is always in your bag. Remember when you accidentally removed your brassiere from your handbag at a dinner with that ambassador?"

My face flamed. "That was different." The unmentionable had somehow crawled into my bag when I was rushing for a train.

"It was such a sight. Your face was a picture!" She bit her lip. "Sorry. I didn't mean to tease you."

"The note is in French." I read aloud:

I have something of interest regarding your designs. Meet on a barge with a red flag on the Seine at nine o'clock tonight. Near Pont Neuf. Only you and your friend, Ruby Dove. Do not bring anyone with you, and do not alert the police if you value your life and the life of your friends.

"Well, I suppose it's foolish to ask if we're going," I said, "but I will ask who slipped the note into my bag."

"Have you had it with you at all times?"

My mind flashed through the past twelve hours. "Someone might have slipped it in at Dr Fischer's, or even at the club. I had my coin purse near me, so I paid less attention to my handbag."

"So that lets out Berthe or Omar."

"Though they both have access to our room." I sighed. "My bag is chock-full, so anyone could have placed something in it, and I wouldn't have noticed."

"No matter. After a few hours' rest, I'm certain everything will become clear."

I JERKED AWAKE, staring into two ice-blue eyes.

"Attila," I murmured sternly, even as I stroked her soft fur. She licked my face, her rough tongue slowly restarting my brain. The memories of the previous night came flooding back, and I squeezed my eyes shut, willing the images to disappear.

As I opened my eyes again, I noticed a figure standing over my bed.

"Ruby!" I whispered.

"Why are you whispering? It's nearly seven o'clock."

"In the morning?"

"At night."

"Selkies and kelpies!" I wiped my forehead. "But I do feel rather better."

"Me too. In fact, I've been arranging my ideas by scribbling a few notes."

"Care to enlighten me?"

She twinkled. "It's still congealing."

"Sounds revolting."

"You know, I've developed quite a superstition about it now. If I tell you, it becomes real somehow. It's a kind of jinx."

"But superstition is my line. Or even Pixley's, on occasion."

"Quite true. Let's say I'm learning from you, Feens."

I laughed. "How can I object? Still...how about a teensy hint?"

"Fake."

"That's what Henriette said. It's scarcely a clue if I already know it. Does it mean fake clothing? A forgery?"

"Partially."

"You are trying sometimes, Miss Ruby Dove."

"I know, but that's why we're such good friends – you trust me."

I sat up, catching a glimpse of myself in the looking glass. "Come to think of it, my hair is also rather trying."

Ruby tossed a black beret that landed squarely on my head. "You can cover your hair with that."

Then I noticed Ruby was still wearing her dressing-gown, and it looked as if it had shrunk two sizes since yesterday.

"Are you wearing something underneath your dressing-gown?"

She untied her belt, revealing black trousers and a black jumper. "We must dress the part, so we'll go as cat burglars to our secret assignation."

"Won't our outfits look suspicious?"

"It's Paris! These outfits are chic rather than suspicious. And before you ask me about evading the police, Omar has agreed to distract our good friend, Albert, whilst we use the backstairs."

"That's jolly kind of him. Why has Omar been so helpful?"

"Perhaps he's just a naturally kind fellow."

"You're not usually so trusting."

"Well, I admit there may be a bit of self-preservation involved in his acts of kindness. You see, Omar is already known to the police."

"What do you mean, 'already known'?"

"He implied as much whilst I was chatting with him at the registration desk. When I asked why he wasn't at his post on the night of the murder, he immediately agreed to help us sneak from the hotel. He doesn't want us to tell the police anything about him."

"And we won't?"

"We don't owe the police anything. We only owe something to the cause of justice."

"Spoken like words from the Ruby Dove manifesto." I chuckled. "But what if the police discover we've left the hotel?"

"He shouldn't need to since Pixley has confessed – the police aren't watching us as closely."

I bit my lip, imagining Pixley in a police cell. "Poor Pix. I wish we could do something for him."

"We must trust he has a plan. So far, his plan has allowed us to roam about, so I'd say it's been successful."

I tucked my hair into the beret and rose. "By the way, did Omar have any theories about Henriette's killer?"

"He and Berthe were among the first to leave the club, right after the musicians. But he did have one juicy titbit for us. He spotted a tall, thin man with flaming red hair at the club before the police raid."

"Reggie?"

"A most curious development, isn't it?"

31

It was nine o'clock, and time to meet our mysterious note-writer. A lonely, derelict-looking barge on the Seine came into view, its tattered red flag fluttering in the moonlit breeze.

"There it is," I said. "Shall I stay behind in case we need to call out a search party?"

Ruby switched off her torch. "The note invited both of us."

"Shouldn't we have left a message for Pixley?"

"I told Omar, remember?"

My back stiffened. "Don't look behind us. I heard a twig snap."

"It's probably a squirrel, or even a tramp finding a place to sleep."

"Squirrels don't live in Paris," I said.

A tiny grin formed on Ruby's face. "You would know that, wouldn't you?"

We tiptoed onto a gravel path, making an unbearably loud crunching noise on this quiet night. The gravel soon gave way to a narrow earthen pathway, and the only sounds became the lapping waves and the flag flapping in the wind.

A milky moon lit our way, recalling Hansel and Gretel's

clever breadcrumb trail used to escape from the witch. I took comfort in the fact we weren't stumbling into a witch's hut. Were we?

Ruby and I climbed aboard, taking a few moments to find our footing. Candlelight flickered through the rear window. Waving Ruby closer, I pressed my ear against the battered door and then shook my head. All I could hear was the water splashing against the boat.

Leaves rustled behind us, and I dared not glance over my shoulder. After all, Paris after dark was full of people engaged in both innocent and nefarious activities.

A sniffing, snuffling noise drew my attention back to the door. I spied the barge's tiny kitchen between a gap in the sun-faded blue curtains. No one sat at the table with two chairs, nor was anyone else about.

After a few more moments of silence, Ruby mouthed, "enter?".

Gritting my teeth, I grasped the cold metal knob.

Almost magically, the turning knob seemed to release its own sound. As if I'd switched on a Victrola recording of a low, menacing growl.

"TIME TO LEAVE," I hissed. "Our friend isn't at home, and I'd rather not tangle with that beast behind the door."

As if to reiterate my point, something scratched the door again.

"But if we leave now, we'll be none the wiser," whispered Ruby. "And we must solve the murder – for Pixley's sake."

"Maybe they've already released Pixley and he's waiting for us at the hotel."

"But then we'd be under suspicion again!"

Our argument resolved itself as the barge door swung open, sending a tiny, growling wire-hair fox terrier scampering out. I sighed with relief at the sight of such a small dog.

A dulcet voice floated towards us. "Marcel, mind your manners! Our honoured guests have arrived."

It was Omar.

A wisp of smoke from his omnipresent cigarette wafted through the doorway. Though he still wore his suit, he'd removed the jacket and loosened the tie. His Brylcreemed hair was also slightly dishevelled, falling over one eye.

"Come in, come in. Do not be alarmed."

"But you were just at the hotel," said Ruby. "How could you arrive before us?"

He waved his hand. "I know this city better than you."

"But you lied," I said. "Why should we trust you?"

Omar shrugged and turned his back. "You came voluntarily, did you not?"

I stepped over the threshold. Ruby followed, pushing away Marcel with her leg. Though Ruby favoured dogs over cats, she and Marcel had not started their relationship on the right foot.

An estate agent would have described the barge interior as 'rustic ramshackle'. Still, I had to admit the oxidised copper pots lining the walls and the faded furniture had a type of charm.

Omar was completely at home now, sitting on a stool, with Marcel on his lap. Scarcely the portrait of a ruthless killer.

Ruby's face had softened, too.

He regarded us placidly. "Would you like a cigarette? A coffee? Ah yes, perhaps a biscuit or digestive?"

Even under normal circumstances, the rather grimy-looking teacups suggested that a warm beverage would be a poor choice.

But a biscuit would be harmless, wouldn't it? "I'll have a biscuit, but only if you promise it's not one of Marcel's."

Ruby, however, was not interested in easing into conversation. "Look here, Omar. If I may call you Omar."

"As you know, dear lady, I prefer it that way." He casually blew dust off a dingy tin, popped it open, and handed it to me.

Broken, brownish crumbs rattled inside the tin.

"Omar, then." Ruby straightened on her spindly stool. "We're all anxious to clear up these tragedies, so perhaps you'd come to the point."

He sucked on his cigarette, studying Ruby. "The police said your friend Mr Hayford confessed to the murders."

"What of it?" I asked.

"It's rude to accept my biscuits and then reject them," said Omar. "Eat."

I gulped. What if he'd put something in the biscuits? I pictured myself keeling over onto the floor and Marcel licking my face, unable to revive me.

"Can't a girl change her mind?" I asked. "Our conversation has rather dried up my gastric juices."

"Henriette's murder was particularly ghastly." He stroked Marcel's fur. "But she must have known something."

"Why do you say that?" asked Ruby.

"Unlike Yvonne's murder, Henriette's murder seemed a rather haphazard affair."

Might as well make the best of Omar's sudden chattiness. "What did you see at the club?"

"I followed the musicians in the club to the exit, though at a slower pace than most. Berthe was a few metres in front of me."

I smiled inwardly, picturing Omar languidly strolling through the backstage maze as people shrieked in a frenzy all around him.

He winked at me, sending a little chill down my back. It might have been fear, or maybe a bit of excitement.

"I glanced over my shoulder and saw Henriette and Virginie racing towards me. But they never actually overtook me."

Remembering the backstage layout, I said, "But they couldn't have simply exited another way. They must have stayed behind you."

"Well, at least one remained permanently," he said grimly.

Ruby shifted on her stool. "Do you think Virginie killed Henriette?"

"Quite possibly." Omar flicked a bit of cigarette paper from his lip. "She's implicated in this dress business, so it's plausible."

"Which was the pretext for inviting us here," said Ruby. "So perhaps you'd tell us about this 'dress business', as you call it."

"Impatience isn't a virtue, Miss Dove. And I'm quite enjoying our discussion. How did you first become acquainted with Madame Lafitte – or rather, how did she become acquainted with you?"

Ruby looked as puzzled as I felt. She stretched her neck from side to side. Then she said in a steady voice, "Why should I tell you? You said you had information for us, not the other way around."

A brown curtain fluttered at the front end of the room. I scanned for an open door or window but saw none.

Someone was behind that curtain.

I motioned to Ruby, slewing my eyes side to side. She pursed her lips, signalling that she understood.

Swinging my legs in the air, I said casually, "Mind if I sit on that comfortable bench if we're going to continue? This stool makes me feel like a hen on a griddle."

I pointed to the hard wooden bench in the corner, near the fluttering curtain.

"Stay where you are," said Omar.

Marcel growled, emphasising the point.

I held up my hands. "Fair enough, but as Ruby said, we're here because you promised information about the thief."

"As dear Miss Ryland would say, there's no such thing as a free lunch," said Omar coolly.

Ruby rose from her seat. "This is ridiculous – let's leave. We'll carry on sleuthing on our own."

"You're most welcome to leave, but you'll be sorry when I have a little *tête-à-tête*

with Inspector Toussaint about your past escapades. Particularly your espionage activities?"

Ruby blinked.

My mind raced – how had he discovered our support of independence movements in the Caribbean? I stared at the threadbare rug, trying to organise my thoughts amidst rising panic.

"I'll take that cigarette now, if you don't mind," said Ruby.

Omar smiled and handed her a cigarette from the pack of Gitanes in his breast pocket.

Cigarette in mouth, Ruby leaned over as Omar struck a match on his shoe.

She inhaled. "What do you want from us? Money? Our undying loyalty?"

"You fool," came a voice from behind the curtain.

Omar turned, clearly mesmerised by the voice.

In a flash, Ruby seized her smouldering cigarette and jammed it onto Omar's hand.

His cry of pain ricocheted around the room, triggering a series of howls from Marcel, as if the little dog were feeling Omar's pain, too.

I had already run to the door and jiggled the knob.

"It's locked," I groaned.

32

There was only one way out.

Focusing on the door and the window next to it, I yanked the tattered curtain and wrapped my hand in it. Then I squeezed my eyes shut and shot my fist through the window. As glass tinkled on the floor, a terrific pain whizzed from my fingertips through to my shoulder.

Ruby angled her arm gingerly through the broken window and around to the front. Her face contorted as she stuck out her tongue.

"Almost there," she gasped.

The door popped open abruptly, sending the yapping Marcel through it and into the darkness beyond. I followed, stumbling over the threshold behind Ruby.

"Stay right where you are, Miss Aubrey-Havelock," breathed a familiar voice from inside the barge. "Don't move. And tell your friend Miss Dove to return to the boat."

I held up my hands and moved backwards. Ruby followed suit, somehow managing to avoid tripping over the doorframe.

"You think you're quite clever, don't you?" said Berthe in a low voice.

Something hard jammed into the small of my back. "Yes, that's a revolver. Don't move."

Though it was definitely Berthe's voice, it had changed – she was no longer speaking English with a French accent. It was the sound of an Englishwoman.

"Omar. Tie them up."

"You'll need to help me. Miss Dove injured my hand." His voice held amazingly little rancour.

We soon found ourselves bound up to rickety chairs, complete with a fetching view of the Seine between the curtains. But my mind wasn't concentrating on the scenery.

Omar rhythmically dunked his hand in a basin of water.

Marcel had returned and sat in the middle of the floor, looking from Berthe and then to Omar.

"He's hungry, Berthe. We'd better feed him."

Marcel's ears perked up.

She sighed and set the revolver on the counter, handing the dog a few brown bits of dried meat. Then she held the meat above his head, making him hop up to snatch it. She snickered as he grabbed the bits and chomped them with gusto.

I could barely turn my head, but I could see Ruby gawking at this spectacle. Was this some sort of circus?

"Marcel is adorable," I said, "But I'm utterly at sea. What have we done to deserve this...and why on earth do you have a plummy English accent?"

Berthe continued to feed Marcel, ignoring my question.

Ruby took over. "I noticed odd lapses in your speech before. Does it have something to do with the initials on your ring? B-S, I believe?" She motioned with her chin towards Berthe's silver ring.

Berthe's small, shrew-like eyes squinted at Ruby. "You're right about my accent, but you're lying about noticing the difference. I'm excellent at languages."

Then she shrugged and sighed. "You see, I was part of the British aristocracy once – the Brocklehurst-Smythe family in Sussex. We were a rather grand family."

Twisting her ring, she continued, "But that came with consequences. We were such a grand family that any hint of impropriety or scandal meant family shame."

Even in my addled state, I realised Berthe must have shamed her family. My own family history made me well aware of how silver-spoon gossip sold newspapers. Journalists had a special knack for sniffing out any whiff of scandal around any minor or major members of the aristocracy. I rarely understood their complaints as a class, but I did have some sympathy for individual stories of all-too-human failings.

"Whilst at a finishing school in Switzerland, I met a man. As you might imagine, the rest of the story is rather predictable." Berthe waved a hand. "And so, I was disinherited for becoming pregnant, even though the child was never born. Since I loved France, I returned here believing I could find footing in the fashion world by working at Madame Lafitte's. But that, too, proved illusory. The only way I could find a job was by pretending to be French. And even then, it had to be a rather stupid French girl. Nevertheless, I started in Lafitte's so-called workshop."

"Sparkle." She rubbed Marcel's ear absently. "That's what my sewing could have brought to her shoddy little collection. But she didn't deserve my talent. At every turn, my master seamstress skills were disrespected."

She released her clenched jaw with a sigh. "Omar helped me find a job at the hotel. It was simple and less demanding than the workshop since I was an excellent maid and seamstress. Soon, however, I began to resent the rich women and men flaunting their wealth in my face."

"So you began to pinch their belongings," I said.

Berthe clicked her tongue. "Nothing so vulgar. But the fact you think so confirms my suspicions of you."

I made another attempt at Berthe's guessing game. "It must be extortion, then. Guilty secrets: gambling, affairs, and various proclivities."

"My, you are persistent! You're closer to the truth, yet still so far away."

Ruby tried another tack. "What did you mean by your 'suspicions of us'? And why all the secrecy around your nightclub activities?"

Despite myself, I gushed, "You and Omar were absolutely marvellous last night. Why don't you quit the hotel and pursue musical careers?"

Berthe snorted. "Such a romantic, Fina. But romanticism doesn't pay the bills, and neither do a few nightclub acts. Even if we are the best. The fools running the club are blind to that, and so they pay us a pittance."

"The money is a pittance, but we both wish it would pay our bills," said Omar quietly.

"Yes, in an ideal world. Unfortunately, we live in this rather sordid, grubby world instead. The world of exploitation."

"Who's being exploited?" asked Ruby.

"Haven't you guessed? Aren't you a great detective?"

Ruby and I strained our necks towards each another, but I couldn't make eye contact. We both shook our heads, puzzled.

Berthe spat out, "You two – and probably your other sidekick, Mr Hayford, were sent here as spies."

"I'm afraid you have the wrong end of the stick." Ruby rocked in her chair. "If you'd just untie us, it would be much easier to discuss."

Omar moved towards us, apparently to follow Ruby's request.

"Stop, Omar," barked Berthe. She peered into Ruby's face. "Look me in the eye and tell me you're not spies."

Ruby threw back her head. "I'll do no such thing until you tell us what you mean by 'spy'."

Omar returned to his chair. "Our contact in the police said you were spies. We have certain friends, shall we say, who frequent the nightclub and pass us information."

Berthe crossed her arms. "And Madame Lafitte's announcement of you as her successor, Miss Dove, confirmed your dubious status."

My mouth hung open. What were they rabbiting on about? When Omar had mentioned our espionage activities before, I thought he meant our subversive political activities, and certainly not anything to do with the world of fashion.

"Go on," said Ruby. "You think we're industrial spies of the fashion world. And so you intend to kill us in cold blood."

"You do have a flair for the melodramatic, Miss Dove." Berthe shook her head. "We have other ways to silence you."

My shoulders relaxed. Whatever it might be, it would be better than death.

Berthe eased herself onto a stool. "Tell us why we shouldn't believe our friend from the police."

She paused. "If you're tempted to lie, please remember that Omar and I will supply Inspector Toussaint with witness statements implicating both of you in Henriette's murder."

Ruby pursed her lips. "Very well. We might be called spies, but our goals are political, not sartorial."

Berthe put her hands on her hips. "Well? Spies in service of what?"

"You mentioned 'exploitation' earlier. Well, we're in service of people fighting exploitation."

"Where?" asked Omar.

"All over the world, but mostly the Caribbean. Is that

enough?"

Berthe and Omar glanced at one another.

Omar began to speak, rhythmically stroking Marcel. "Two years ago, my sister had an accident. She was a seamstress for Madame Lafitte in a workshop – not working directly for her, but in a factory. My sister lost both her hands." His voice cracked. "If it hadn't been for Berthe's keen eye, she would have lost a great deal more – her life."

I couldn't help myself. "I've been in terrible workshops, but Madame Lafitte's was among the best I've seen."

Berthe snorted. "That's just for show. You haven't seen what goes on in a cellar in a nearby building, where the real work takes place."

I lowered my eyes, remembering a friend who'd lost two fingers because her employer had sacrificed safety measures to save money.

"I'm heartened by your reaction, Fina," said Berthe. "You're not a talented actress, so your face tells me you understand these horrid conditions."

Despite my general discomfort, I was gratified by this back-handed compliment.

Omar continued. "Soon after the accident, I met Berthe. I was indebted to her, and our love of music soon brought us even closer together."

Were they lovers? Surely not. They certainly didn't act like lovers.

"Fina, I believe the English expression is that 'your mind is like a sink'." Omar twinkled. "No, we became like siblings. We started the nightclub act to earn money for my sister, who I still look after now."

A little jolt of pleasure crept up my arm. That shopping list I'd seen at Omar's desk was for his sister, not for a secret wife or lover.

"By lucky happenstance, the manager position at Madame Lafitte's hotel was vacant, so I applied. After I began work there, I convinced Yvonne to hire Berthe."

"Didn't Yvonne recognise Berthe from the workshop?" asked Ruby.

Berthe cocked her head. "Yvonne had little to do with us, and I'm not certain she was even aware of that subterranean factory."

"How is that possible?" I asked. "She ran Madame Lafitte's business affairs."

"It's not so simple," said Berthe. "You see, the factory wasn't run by the fashion house itself. The big houses contracted sewing jobs with this dodgy group operating the factory. The group has secret workshops all over the city: underground burrows with no air, no light, where we worked like moles, sewing clothes for Paris's finest *femmes haut monde*. I only discovered these connections by chance. The factory actually makes clothes for several fashion houses, though Madame Lafitte's has by far the greatest share."

"So once you discovered this, you and Omar decided to snoop," said Ruby. "Hoping to uncover the responsible party."

"Just so," said Omar. "That's why I eagerly assisted Yvonne with the accounts, though those proved completely baffling. Just as well, since Maurice soon turned up. But once we determined the responsible party, we were prepared to exact our revenge."

"By murdering them?" I blurted out.

Omar chuckled. "That was the last thing on our minds, dear Fina. We're still uncertain about who is responsible. Besides, we wouldn't take our revenge through such violent means."

"Of course," said Ruby. "Instead of violence, you planned to snatch what was most precious to them – their reputation. To shame them publicly."

"Very astute of you, Miss Dove," said Berthe. "That's why we became nervous when two journalists unexpectedly appeared along with the two of you. "It was perfect camouflage for spying on behalf of whoever is behind these factories. Then, when Madame Lafitte announced Ruby would take her place, it became a conspiracy."

"But surely no one would go to such lengths—" I said.

Berthe's eyes flashed at me. "You're a pet, but rather naïve. Fashion is awash in scandal, exploitation, and greed. There are lovely aspects to it, naturally, but when you pull back the proverbial curtain, it's grim."

I stuck out my chin. "I'm just surprised by how far you think they'll go to cover up these conditions. After all, they treat young women in the factories as disposable, so they could simply hire more if they were exposed in some way."

Omar lit another cigarette. "You're not incorrect, Fina. Though it's difficult to buy a new reputation if yours has been tarnished publicly."

"And my designs?" asked Ruby. "Are you saying you haven't a clue about who is responsible for copying my designs?"

Berthe and Omar shrugged in unison.

"Nothing goes on at Madame Lafitte's that gets past me," Berthe said. "But that doesn't interest me, as it has nothing to do with working conditions, nor for that matter, with the murder."

"*Au contraire*," said Ruby.

My wrists and arms ached, distracting me from whatever Ruby meant by this last statement. "It's been a most stimulating evening, but we must toddle. May we leave?"

A light tap came from the doorway.

Berthe picked up the revolver and crept towards the door, like a mother bear ready to maul a rambler bumbling through the woods.

33

The soft tapping became louder.

"Hullo, hullo, anyone home?"

Omar held a finger to his lips.

"Hullo?"

It was Pixley.

Taking advantage of this diversion, I inched my chair to the right. Now I could see Ruby better, and what I spied in her hand warmed my soul. She moved a nail file rhythmically against the rope on her wrist.

Berthe, however, was focused on the door. In one swift movement, she flung it open and levelled the revolver at Pixley's forehead.

His hands shot up. "I've come in peace, and I've come alone."

"Get in here." Berthe waved the gun.

Following this command with alacrity, Pixley still held his hands high above his glistening head. But he soon relapsed into his playful, leisurely speech, a disarming tactic that had proved useful in the past.

"I say, it's a perfectly ripping space you have here – the decor is most charming. The only item marring this cosy scene is your rather distasteful revolver. Much too vulgar."

"Enough," Berthe said.

Marcel scuttled towards Pixley, growling and bouncing up and down.

"Mind your manners, Marcel," said Omar. "Shall we offer our new guest a chair?"

Berthe smirked. "An excellent idea. Last I heard, Mr Hayford, you had confessed to the murder of Henriette. Now, if there's one certainty in life, it's that the police wouldn't have let you go without someone else confessing or you agreeing to cooperate. I expect it's the latter."

Omar gently pushed Pixley's arms down behind his back, lacing rope around his wrists as he did so.

"I assure you I came alone," said Pixley. "I simply retracted my confession and told the police they'd no reason to detain me any longer. They graciously allowed me to ring up my solicitor, but I chose to wire my editor in London instead. He's a most obliging chap when a story is on the line. He spoke with Inspector Toussaint and explained the potential negative fallout from holding me any longer. Poor Toussaint is already in the soup with the bigwigs at the Sûreté for his unconventional methods, so he had no choice but to release me."

After Omar had finished trussing Pixley on a chair like a Christmas goose, Berthe handed him the revolver. "Omar, check outside for any suspicious characters. Meanwhile, I'll consider what to do with our guests."

"Look here," said Pixley. "You should know that Inspector Toussaint's become rather curious about your vanishing act, let alone the disappearance of Ruby and Fina. In fact, your absence has thrown the hotel into utter chaos. The police have gathered all the suspects there, and they're all wondering where you are."

Berthe twisted her silver ring around on her finger. "You put me in a difficult position, Mr Hayford."

"Me?" He fairly squawked the words. "If I hadn't confessed, the police would be all over you and your sidekick like a cheap suit."

"Quiet!" said Berthe. "I must think."

With lowered eyes, I saw that Ruby's filing had loosened the rope. Marcel, however, was sniffing around Ruby's chair, trying to ferret out any unorthodox activities.

Her brow furrowed as she surveyed Marcel rubbing his nose on her shoes. Then a wide smile spread across her face. I followed her gaze towards Pixley and then towards me. Berthe's back was slightly turned, so Ruby's facial acrobatics wouldn't be noticed. She scrunched her cheeks, moved her lips rapidly, and lightly bounced her head from side to side as if she were scolding someone.

Pixley and I continued to stare at Ruby, trying to understand her miming signals. As per usual, Pixley was first off the mark.

"I say, where'd you find that mangy little blighter? I wouldn't let him near me without a vigorous bath, and even then, I'd think twice about it. Why don't you just toss him overboard?"

Berthe's face twisted into the angry, puckered countenance of a bulldog. Before she could reply to Pixley's opening salvo, Marcel did his best. He barked and growled at Pixley, leaping up at him for good measure.

"Jolly good, you mangey mutt. Go on. As soon as I get my hands untied, I'll throw you overboard myself!"

Crouching down, Berthe hummed the Old Mother Hubbard nursery rhyme, clearly trying to calm the beast. Marcel's rear quarters lowered onto the floor as he stared in awe at Berthe. Soon, he took up a kind of whining singing in unison with her, punctuated by the occasional approving yap. He seemed oblivious to the song's line about the poor dog dying.

Berthe's head bent closer and closer to Marcel. In a sudden movement, Ruby yanked her arms from the chair and hurled herself forward. She leapt onto Berthe's back, locking her legs and feet underneath and lacing her arms around her shoulders.

The low groan coming from Berthe soon turned to a snarl. She rose from the floor, carrying Ruby on her back, ineffectually scrabbling at her with her hands. Ruby had her in a straitjacket position, so all she could do was lumber about with Ruby in tow. Marcel aided his mistress by nipping at Ruby's heels.

But Berthe couldn't lumber very far, giving Pixley and me a few seconds to consider our next move.

Unlike his handiwork with Pixley, Omar had skipped the step of tying up my calves and feet, probably because my legs didn't quite touch the floor.

I was in the best position to make a move.

"Do something!" yelled Ruby.

She had avoided Marcel's nipping at her heels by simply lifting them upward, but Berthe had now gained her footing and was slowly moving her load towards a hanging bookcase jutting out from the wall.

She was going to use the bookcase to dislodge Ruby.

I had to act.

Rocking back and forth on my chair gave me momentum. If I could just propel myself forward enough to let my toes touch the ground, I could lift the chair off the ground to move about on my tippy-toes. The next rocking movement let me brush my toes against the floor. Assured that I'd soon be walking, albeit in a rather compromised manner, I became a little careless with my rocking. The hind legs of the chair buckled just as I was leaning back, and I tumbled backwards, crashing onto the floor.

The slats of the high-back chair saved me from a sizable dint in my head. I shook myself, both in frustration and in an effort to clear my mind. Now I was even worse off than before: like Pixley, I was a Christmas goose ready to be slid into the oven.

"Push yourself over, Red!"

Thank goodness Pixley's yelp hadn't yet attracted Omar's attention outside.

"Easy for you to say," I retorted.

"That's right, Red. Get angry, so angry you'll just push yourself over."

Finally, I had instructions I could follow. In a fury, I strained every muscle towards leaning over onto my side. When I had tumbled to the floor, the rope had loosened, allowing enough give for me to flip onto my side and then onto my knees, in a ridiculous parody of Berthe's lumbering position. Except my load was a chair rather than a human, so moving about proved easier.

I struggled to my feet and waddled towards Berthe and Ruby. They edged closer and closer to the hanging bookcase. With all my might, I twisted to one side and then spun on one foot. Ruby could see me, and I hoped she understood what I was about to do.

The chair rammed into Berthe, just as Ruby relaxed her iron grip. The combination of the two forces propelled Berthe forward, right through a large window. She plunged into the Seine, yelping and screaming.

In a flash, Ruby had already begun untying Pixley, so I rushed to her side and also began tugging at his rope.

"Omar! Omar!" gurgled Berthe. Her splashing and thrashing muffled Marcel's yapping as he peeked over the broken window.

"Should we rescue her?" I asked.

"I expect she's a strong swimmer." Pixley winced as I removed the rope from around his wrist.

"And if not, she'll learn," put in Ruby. "The water isn't deep, and her overcoat protected her from the shattering glass."

"Where's Omar?" I asked.

"Must have done a runner," said Ruby. "I certainly would if I were in his shoes."

"Let's vamoose," said Pixley. "Before Omar changes his mind."

34

On the street behind Hôtel D'Escalier, all was quiet.

Well, almost quiet.

Gas lamps hissed gently, like a teakettle without a stopper, and a bleary-eyed man pushed a rickety cart marked 'Pain Grillé Jacques', squeaking by us, leaving behind the smell of warm, fresh bread. The scene was a welcome respite from our frenzied escape from the barge. I looked behind me longingly as Pixley mounted the steps of the hotel.

"Must we go in?" I asked tentatively, not wanting to break the spell of this tranquil scene.

Ruby looked over her shoulder. "I'm afraid so."

"Prepare yourself for an irate inspector," put in Pixley.

Our footsteps echoed on the marble floor of the empty lobby.

I heaved a sigh of relief. "Thank goodness you were wrong, Pix."

Then something moved in the shadows.

The balding white head of Inspector Toussaint emerged from the darkness, puffing on a cigarette. "Wrong about what, Miss Aubrey-Havelock?"

My stomach clenched. "Oh, I was saying thank goodness he was wrong about the hotel door being locked."

"We were waiting for the three of you, and now we may begin," he said in a low, measured tone. The rather jovial version of Inspector Toussaint had vanished.

He looked at Ruby. "Are you ready?"

In unison, Pixley and I said, "Ready for what?"

"I asked the inspector to tell all the so-called suspects how Yvonne was actually murdered and to be ready to gather everyone at a moment's notice."

"But how could you know when we'd return from that blasted barge?" I asked. "Did you tell him where we were going?"

"And why tell everyone about the electrocution?" asked Pixley.

Ruby held up her hands. "I wanted the murderer on edge. First, they'd know that we were on to their dastardly electricity scheme. Second, they'd be as jumpy as a cat on hot bricks if they knew the police might wake them in the middle of the night."

"I agreed to Miss Dove's plan not to follow you two on your little escapade," said Toussaint. "Though she didn't tell me what to do after we released you from police custody, Mr Hayford."

The front door slammed. Three uniformed officers appeared out of the gloom, escorting Berthe and Omar. Berthe's wet clothes hung limply on her round frame. With her teeth chattering and hands trembling, she cradled herself, probably from a mixture of cold and shock. Omar was dry, but mud covered his shoes and trousers.

A young, wiry officer said, "After following Mr Hayford, sir, we accosted these two near a barge on the Seine."

"Good work," said Toussaint. "Take them into the ballroom and give them something warm to drink. Bring blankets for Mademoiselle Dumont. Albert will inform you later if they ought to join us."

THUNDER RUMBLED outside the book-lined hotel library, daring the fire in the grate to continue crackling away. Albert poured cups of tea and coffee at a makeshift sideboard near the door, handing them to bleary-eyed guests stumbling into the room. Beverages in hand, each guest stepped gingerly into the tight circle of chairs around the fireplace.

Elizabeth sat bolt upright in a stiff cambric dressing-gown, her hand quivering as she lifted a teacup to her lips. She glanced at me, grimaced, and quickly looked away.

Reggie sat next to Elizabeth, toying with the cord on his jaunty striped dressing-gown. His usually slick red hair stood in tufts all over his head, creating a fiery halo. Though I now knew Reggie was anything but angelic.

On Reggie's right sat Dr Fischer, grinning to himself in a red silk gown sporting a puffy emerald ascot. I found it decidedly unnatural to be so pleased with anything at this ungodly hour and under these trying circumstances.

Next to the purring Dr Fischer sat Virginie. Or rather, she lounged. One arm stretched lazily over the back of the sofa, whilst the other held a cigarette. She was wearing full makeup, her blood-red lipstick shrieking for attention against her pink silk gown.

Stationed at the other end of the sofa, Maurice sat hunched over, with his hands in buried in his lap. His trousers had ridden up, revealing mismatched argyle socks that I expected were an accidental rather than sartorial decision.

Finally, Madame Lafitte perched placidly on the edge of her chair, her knitting needles clicking away. There was something deuced peculiar about Madame Lafitte, and her knitting only added to my sense she could be a Madame Defarge. Every time I thought I managed to pigeonhole her, she did something unexpected.

Pixley sat next to me, enjoying yet another cup of coffee. His hand trembled like Elizabeth's, but in his case, I suspected it was due to an oversupply of caffeine.

Inspector Toussaint ambled in through the large doors at the far end of the room. A revived Ruby followed, her eyes sparkling.

Pixley nudged me. "Ruby knows who did it. Look at her – she's as pleased as punch."

Dr Fischer suddenly leapt up. "What is the meaning of this, Inspector? We've been harassed, kept prisoners in this hotel, and now you wake us at an ungodly hour." Despite his outrage, he retained a curious sense of self-satisfaction.

"Yes, yes, Dr Fischer." Toussaint rubbed his eyes. "That's why you're all going to listen to what Miss Dove has to say. Then *some* of us can return to bed."

Virginie gave a light, tinkling laugh. "Didn't she murder Henriette?"

"Hear, hear!" Reggie croaked. "What kind of farrago is this, Inspector?"

I spied Albert smirking from across the room. *The smarmy devil thinks Ruby and the inspector are going to fail*, I thought.

Toussaint reached the fireplace and spun round. "You will all cooperate. Otherwise, you will find yourselves enjoying the hospitable conditions of a damp police station, run by rather inflexible and prejudiced men with certain unsympathetic views of other nationalities."

He bent over, his head moving slowly from person to person. "Do I make myself clear?"

"Thank you, Inspector Toussaint." Ruby slid her arm along the top of the mantel and let it rest in place. "In the fashion world, people dress up and play pretend. Fashion hides, but it also illuminates. The same applies to these two murders. Many of you are playing pretend, but only one of you is the murderer."

My chest tightened, and my legs tensed, sure signs of an atmospheric change in the room. Everyone was holding their breath.

"We'll begin with the facts," Ruby continued. "On the night or early morning following Madame Lafitte's retirement dinner, the first murder occurred. Mademoiselle Dumont discovered Yvonne Jourdain's body in Dr Leo Fischer's room at 7:15 in the morning. The body was fully made up and wearing a gown originally meant to be worn by Mademoiselle Giroux at the previous afternoon's show. Mr Hayford was the second person on the scene, as he happened to be wandering downstairs."

"I say, he was snooping. I'm a journalist, too, you know," protested Reggie.

"Ah yes, we'll discuss your rather dubious journalism credentials later, Mr Barrington-Loftus."

"What the devil do you mean by 'dubious'?"

Ruby ignored him. "Inspector Toussaint and I both suspected foul play from the start, despite Yvonne's apparent heart attack. However, we soon discovered that Yvonne had suffered an electrical shock in her bathtub, leading to her death. And, of course, Henriette's murder only confirmed foul play."

"And the most likely murderer is *you*, isn't it, sweetie?" quipped Elizabeth.

Ruby gazed steadily at her. "I was framed for Henriette's murder on purpose or by accident. And Fina might have been framed as well."

Albert shuffled his feet, his head downcast. "We've just had reports that the blood on Miss Aubrey-Havelock's arm was indeed her own, sir."

Pixley clapped his hands. "Fantastic news, Red!"

I gave Pixley a weak smile and heaved a sigh of relief.

Ruby grinned. "That is indeed a relief, though I never suspected Fina in the first place. Indeed, everyone else was also a suspect, based simply on their opportunity to commit the second murder."

Madame Lafitte raised her finger. "You forget that Mr Barrington-Loftus and I returned to the hotel after my husband's soirée. Neither of us are suspects."

I was about to mention Omar's spotting of Reggie when Ruby shot me a quick, knowing glance.

"Could Monsieur Abelli or Mademoiselle Dumont confirm your return to the hotel?" asked Ruby.

"Absolutely. Monsieur Abelli was at the registration desk."

"It pains me to say it," said Ruby quietly, "but that couldn't possibly be true."

35

Madame Lafitte set down her knitting needles and gazed at Ruby. Her eyes gave nothing away.

Ruby flicked a speck of dust from the mantelpiece. "Omar and Berthe were seen at the club, so they cannot provide you an alibi."

Reggie held up his chin. "Well, I can provide Madame Lafitte with a bally alibi, remember? We shared a taxi to the hotel."

Maurice cleared his throat. "Omar said he spotted someone at the club with fiery red hair, your build, and your height."

"Balderdash," spit out Reggie. "After all, I was blotto. I couldn't have possibly toddled to the club in that state. End of story. *Fini.*"

"Be that as it may," said Toussaint, "we've questioned all the taxi drivers in the area, and no one remembers you two. After all, you make quite a memorable couple."

Dr Fischer jabbed his pipe at Toussaint. "I must protest, Inspector. My wife is a respected designer and business-woman. I warn you, I shall lodge a complaint with your superiors."

"Leo, my sweet, please," said Madame Lafitte. "You see,

Inspector, I didn't want to embarrass young Reggie, so I agreed to his story."

"Continue, Madame."

Toussaint's eyes remained fixed on Reggie.

Reggie drummed his fingers on the arm of his chair.

"Mr Barrington-Loftus was in a regrettable state that night," said Madame Lafitte. "I was also in a regrettable state, but one due to emotion rather than drink or drugs. After we'd left the soiree, he said he'd stroll back to the hotel to clear his head, which seemed eminently sensible. So I also meandered back to the hotel, stopping only for a bite to eat at a cafe."

"Is this true, Mr Barrington-Loftus?" asked Toussaint.

"Yes, Inspector, though my memory remains a bit hazy."

"Whilst I appreciate the explanation," said Toussaint, "your alibi is still shaky since either of you still could have taken a taxi to the club and murdered Mademoiselle Giroux."

"Quite right," said Ruby. "So let us turn to the *why* of these murders."

"That's easy," said Virginie. "Yvonne had simply oodles of enemies. In French, we say there is no such thing as an insignificant enemy."

So, little Virginie isn't as vapid as she appears, I thought.

"Thank you for volunteering yourself, Mademoiselle Corbin." Ruby licked her lips, clearly relishing the chance to interrogate Virginie.

"On the surface," Ruby continued, "Mademoiselle Corbin might have murdered Yvonne to keep her modelling job, even though she might have found work elsewhere. If we look deeper, however, Virginie *did* have a more pressing reason to commit murder."

Virginie's mouth twitched, her teeth barely showing through her glistening red mouth.

"She's part of an elaborate theft and forgery scheme with

Elizabeth Ryland and Reggie Barrington-Loftus," said Ruby. "A scheme Yvonne might have discovered."

Toussaint broke in. "It's a lucrative counterfeit fashion scheme. My colleagues have been pursuing an international web of fashion copyists based in Paris. Most involved are unaware of the others' identities, so the web stays intact should any one person be exposed. The French government has created stricter penalties for such activities, but this particular gang has become bolder recently, and I suspect the mastermind may be in this room."

"Tell us how it works," said Pixley.

"Designers have gruelling schedules," said Toussaint, "and often cannot produce enough high-quality designs each year. The demand from New York alone is so voracious that buyers, such as Elizabeth Ryland—"

"Hey! I resent that," Elizabeth said.

"—will purchase copies of designs on the illegitimate market."

"So everyone in fashion is part of it or turns a blind eye," I said.

"Precisely," said Ruby. "Even the *premières,* or seamstresses assisting designers directly, make a tidy sum at a fashion house by day and then copying their work by night at a copy house. Copy houses can be independent of a couturier, or they can be run in parallel. When they're part of a legitimate house, the house keeps double accounting records, one legitimate and one illegitimate. These copied designs are in the shops or displayed elsewhere for short periods and then taken home or given to friends."

"How does it actually work?" asked Pixley. "Does someone just swipe a dress and give it to someone else?"

"Sometimes," continued Ruby. "Even clients can purchase a dress and then 'lend' it to a copyist for a fee. But the devilishly troublesome cases involve trading sketches of clothing. Copyists are often artists who draw frocks they see at shows, or even from second-hand descriptions from a client, a buyer, a seamstress, or a model."

"A model, you say?" Dr Fischer's eyebrows rose.

All eyes shifted back to Virginie.

"In a falling-out among thieves," said Ruby, "Fina and I saw Virginie, Elizabeth, and Reggie quarrelling at the Ritz."

"*C'est une sottise*," bleated Virginie. "Perfectly ludicrous. Why should I need to copy, as you say? I'm a model, and I earn a great deal."

"Dining at the Ritz and wearing a fantastic emerald ring do indicate great wealth. When Henriette said how little she earned, however, I realised you must have another source of ready cash."

Virginie treated us to a perfect Gallic shrug. "I am a better model than Henriette."

Toussaint said, "We checked your bank, and I doubt any model in Paris might command even a fraction of that amount."

"I inherited the money, and you cannot prove otherwise." Virginie sniffed. "Besides, a former lover gave me the emerald ring."

"If your wealth *did* come from this copying scheme," said Ruby, "you likely passed along details about the clothing you modelled. You have an excellent memory, as we discovered when you recounted your story about the night Henriette was murdered."

"A sharp memory proves nothing."

Virginie's chirpy voice had vanished.

Pixley pulled up his trouser leg and leaned forward, his elbow on his knee. "You said Virginie would give the details to a copyist. Would the copyist then sketch the designs?"

Ruby cocked her head. "Yes, and who is an excellent sketch

artist among us? Perhaps someone seen doodling at the retirement dinner?"

My mind flashed to Reggie's shark sketch at Maxim's. But that wasn't all. I leapt up. "That's it! Reggie was the doodler, and he also had dirt on his sleeves. I thought it was mud or soot, but it was charcoal, wasn't it? Charcoal used by artists for sketching. I've seen Ruby use charcoal a thousand times."

Despite his clearly strained affability, Reggie swung a crossed leg and flicked a speck of dust from his trousers. "Frightfully sorry and all that, but I haven't a clue what you're on about. I keep my clothes in the most spectacular sartorial condition."

"Then why were your sleeves smudged at such an important dinner?" I persisted.

Toussaint leaned forward over Reggie. His frown turned to a quick, disconcerting baring of teeth. "Shall we search your room for these charcoal pencils?"

"Suit yourself, Inspector. Even if you find such materials, it only means I have an artistic hobby."

"Nevertheless." Toussaint lifted his chin at Albert, who scurried from the room.

"I must say, old man," Pixley turned to Reggie. "you're a splendid chap, but you're no journalist."

"I didn't claim to be one." He paused. "*Old man.*"

Pixley's spectacles bounced as he wriggled his nose. "I know Nashie, and I was astonished he'd let a rookie take over his post, even temporarily. He's a thoroughly competitive bloodhound. So, I wired him in London today, asking him about you."

I was certain Pixley hadn't wired Nashie or anyone else today. A crafty fox, that Pixley Hayford.

Ruby's eyes flashed her approval.

Reggie gulped. "It was just a joke, a rib, though perhaps a poor one at that. A friend of a friend told me this Nash fellow couldn't go to Paris. This friend wagered I wouldn't be able to pose successfully as a journalist."

A sheen of sweat appeared on his forehead. "But it was just a bit of fun. I didn't know anyone was going to be murdered..."

He trailed off into incoherent mumbling.

Elizabeth stood up. "Miss Dove, you've been throwing around my name without actually accusing me directly. Just tell it to me straight."

Ruby turned her best false smile on Elizabeth. "Of course, Miss Ryland. Did you think I'd ever forget you?"

36

Still standing, Elizabeth crossed her arms. "Let's clear this up right now."

"Of course," said Ruby. "After Virginie helps Reggie with the sketches, he sends you the drawings, and you sell them in New York. The three of you share a cut of the proceeds, but you're the only one with the brains to mastermind the operation."

Elizabeth clapped. "Your imagination is very cinematic."

Ruby's voice became low and dangerous. "You killed Yvonne, fearing she'd expose you. Or you killed her simply as a warning to Reggie and Virginie."

"Baloney."

"Your precious scheme became more vulnerable by the day, didn't it? You saw Yvonne rushing off to consult Maurice at the fashion show, and when you noticed he'd brought an empty briefcase, you put two and two together and realised that *he* was watching the accounts, not Yvonne. You knew Yvonne wasn't crafty enough to keep two sets of books, one legitimate and the other under-the-counter. Maurice could hardly miss the extra cash flow that your fraud was generating. And word was spreading: even Henriette, who was only a model, had an inkling of the covert deals going on at House of Lafitte."

"So these three also targeted Henriette?" I asked. "Was it connected to her fall at the show?"

"In all probability. Remember, Henriette had lunch with Elizabeth and Reggie before the show. They might have slipped something into her food."

"But they all had oysters and the same drinks."

Ruby shrugged. "It wouldn't have been difficult to sprinkle some concoction on the oysters when Henriette was distracted. After all, most people swallow them whole. Or they could have slipped something into her glass."

"But why didn't Henriette die, then? Was it a mistake?" asked Toussaint.

"They didn't want to kill her – at least not at that point," said Ruby. "Whatever drug they used was to ensure she was so discredited that she'd never model again. As for the Ritz show, I expect she'd already been hired for that before Madame Lafitte's show."

"But how could they time the drugs to take effect at just the right moment?" I asked. "What if it took effect earlier?"

"It was risky, but Henriette must have told them what she told us – that Yvonne wanted to sack her anyway."

"When I saw Henriette at the Ritz," I said, "she had clearly spotted Elizabeth, Virginie, and Reggie. Did she discover something about their activities? After all, she did think the gown you wore at the club was Madame Lafitte's, not your own design."

"Henriette must have had at least an inkling about the copying fraud. Virginie might have even asked her to join the gang to keep her quiet."

"Preposterous," said Virginie.

"The dress mix-up at the first show was probably enough to confirm Henriette's suspicions of a copying scheme. Both Henriette and Omar said that last-minute gown switch at the show was puzzling. The velvet gown was a gorgeous piece, so why didn't anyone model it?"

Madame Lafitte shifted in her seat. "Yvonne might have discovered it was defective, or that it was meant to be shown later in the season. Or..." She sighed the sigh of someone exhausted for years rather than days.

"Or," said Ruby, "Yvonne realised the gown was a copy, or that someone in the audience might recognise it as such. Therefore, she might have hidden it in her room."

Madame Lafitte buried her face in her hands. "It's a wicked, wicked business. I've just pretended it doesn't happen."

"This seems to implicate Mademoiselle Jourdain in this copyist business, a business that led to her untimely demise," said Toussaint.

"On the contrary, Inspector," said Ruby. "I believe the opposite to be true."

37

The library erupted into a crescendo of murmuring disbelief.

"It's impossible!" Toussaint shook his head. "Mademoiselle Jourdain must have known – she ran Madame Lafitte's business."

He gazed at Reggie, Elizabeth, and Virginie. "How about it, you three?"

They all shook their heads, unwilling to speak.

Practised in the art of surprise, Toussaint suddenly pointed a finger at Dr Fischer. "You were having an affair with Mademoiselle Jourdain. She must have said something about it."

Dr Fischer rose from his seat. "Inspector, I—"

Then he plopped back into his chair and stared at the floor. "It meant nothing, nothing at all. Besides, our affair had ended before she was murdered."

"That's not true," I said. "Your secret embrace at Maxim's was not one of former lovers."

"I was merely comforting her."

"If so, why were you arguing?"

He removed his spectacles and rubbed his eyes. "I made promises, the kind lovers regret later."

"Such as?" asked Toussaint.

Dr Fischer waved a dismissive hand. "I said we'd soon be together."

Madame Lafitte aimed a look of utter disgust at her husband.

"And you're saying you never meant it, even though you insist the affair was over," said Toussaint.

"You know how women are, Inspector. They become hysterical."

"She didn't seem to be the hysterical type, as you call it."

"She was under much strain, what with the business and the retirement."

Toussaint was relentless. "Talking of strain, Yvonne could have threatened to tell Madame Lafitte about your affair, and then your life of soirees – not to mention your research – would have come to an end."

"I already knew about it," said Madame Lafitte. "I believed him when he said it was over."

"And you knew this when you made Yvonne director of the House of Lafitte?" asked Toussaint.

Madame Lafitte nodded.

Why was she protecting him? Was she lying? I had to say something.

"You're lying, Dr Fischer."

"What, what do you mean?" Little flecks of his spittle flew onto the rug.

"After Yvonne expressed her doubts, you responded: 'Maurice will take care of it. You know he will.'"

Dr Fischer's mouth moved, but he was unable to speak.

Toussaint turned to Maurice. "How about it, Monsieur Neuville?"

Maurice rubbed his nose. "I just helped Yvonne with her accounting."

"Were things missing in the accounts?" asked Toussaint.

Maurice doubled over as if he felt ill. "I–I–I don't know."

His whole body heaved in an enormous sigh. "The accounts were dreadful. An absolute nightmare."

"Why?" asked Ruby.

"Maury gets in over his head, don't you, darling?" Virginie twittered, returning to her earlier persona.

"Were they a nightmare because you couldn't manage or because something else was wrong?" asked Pixley.

"Something else was wrong," said Maurice. "Figures were always jumbled. Yvonne always told me to add in last-minute sums. Nothing was ever quite right."

"We found a list of horse or dog races," said Ruby. Was she in debt?"

So that was it. Of course, Ruby had made sense of those lists I'd found in Maurice's room. Even if she were wrong, it was still a brilliant shot in the dark.

"Yvonne was a born gambler." Dr Fischer was clearly eager to distract attention from himself. "She'd even place a wager on small, irrelevant matters."

I remembered Yvonne's strange use of an "I'll wager" phrase repeatedly. Was it a subconscious wish? She certainly took risks, like nearly sacking the entire hotel staff.

"So she was in debt and potentially fiddling the books," concluded Pixley. "And she was killed for that?"

"She may have been in debt," said Ruby, "but I don't believe she was fiddling the books."

She spread out her arms towards the gathering. "Let's play a little game. When I say Yvonne's name, tell me the first word that pops into your mind."

"Mercenary," said Elizabeth.

"Cool customer," said Reggie.

"A shark," said Virginie.

"Efficient," said Madame Lafitte.

"Overbearing," said Maurice.

There was a brief, awkward pause.

"Dr Fischer?" asked Toussaint.

Dr Fischer tugged at his beard. "Pathetic."

"Most interesting, Dr Fischer," said Ruby. "Your word is quite different from the others. Why did you say 'pathetic'?"

"The other words are accurate, but only describe her façade. She was helpless, really. She'd put on a good show, as you say, but underneath, she was like a frightened child."

"Why was she frightened?" I asked.

He stared at the ceiling. "It was as if everything was just out of her grasp, and she couldn't keep it under control. Accounts, dates, shows, the running of the hotel. She wanted to do it well, but she just couldn't."

"So how did she fool everyone into thinking otherwise?" asked Pixley.

"She bullied, she cajoled, she threatened, and she also took people in, promising them things," he said. "They thought they'd receive something in return, or they thought the job would be easy. But neither turned out to be the case."

Maurice leaned forward. "At first, I thought she was efficient, just like Madame Lafitte said. Then I realised her efficient appearance hid her incompetence. I started to believe I was going mad when she blamed me for accounting irregularities."

The small figure of Madame Lafitte stepped forward, looking utterly bewildered. "Since Yvonne died, I've been searching for some missing business documents."

She looked at Maurice. "Any time I asked Yvonne an accounting question – which was admittedly rare – she told me not to worry about it."

Ruby nodded. "Bullies develop out of habit, a thirst for power, or from fear – or perhaps all three. You all knew Yvonne was a bully, but it seemed to be driven from a need to control others."

Maurice snapped his fingers. "That's it. She was actually driven by fear. She couldn't control anything in her life, so she tried to blame others or pretend something was wrong with them."

"I expect she sacked the staff in a desperate attempt to reassert control," said Ruby. "My entry as a possible new partner also threatened her."

Pixley held up a protesting hand. "Half a moment, Ruby. Are you saying Yvonne was a victim?"

"Injustice is a peculiar emotion, and many feelings underlie it. I expect Yvonne had a story about experiencing some injustice to explain away her incompetence."

"I appreciate the psychology lesson, Miss Dove, but how does this help us understand her murder?" asked Dr Fischer, regaining his patronising tone.

"It confirms what Pixley said: she was a type of victim. Her veneer of control and authority masked a completely chaotic life beneath it. That chaos, particularly in her line of business, made her vulnerable to anyone on whom she relied, whether it be an accountant, a lover, a business partner, a buyer, a journalist, or a model."

"Or even a hotel manager and maid," said Dr Fischer with a wry smile. "Where are Omar and Berthe, by the way?"

Ruby leaned over and whispered in Toussaint's ear.

"I'm the one who asks the questions," snapped Toussaint. "It's time to see how Albert is getting on. Please follow me upstairs, everyone."

38

As we reached the first-floor landing of the grand staircase, I spotted Albert holding a sketchbook and a small tin under one arm.

"Looks like Albert has discovered Reggie's sketching habit," whispered Pixley.

Toussaint bounced on the balls of his feet. "In the name of fairness, I thought everyone should experience the same search treatment as Mr Barrington-Loftus, who does indeed appear to be a budding Rembrandt."

"Very amusing, Inspector," said Reggie. "But as I said before, it proves absolutely nothing."

Toussaint held out his arm to Ruby. "Miss Dove, would you kindly explain the search we're about to perform?"

Elizabeth jabbed a finger at Ruby. "Excuse me, but what does Miss Dove have to do with it? I can tell you the police don't work like this in the States, Inspector."

"I have little doubt the New York Police Department is remarkably different," said Toussaint drily. "But this is Paris, and we follow our own procedures."

Albert smiled into his moustache. He no doubt believed his

chief followed his own procedures more often than not, regardless of whether he was in New York or Paris.

"Now then, we're going to search your rooms. I'm asking the assistance of Miss Dove, Mr Hayford, and Miss Aubrey-Havelock, as the last search took Albert too long to conduct, and my men on the ground floor must stay where they are."

He held up both hands, forestalling any possible additional protests at this highly unusual procedure.

Our trio and the two policemen soon found ourselves in Dr Fischer's room. The air was close, and I closed my gritty eyes, trying to avert my gaze from the bed where Yvonne's body had lain.

Toussaint said, "We're going split up for the search."

"What are we searching for?" I whispered to Ruby.

"I told him we needed to search for the electrical appliance used to electrocute Yvonne," said Yvonne.

I nodded, though I couldn't quite understand why the murderer wouldn't have just disposed of the item elsewhere, such as a rubbish bin in a park.

"Try to remain focused and remember that although we're searching for a lamp with a cut flex, almost any electrical appliance might have been used. I expect that whatever it is could be shoved in a cupboard or drawer. My men have already searched the rubbish bins."

Pixley unbuttoned his jacket. "Right. We'll find it before you can say Jack Robinson."

The first room we searched was Virginie's. Besides the largest collection of lipstick tubes and pink clothing I'd ever seen, little was of interest, either in terms of the lamp or other suggestive items.

The second was Elizabeth's. Unlike the chaos of Virginie's room, Elizabeth's evoked the military order of her clothes. Rigid, tight, and proper. She had apparently succeeded in her request to have the largest room available, or perhaps Omar had helped her to switch rooms after another guest's departure. The other guest rooms had one bank of windows, whilst this one had two, both festooned with potted red geraniums on the windowsill – a rather frivolous touch for the business-like Elizabeth.

My eye was drawn towards her bedside lamp, not because it was missing a flex or had been otherwise altered, but because I spotted a tiny piece of paper protruding from underneath its base. I lifted the lamp, revealing an American passport. It was an odd place to keep it.

I flipped through, noting the places she'd been, from Tokyo to Warsaw to Lagos. Interesting. Those were places I'd love to visit, but they were scarcely the fashion capitals of the world. However, that surprise was nothing compared to what was on the first page.

The photo was of Elizabeth, dated five years ago.

But it wasn't Elizabeth.

It was someone named Lucia Alessandri.

39

Toussaint held out the passport to Elizabeth. "Would you care to explain this, Miss Ryland?"

True to type, she waved a dismissive hand and leaned back against the bannister, steadying herself with her arms. "Ah, I was waiting for the right moment, but I suppose this will have to do. When Reggie yammered on about how we met in Berlin, I figured it was only a matter of time before you discovered my identity. I didn't have much time to hide my passport properly."

"Are you Lucia Alessandri or Elizabeth Ryland?" asked Ruby.

"Crikey," breathed Reggie. He shot a quick glance at Virginie, who had the good sense to look away.

Madame Lafitte's shrewd eyes narrowed. "I thought something was peculiar about her, but I assumed it was because she was American."

"Hey – enough with the knocks against Americans," said Elizabeth. "I am American, though my mother was from Italy. I used the name Lucia Alessandri because my great-grandmother was Lucia, and an uncle's last name was Alessandri. My real name isn't Elizabeth Ryland, either, but that's neither here nor there."

I suddenly remembered her saying *grazie* to Pixley at the Barrelhouse on that fateful night – I had just assumed it was a result of her tipsiness.

Toussaint puckered his lips in a gesture of exasperation. "Please come to the point, Miss Ryland. Or Miss Alessandri."

"Sure, Inspector. I work for the New York police. Actually, it's a special division of the police, dealing with forgery. I've been undercover for years. So long, in fact, that I feel more like Elizabeth Ryland or Lucia Alessandri than like my old self."

Reggie and Virginie had a sharp intake of breath.

"Yes, that's right, you two. You've been dealing with a police spy."

"Selkies and kelpies," I breathed.

"I don't understand what you're saying, Miss Aubrey-Havelock, but yes, I've got plenty of dope on these two. Enough to send them up the river for a long time."

"So we were right about your scheme," said Ruby.

"Yep. That's also why I needed this large room in the hotel. It was the only one with two windows, which was a signal for my contact in Paris."

"With the red geraniums in the window," I said.

Elizabeth cocked her head. "Say, you're almost as sharp as your friends. But signalling to my contact was pretty much a moot point because these two tried to cut me out of the deal. I'm pretty sure it was Yvonne who saw to that. I'm still not sure why she decided to do it. She either got cold feet or pulled out for some other reason. Maybe she was just in over her head."

"That's why you were so anxious when she refused to sell you any dresses," I said. "And when you realised Maurice was auditing the accounts."

"Bingo. Our deal had gone pear-shaped, as I believe you say in your country."

She turned to Reggie and Virginie. "I suggest you two speak

up soon. As I said, I have a list of charges as long as my arm for each of you. We will help you if you cooperate."

A visibly deflated Reggie croaked, "Even though I desperately needed the extra cash, we were ordered to cut you out of the deal."

All heads turned towards the doorway as Albert entered, looking triumphant.

He pulled a lamp from behind his back. A lamp missing its flex. "I found this in one of the rooms after Miss Aubrey-Havelock discovered Miss Ryland's passport. It was well hidden."

Pulling on a pair of gloves, Inspector Toussaint strode forward and took the lamp.

"But whose room, man?" Pixley demanded.

"The room of Monsieur Maurice Neuville."

MAURICE RAN his tongue around his lips. "But it isn't mine. It isn't. I swear." He put both hands to his face and raked them downward.

"Well done, Albert," said Toussaint.

Albert removed a pair of handcuffs and advanced on a trembling Maurice.

"Wait," said Ruby.

"Sir?" Albert looked inquiringly at Toussaint.

He waved two calming hands. "Do as she says, Albert."

"I'm with Albert, here," said Reggie. "Lock him up. Maurice did it."

"Quiet!" Without looking at Ruby, he said, "Continue, Miss Dove."

"The search has been most revealing, but I'm afraid we're not finished," said Ruby. "Not quite yet. We must first understand *how* Yvonne's body was put in Dr Fischer's room."

My mind whirred. If we knew Yvonne had been murdered in her bathroom on the ground floor, then the murderer had to drag the body to the first floor without being seen. But how?

"The hotel backstairs have a pulley system for the laundry bin. Under cover of darkness, thanks to the power cut caused by Yvonne's electrical shock, the murderer could sneak to the backstairs. Remember, the outage happened on the ground floor, so only Berthe would have noticed, but not if she slept through it, as she claimed. Omar might have noticed, too, but not necessarily if he were at the front desk."

"Picture the scene," said Ruby. "It's quite late, and whilst the murderer may have moved the body to the backstairs, they cannot yet stow the body in Dr Fischer's room, as he is presumably asleep."

"Why do you say presumably?" asked Pixley.

"Because contrary to Dr Fischer's claims, he hadn't slept in his room that night."

Dr Fisher removed his spectacles, his eyes boring into Ruby. "Absolute *quatsch*."

"I say..." breathed Pixley. "Where was he?"

"Canoodling with another woman," said Ruby. "But not Yvonne."

Without warning, Madame Lafitte exploded. Her arms outstretched, legs wide, she hurtled towards her husband, a little brown and white ball of fury. She spewed French invective involving a badger.

Dr Fischer held Madame Lafitte's arm steady in mid-air, preventing her from striking him. "Calm yourself, dear. It was a harmless flirtation. Nothing happened, I promise."

I had a sudden brainwave. "At breakfast, Henriette intimated that Virginie had been out all night with a lover. But why wouldn't she have just said 'Maurice'?"

Pixley nodded. "That's why he wanted to end his relationship with Yvonne."

He turned to Dr Fischer and Virginie. "How about it?"

Virginie shrugged. "Fishy and I are having an affair. He comes to me for his needs."

I rose in anger. "You mean she'd been dallying with Dr Fischer when she disappeared? And that's why I had to replace her at the show?"

Madame Lafitte suddenly pushed her arms hard against her husband. His hand slipped, and her fist hit him squarely in the jaw. I felt a wave of satisfaction wash over me.

"*Arrêt!*" yelled Toussaint, stamping one foot. "Behave, or I'll have Albert handcuff you."

In an effort to redirect, Pixley asked, "What if the murderer were recognised when they were moving the body?"

"Remember the staff uniforms we saw in the laundry bin? No one would have thought twice about staff wheeling about a laundry bin – even late at night."

"Well, blow me over," breathed Pixley.

Albert snorted. "It's obviously Monsieur Neuville. We found the missing lamp in his room."

The beads of sweat dripping down Maurice's forehead made everyone sit up a little straighter. It was not the look of an innocent man.

"Ah yes, Maurice." Ruby leaned against the bannister. "He may have had his fingers in the till, and Yvonne discovered his pilfering. And his peculiar behaviour towards Virginie only makes matters worse. From the start, their relationship seemed odd—he'd flirt with me and act as if Virginie weren't his girlfriend. Perhaps she had a hold over him, one not involving love."

Virginie raised one eyebrow.

Taking pity on Maurice, Pixley handed him a handkerchief. Like the breaking of a dam, the words finally gushed from his lips. "Soon after Virginie and I ended our relationship a few months ago, she overheard me speaking to Yvonne. Yvonne accused me of stealing, though the irregularities were actually due to her incompetence. Virginie decided to extort money from me and use me as a 'cover' – her boyfriend only in name. Then no one would suspect her of having a relationship with Dr Fischer, though I didn't know he was the boyfriend until just now."

Toussaint groaned. "I appreciate your honesty, Monsieur Neuville. If your story is true."

"It is true enough," said Ruby quietly. "You see, the fact Albert found that lamp Maurice's room is enough to clear his name."

40

Even Inspector Toussaint looked baffled, rubbing his forehead. "Let's sit down a moment."

He looked around and soon settled into a soft chair in the corner.

Ruby moved the only other chair on the landing and patted its seat, beckoning Madame Lafitte to take it.

"I say, are we all supposed to sit on the floor now?" asked Reggie. He glowered at Ruby. "Must be part of Miss Dove's plan to make us uncomfortable."

Inspector Toussaint leaned back in his own comfortable chair. "Might as well make yourself comfortable sitting or standing, Mr Barrington-Loftus. I expect the murderer will be deuced uncomfortable either way."

"Now, Miss Dove," he continued, "tell us about your cryptic last remark."

Ruby stood with one hand on the back of Madame Lafitte's chair. "That search had two purposes. One was to find the lamp or other appliance with a cut flex. As I said, I knew the murderer hid it there to implicate someone. In this case, Maurice."

"And the second purpose?" I asked.

"I always suspected Elizabeth Ryland wasn't whom she said she was, and I needed a pretext to search her room."

"Hey!" said Elizabeth. "I wasn't that obvious."

"Now that we know how Yvonne died and how she was moved to Dr Fischer's room, let's discuss the curious matter of timing," said Ruby. "The killer needed access to Yvonne's room right before the dinner at Maxim's, or immediately following it – before Yvonne returned to her room."

She turned to Pixley and me. We were sitting on the floor. "When did you see Yvonne at the House of Lafitte that evening?"

"I remember it was 7:30," said Pixley, "because I didn't want us to be late to the dinner. From there, it took 20 minutes to arrive at Maxim's at 7:50."

He smiled sheepishly. "Journalist's habit, I'm afraid. Must remember times and places."

"Madame Lafitte, how long does it take to get from the hotel to your workshop?" asked Ruby.

She put a finger to her lips. "Five minutes at a minimum in a taxi, though ten on average."

"Thank you," said Ruby. "What time did Yvonne arrive at the workshop?"

"I'm not certain – I was too engrossed in my designing." Then her finger poked the air. "I *do* remember sounds coming from her office next door, shortly before Mr Hayford and Miss Aubrey-Havelock arrived."

"Our conversation lasted only a few minutes," I said. "So 7:20 would have been the latest Yvonne would have arrived at Madame Lafitte's workshop."

Ruby rested her head against the doorframe and stared at the ceiling. "Then let's say she left the hotel at 7:10. She'd prepare before that – maybe a minimum of 30 minutes? That puts the time at 6:40. Since it's at least 30 minutes from the hotel to Maxim's via taxi, the murderer would have had to slip into

Yvonne's room between 7:10 and 7:30. But I cannot believe the killer would have had enough time to sneak into her room unnoticed to set up the live-wire device, especially because they would have been foolish to enter her room at precisely 7:10."

"Why?" I asked.

"Because even if they saw Yvonne leave the hotel, they couldn't be certain she wouldn't forget something and return in those first few minutes. They'd need to wait at least five minutes to ensure she had actually left. That leaves only 15 minutes to do the deed and then appear with the group to take taxis to Maxim's."

"Couldn't they have set up this bally device after dinner?" asked Reggie.

"No," I said. "We all arrived back together, albeit in different taxis. After that, the murderer couldn't know when Yvonne would be in her room."

Pixley pinched his bottom lip together. "Then the murderer must have arrived late to dinner, which leaves Ruby, Maurice, or Virginie."

"I'd spotted Maurice coming from House of Lafitte, so it wasn't him," said Ruby. "Both of us were only 10 minutes late, so even if we had conspired, we'd still be short on time. As for Virginie, she hadn't been seen all day – remember? She would surely have been noticed had she appeared at the hotel."

I suddenly recalled that peculiar sensation of standing near the water's edge at the seashore. Of wet sand shifting beneath your bare feet. "But then no one could have done it!" I protested.

"Not quite. Because the murderer wasn't at Maxim's."

41

A shocked silence fell, broken only by the appearance of two figures in the bedroom doorway. A haggard Omar and defiant Berthe entered reluctantly, escorted by Albert behind them.

"Jupiter's teeth!" cried Reggie. "I knew those two were shifty."

"Silence, Mr Barrington-Loftus," said Toussaint. "I've had enough of your antics, and I'm certain the courts will take a dim view of your activities, even if they aren't violent."

"They sure will." Elizabeth folded her arms and grinned with satisfaction. "I'll see to that."

Toussaint said, "Miss Dove, please tell everyone about your adventures with Mademoiselle Dumont and Monsieur Abelli."

As Ruby related our encounter with the multi-talented Berthe–Omar duo, I revisited their alibis. We assumed they had lied about their whereabouts for Yvonne's murder, but for a legitimate reason – they were playing at the club. And as for Henriette's murder, well, anyone could have done it.

Slowly, I returned my attention to Ruby's story.

"And so, whilst they had the best opportunity to commit the first murder, I was less sanguine about the second," she said.

"Why?" I asked. "Surely, the two of them were the *only* ones capable of committing the first murder, given what you've told us."

"Quite possibly, but there was still a slight possibility a potential murderer could have used those fifteen-odd minutes to slip into Yvonne's room before the dinner. Highly unlikely, but still possible."

Pixley snapped his fingers. "We've forgotten something. What about Henriette herself? She was the only other one in the hotel during the dinner. Could she have killed Yvonne and then been murdered herself?"

Ruby gave out a long sigh. "I was all wrong about Henriette. She was my prime suspect, particularly after we found her rooting around in Yvonne's room."

"Did it have something to do with her dying clue? Something fake?" I asked.

"She probably did know something, but not enough to make any accusations about the murder. I expect she was doing a bit of sleuthing herself when she searched Yvonne's room."

Then she shook her head. "I regret that I didn't seriously consider the psychology of the first crime. That would have told me Henriette wasn't the murderer."

"She was very impulsive, dear Henriette," said Madame Lafitte.

"Precisely," said Ruby. "If Henriette had murdered Yvonne, it would have been straightforward and much less elaborate."

"And then she was killed, putting a final end to the matter," said Pixley quietly.

"That's why I returned to Henriette's murder to align suspects and alibis more carefully. The puzzle was that both Monsieur Abelli and Mademoiselle Dumont had the opportunity to commit the crime, but they had provided alibis for one another. The same proved true for everyone else – they all relied on someone else to vouch for them."

Ruby twitched her nose. "Yet only one pair had access to vital information that provided the opportunity to murder Henriette."

"I've got it!" cried Pixley. "The police raid. It has something to do with the police raid."

"Although Henriette suggested we go to Barrelhouse," said Ruby, "Someone at the hotel had recommended it. Omar would be the natural person to offer such a recommendation. Furthermore, since Omar and Berthe worked at the club, they would also be the most likely persons to know about a potential police raid."

She hesitated. "Omar gave me this idea when he mentioned their 'friend' in the police."

"But why plan a murder during a police raid? It's absurd," I said. "Isn't it?"

Maurice scratched his cheek. "The Barrelhouse is raided regularly because it ignores the colour bar practised by some other clubs. Unsurprisingly, the police once hauled me off during a raid a year ago."

He levelled a steady gaze at Toussaint, who shifted uncomfortably on his feet. Albert smirked.

I persisted in my assertion. "It's appalling, yes, but the assertion still stands. Why plan a murder with police present?"

"You saw it for yourself," said Maurice. "Complete bedlam. Chaos."

"Maurice is right," said Ruby. "A police raid creates exactly what a murderer wants: utter confusion."

"So it was Omar or Berthe," I breathed. "But why?"

Ruby nodded at Omar. "I considered that Omar's casual exterior could be a pose. Perhaps he had a hidden passion. He did at that, but it was a passion for justice for his sister."

As Ruby related the details of her tragic accident to the crowd, I watched Omar.

Finally, he'd raised his chin, his cigarette bouncing up and down in the corner of his mouth. "My sister is my only concern, and I am eternally grateful to Berthe for helping me."

"Unfortunately, your loyalty is misplaced," said Ruby. "In a curious turn of events, Reggie's comments helped me realise that."

"Me?" Reggie gulped, clearly uncertain if the compliment hid an accusation.

"When I met Reggie at the show, he told me about how he'd been falsely accused of sticking treacle on a schoolteacher's seat."

"The little blighter Darrington did it. Not I."

"Your long memory of this injustice reminded me how so many of us cling to such stories. We can all recount some childhood slight that still stings. If it happened when we were young adults, the sting can be even greater."

Ruby turned. "Isn't that true, Berthe?"

For once, Berthe was at a loss for words. Then she folded her arms and sneered. "You haven't a shred of evidence."

"Why is she speaking with an English accent?" asked Reggie.

"Perhaps you weren't listening earlier," said Ruby. "Berthe has created a rather grand victim narrative about herself. She shares this quality with Yvonne, and both were 'fake' in that they were hiding something. In Yvonne's case, she used her victim story to cover her incompetence. In Berthe's case, it covers something simpler and more terrifying."

42

"Must be greed," said Maurice.

"No, it's more troubling than that: a sense of her innate superiority," said Ruby.

"She thought she was better than Yvonne and Henriette, and ergo she had to murder them?" asked Toussaint. "It's a bit too pat, Miss Dove."

"If anything, it's actually more complex. Berthe's life story is chock-a-block with misunderstandings and revenge. In each case, she says she's motivated by justice, or more specifically, vengeance for a wrong she's suffered. These perceived wrongs come from her sense of superiority. I became certain of it when we were on the barge tonight."

"When she doubted that you already knew she might be English?" I asked.

"Yes, and how every story she told featured her as the victim. She is also remarkably self-possessed."

"I am self-possessed." Berthe held her button nose high in the air. "But victims are passive. I act. I make things happen. Victims don't do that. I was *betrayed*, which is a different kettle of fish."

Ruby half-closed her eyes. "It's the perfect logic of a victim. 'I'm not a victim like everyone else. I'm special because I was betrayed.'"

Omar cleared his throat. "But Berthe was betrayed by her family, then by society, and then by whoever was running this ghastly workshop where my sister was injured."

"That's how she tells it, but the first proverbial crack in her narrative was revealed when Fina asked why she'd been kept on as hotel staff. She said she was 'better'. Not 'better at it', but 'better', full stop. In fact, she focused on how she had to do everything, leaving aside how Omar was obviously also stretched thin. She also called the hotel cook 'stupid'."

"Typical British misunderstandings of confidence," said Berthe. "The French don't have false modesty."

Ruby waved this away. "Later, when she described being victimised in the workshop, it simply didn't ring true. Berthe only takes on lesser roles – at least that's how she thinks of them – such as maid or apprentice seamstress when she has a reason to do so."

"Ah." Pixley held up a hand. "So why would she have worked in such a frightful factory?"

"She wanted revenge and perhaps to pad her pocket along the way," said Ruby. "And her bubbling hatred boiled over when her application for a special seamstress position at House of Lafitte was rejected."

The cigarette hanging from Omar's mouth dropped to the ground. "I don't believe it." He shook his head. "She wouldn't double-cross me."

"Berthe wanted revenge on high society, specifically the fashion world. She felt snubbed, so she hatched a plan for revenge on one particular individual: Madame Lafitte."

"If it were true, why wouldn't I just kill her?" asked Berthe.

"You wanted her to suffer," said Ruby. You wanted to destroy

Madame Lafitte's reputation by destroying anyone with any connection to her."

"Rubbish. You're talking pure gibberish," said Berthe.

Ruby was relentless now. "You took a job at that dreadful factory to learn more about the underbelly of fashion. You bided your time, knowing an opportunity would come your way.

"*Mon Dieu!*" Toussaint's eyes lit up. "The accident. Omar's sister."

"How lucky you were to find such a loyal and willing friend in Omar," continued Ruby. "You fuelled his anger by blaming Yvonne for speeding up production, creating conditions that would surely cause an injury or death. No matter that you had no evidence it was Yvonne."

"Absolute rubbish," said Berthe. "She's lying, Omar."

"Omar agreed to infiltrate the hotel, with an eye towards eventually exposing the terrible workshop conditions, with the hope of gaining injury compensation for his sister. He didn't realise your *real* goal was much larger: the complete and utter abasement of Madame Lafitte via the destruction of anyone who dared to be part of her coterie of fashion acolytes."

"Well, I'll be a..." Pixley trailed off.

"You see, Yvonne's death itself exposed everyone and everything around Madame Lafitte, including her husband's affairs, Yvonne's shoddy book-keeping, and high society types like Reggie."

Looking into Omar's face turned my stomach. He was a gentle soul, but his fierce loyalty had rendered him vulnerable to this tragic situation. His lighter slipped as he tried to light a new cigarette with his long, quivering fingers.

"I see you're still unconvinced, Omar, so let me ask you this," said Ruby. "Why didn't Berthe scream when she first found the body? Why did she scream only *after* Pixley entered the room?"

"Then I remembered Berthe said her father had been an undertaker, and she had seen many dead bodies," said Ruby.

"Then why would she scream at all?" Then Pixley slapped his forehead. "Her father isn't really an undertaker at all, is he? She said as much on the barge when she told us about her aristocratic family. Her scream must have been a reaction to me discovering *her*, precisely because she already knew *why the body was there*."

Omar stared at the floor, still silent.

In a rather cruel twist of logic, Toussaint said, "Who will care for your sister if you are in prison – or worse?"

Running one hand over his face, Omar sighed. "I didn't see Berthe at the club after the raid. I said I had because it was part of our plan, as it was to lure Ruby and Fina to the barge. Clearly, I've been a fool."

"I'm the fool for ever having trusted you." Berthe pointed a finger. "Omar planned it all. I'm the one who lied for him about the club."

Slowly, her accusation seemed to register on Omar's face. "You planned I should take the fall for this. My God, what would happen to my sister?"

"Curse your weakling sister. She had no spirit. No fighting spirit. She's just like you, a namby-pamby, snivelling, untrustworthy snake."

"Come now, Mademoiselle Dumont," said Toussaint quietly. He nodded at Albert, who moved towards Berthe with a pair of handcuffs.

Omar coughed. "Inspector, I beg you to stop." He began to shiver and shake like a freshly caught trout.

I spied a flash of silver between Berthe's hand and Omar's back.

"She has a knife!" I screamed.

Pixley grabbed Berthe's arm and thrust it in the air. He was only an inch or two taller than her, and his arms were considerably shorter. They struggled, arms outstretched in a kind of maniacal tango of death, side to side, until Omar spun on one foot and joined the melee. He finally grasped Berthe's wrist and wrenched the knife from her hand.

It clattered to the floor, but Berthe had already leapt away, somersaulting over Albert's outstretched foot and dashing down the corridor.

"After her!" yelled Toussaint.

We all rushed after Berthe, sliding on the slippy floor tiles, worn smooth by years of use. Pixley led the pack, followed closely by the long-legged Reggie.

We all stopped short once we reached the backstairs. She'd already slammed the door behind her, though we could hear her running up the stairs.

How would she exit from the second floor? She could climb down the drainpipe, but she had said they had been under repair. Perhaps she knew about a secret passage? Or a garret?

Reading my thoughts, Ruby leaned over. "Do you think there's a hidden garret?"

Berthe soon disappeared from sight.

Maurice began to climb the stairs, but Toussaint held him back. "Wait. Let's listen to see where's she's going."

We heard running footsteps above us, so we all dashed back towards the first-floor landing.

Berthe's round figure lumbered slowly onto the second-floor landing. Her head was bowed, and her bottom lip stuck out as she advanced steadily to the stairs. Her legs seemed to be moving of their own accord, like a clockwork toy.

"That's right, Berthe, just come downstairs, and then we can talk," said Toussaint.

"I have nothing to say. I've accomplished my task. The House of Lafitte will crumble, and along with it, every snob who ever dared to snub me. Me! The daughter of a Brocklehurst-Smythe."

Ruby stepped forward. "This is madness, Berthe. You'll only bring dishonour to your family. You don't want that, do you?"

She snorted. "They don't care about me – never have and never will."

Omar held up his hands, pressed together. "Please, Berthe. You don't have to do this. Isn't it better to end this all with dignity?"

Berthe's scrunched face loosened, and she held her chin high. "You've never spoken truer words, dear Omar. It's much better to end this all with dignity."

She flung herself over the bannister.

Into oblivion.

43

A few weeks after the tragedies in Paris, Pixley rang me up in Oxford.

"I say, it's time for a spot of tea and sympathy. Or a pint and explanation. I've been absolutely thirsty for the truth, but I've wanted to respect Ruby's finer feelings."

"What about my finer feelings?" I asked. "I'm the sensitive one, remember?"

Pixley chuckled. "Especially if you haven't eaten."

"Can't you be serious for a moment?"

The line went quiet. His lip-licking pause expressed what words could not. "Yes, Red, I play it all over and over in my mind. Berthe was horrid, but she shouldn't have died like that."

"Better than the guillotine."

"Now who's insensitive?"

"Touché."

The following afternoon, we ensconced ourselves at Oxford's Lamb & Flag, home to students from around the country and the world for generations. Our Paris adventure seemed to fade amidst the comforting hum of background chatter and glasses clinking.

Pixley sipped his bitter. "I always picture old Thomas Hardy scribbling away in this fine establishment. Didn't he write *Jude the Obscure* here?"

"Never read it," I said. "Though I have had obscure feelings since Paris. A sort of in-between-worlds sensation. Too many loose ends, I expect."

I turned to Ruby, just as she was taking a gulp of her pint. "What do you say? Are you game to explain?"

Though Ruby's face had grown thinner, her brown eyes began to glow. "I'll answer your questions, but first answer mine."

She slid an envelope addressed to me across the pock-marked table.

Pixley rubbed his hands together. "Marvellous. I love beginning with a mysterious envelope."

I was less sanguine about such missives, but I opened it anyway and smoothed out the letter.

"Dear Fina," I read aloud and then looked up at Ruby. "Why did you receive my letter?"

"Some sort of mix-up with the post. You know how it is with the scouts."

"Dear Fina," I continued. "I'm grateful to you and your friends for cracking the case. If you ever want a job with the New York Police Department, it's yours."

I stuck out my tongue. "If pigs fly."

Pixley frowned. "That's in the letter?"

"No, no, that's what I think," I said.

Ruby chuckled. "Pix is pulling your proverbial."

"You are maddening, Pixford." I turned to Ruby. "That's what Elizabeth called him at the club."

"Aha, a new nickname. Excellent."

Pixley waved away our comments. "What else does Elizabeth say?"

"That's it, except for a postscript."

My face flamed as I set down the letter.

Ruby scooped it up. "It says, 'P.S. I knew you'd spiked my drink at the club. Can't put one over on Elizabeth or Lucia, sweetie. But nice try'."

Pixley spluttered, "You put alcohol in her drink, Red? Her tonsils must have been toasted!"

He slapped the table. "You are a one, aren't you?"

"Ignore him, Feens – he's just egging you on."

"I just thought it might loosen her tongue a bit," I said. "Besides, you two had abandoned me."

Pixley moved his hands up and down, mimicking a violin.

"Talking of mimicking, did Berthe pretend to be me during the raid? And how did you know, Ruby?"

Ruby twisted her glass. "Two people had shown off their mimicking talents before."

Pixley snapped his fingers. "Old Reggie did a credible impersonation of Elizabeth at Maxim's. Was that the first?"

She nodded. "Yes, and as for Berthe—"

"I know!" I leapt in my seat. "Ivie Anderson."

"Precisely," said Ruby. "Remember Berthe's red-hot rendition of *It Don't Mean a Thing*? It was a perfect copy of Ivie Anderson from the famous Duke Ellington recording. I expect she mimicked Fina's voice to confuse me—quite successfully, I might add."

A young woman with tiny eyes and a broad smile approached our table. "I do apologise for interrupting, but I just couldn't help myself. Might I have a word?"

Pixley pushed his spectacles on his nose. "Of course. Did you have someone in mind?"

"Oh! How frightfully embarrassing." She pulled down her hat over her ears. "It's with you, Mr Hayford."

"Let's go to that table, shall we?" He rose, and they padded to a tiny hidden table in the corner.

"I'll just powder my nose," I said.

"I'll come with you," said Ruby.

Though I didn't exactly powder my nose, I did brush my hair whilst in the toilet. As I watched myself arranging my hair in the looking glass, a sudden rush of images flooded my mind.

Makeup. Hair. The velvet gown.

Ruby surveyed me in the looking glass. "Your eyes are so wide! Did you have a brainwave?"

"Just as I was brushing my hair, one more piece of the puzzle fell into place. Yvonne's makeup. Her hair. Her gown."

"Ah." Ruby's smile looked slightly crooked in the looking glass. "Berthe's undoubted makeup skills."

"She was one of the few people who could have replicated Yvonne's makeup and hair routine, wasn't she?" I looked sideways at Ruby. "But you knew that already, didn't you?"

"I'm afraid so. It did occur to me early on, but it didn't seem that important. After all, anyone *could* have replicated her look."

"But I've tried it myself," I said. "It's hard enough to put on one's own makeup – let alone another's – whilst also remembering exactly how it looked."

"In hindsight, it ought to have been a major clue." Ruby sighed. "After all, Berthe was probably the most skilled makeup artist amongst the suspects – she helped the models prepare for shows."

"I suppose Virginie could have done it, but she was eliminated as a suspect for other reasons," I put in as we walked back to our table.

We found Pixley grinning from ear to ear.

I retook my seat. "You look rather pleased with yourself."

"That young lady was a fan of mine."

"Not possible." I smiled.

Pixley rubbed his jumper. "She'd read my stories on the Ethiopian war and just had to have my autograph."

"Only in Oxford, Pix." Ruby laughed.

He raised a fresh pint of bitter. "She even bought me another pint, but I'm not going to allow my new-found celebrity distract me from the matter at hand."

Ruby spread out her hands. "Please, ask me anything, great Pixford."

"I feel like a positive dunce, but I'm still hazy about Berthe's motives altogether," he said. "I gather she was a supreme egoist or narcissist, but why kill Yvonne and not Madame Lafitte? And Henriette?"

"Berthe's biography is riddled with stories about ruined reputations," said Ruby. "To her, death was preferable to a ruined reputation."

"So to make Madame Lafitte suffer, she killed Yvonne?" I asked.

"Goodness knows it's peculiar." Ruby sighed. "But if there had been a way to expose the secrets of everyone connected to Madame Lafitte, none of the murders need to have happened."

"Murdering Yvonne was simply a means to ruin everyone's reputation around Madame Lafitte," said Pixley, "thereby ruining her own reputation and causing her great suffering?"

"Yes," said Ruby quietly.

I squinted at my pint, trying to comprehend Berthe's twisted mind. "Because a newspaper exposé on that awful workshop wouldn't be painful enough?"

"I'm afraid so," said Ruby. "And Henriette had to die because she clearly knew something about Yvonne's murder. Perhaps she'd seen something."

"Which is the real reason she was in Yvonne's room when we surprised her?" asked Pixley.

Ruby nodded. "Her dying clue of 'fake' ironically meant she

knew something important, but she actually didn't know Berthe had committed the murder."

"Otherwise, she would have just said 'Berthe' instead of 'fake'," I said.

Pixley frowned. "So Berthe probably spotted Henriette leaving Yvonne's room and deduced she must know something?"

"Berthe couldn't take any chances, because Henriette was one of the few people who wasn't at Maxim's and therefore could have seen her doing something suspicious."

"Selkies and kelpies," I murmured. "I just realised that murdering Henriette was also a perfect plan for Berthe because Henriette was Madame Lafitte's niece, which would cause another layer of suffering."

"And conveniently implicated me in the crime," said Ruby. "Which was yet another attraction."

"You were quite the easy scapegoat, weren't you?" Pixley scratched his forehead. "But what about the lamp business? Why did we need to search for it? Did you know it was in Maurice's room?"

"And why wouldn't Berthe have just disposed of the lamp earlier?" I asked.

"The answer is in Berthe's psychology."

I drummed my fingers on the table. "She stowed that lamp in Maurice's room earlier to implicate him, simply because he was a part of the House of Lafitte."

Pixley frowned. "And that's why she moved Yvonne to Dr Fischer's room."

"So it didn't matter to Berthe who went to the guillotine for these crimes," I said. "What mattered was that all the suspects had their secrets yelled from Paris rooftops, ensuring the maximum suffering of the person at the centre of this web: Madame Lafitte."

"Bingo!"

Pixley whistled. "And that's why it was so deuced difficult to finger Berthe for the crime."

Ruby shivered. "She took risks that any other murderer wouldn't have taken."

"But why did Berthe hate Madame Lafitte so much?" I asked.

"Despite Madame Lafitte's humble beginnings, to Berthe she represented the ultimate snobbery of the fashion world. Berthe probably didn't even know Madame Lafitte very well – all she saw was the harshness of the fashion world. As Berthe was from a titled family and accustomed to getting her way, every setback she suffered seemed to stem from this fashion house, especially when she was turned down for a seamstress position by Yvonne. You must remember, Berthe had a grandiose vision of herself, so simple revenge wasn't enough. It had to be grandiose."

"Grandiosely grotesque," I said.

"At least I had a good story out of it," sighed Pixley.

"Pix!"

"No, no, I don't mean that." Pixley laughed in response to my scolding. "I'm speaking of Dr Fischer. It appears his affairs were the only peccadillos that might prevent further research funding. He's solved that problem, so he'll be receiving funds from this Egyptian benefactor for a jolly good cause, even if I don't care for Dr Fischer myself."

"What do you mean, he's 'solved' his problem?" I asked.

"Madame Lafitte wants a divorce. Quite right, too. In even better news, Maurice will be the director of Dr Fischer's plan to return artefacts to their original locations."

Our eyes slewed towards Ruby. How did she feel about Maurice?

"How about it, Miss Dove?" said Pixley, in an exaggerated version of himself. "For an exclusive with the *Daily Perk*. Tell us all about Monsieur Neuville."

Ruby tucked a stray hair behind her ear. "Nothing to tell, Mr Hayford."

"Oh, come now, our readers are positively voracious for your story."

She twisted her now-empty pint glass thoughtfully. "Any possibility of romance has died on the vine."

"How so?" I asked.

"I cannot abide hedgehogs, much less someone who allows them to range around his room!"

"If he loved you, he'd give them up," I said.

"My thoughts exactly, dear Feens. Besides, I'm too busy to traipse after him to Egypt."

She held up a forestalling hand. "And before you ask, yes, I have news about Madame Lafitte's offer. Finish your pints and follow me."

44

"Thrupp?" whined Pixley. "It will take ages to get there!"

"You've become soft in your dotage, Pix," I said.

Ruby dusted the seat of her bicycle with her favourite hand-kerchief. "It's Crickle Hythe, a hamlet near Thrupp. We can cycle to it, or—"

He raised his eyebrows. "Walk?"

"I believe Ruby was about to suggest a contraption with four large wheels and many seats?" I motioned to the bus headed towards the Oxford Canal.

Leaving our bicycles behind at the Lamb & Flag, we paid our fares and began the six-mile journey to Thrupp.

I breathed in the fresh air as the bus trundled out of Oxford, leaving behind the traffic and the stale cigarette smoke of the pub. "I have one more question, Ruby. Why on earth did you suddenly take up smoking?"

Pixley turned around. "You took up smoking? When? Why?"

Ruby broke into a rare belly laugh. "That's why I love you two. No stone left unturned. It was an experiment. I tried smoking once when I was fifteen, but it tasted dreadful and made me queasy. Lately, though, I've wanted to see how it would change my personality."

"You mean to play a role – like an actor?" I asked.

"Yes, I thought my necessary fibs to the police or Berthe would be more convincing if I became *Madame Dove*."

"Ah," I said. "Like some world-weary woman who doesn't care what happens to her. A cigarette would be a handy prop for that role."

Pixley removed his cigarette case from his tweed jacket. "Care for one, *Madame Dove* or *Madame Aubrey-Havelock*?"

We both shook our heads. Pixley was a fair-weather smoker. He'd take it up for weeks at a time, then drop it, and then pick up a pipe. I'd even seen him go in for cigars once, but that only lasted a week.

"Speaking of personas, what ever happened to Reggie, Pix? Have you given him up?"

"I heard he and Virginie will be in a French courtroom soon," said Ruby. "Though I expect they'll be fined rather than go to prison."

Pixley blew a smoke ring out of the bus window. "Reggie was just a passing fancy. Devilishly attractive in a peculiar way, but I'm not keen on bad hats like Barrington-Loftus. You know me. If I fall for someone, it's hook, line, and sinker. Talking of which…"

He winked and withdrew an envelope from inside his jacket. "Not like your attraction, dear Red. I, too, have another letter for you."

"Who's it from?" Without waiting for a reply, I tore open the envelope.

"Omar," Pixley said quietly. "He didn't know how to reach you, but he knew the address of my newspaper."

Ruby suddenly became fixated on the scenery, and Pixley

turned around to face the front of the bus, humming softly to himself.

Blood rushed to my ears, and my heart thumped.

Dear Fina,

I'm not one for sentiment, so I'll be brief. You may have wondered why I tried to divert the police from suspecting you and your friends at first. I'm certain you were even more puzzled by the incident on the barge.

As you know, I was driven to protect my sister and have my revenge on the people responsible for her accident. Along the way, however, I fell for you. That is all. Prison may be my future, or perhaps the court will have mercy.

Since I will never see you again, you deserve the truth.

Yours,
Omar Abelli

With shaking fingers, I stuffed the note into my handbag and stared at the back of Pixley's head.

I had become completely numb.

Ruby patted me on the shoulder. "It will all reveal itself in time, Feens. Trust that."

"Oxford Canal, Thrupp!" announced the driver.

Knock-kneed like a new-born foal, I followed my friends onto the twilight-lit pavement near the canal. The gloaming cast pink and orange shadows against the stone cottage windows holding purple and white petunias. The bucolic scene was completed by the quiet murmurs of patrons sitting outside a pub, enjoying pints and chips.

"Deep breath, Red," said Pixley. "Smell that ocean breeze."

Already moving with a rapid step towards the canal, Ruby ignored Pixley's joke.

"Follow me!"

We wound past the pub, past the row of stone cottages, and finally onto a pathway along the canal. Colourful narrowboats lined the canal, stuffed with hanging flowers, chairs, bicycles, and a few cats soaking in the last rays of light before nightfall. Smells of roasting meat and veg wafted towards us, signalling the coming evening meal aboard many of the boats.

"It's calming, isn't it?" Ruby turned left onto a narrow flagstone path. When we arrived at a low hedge, she halted and drew out two scarves from her handbag.

"Cover your eyes, please."

Pixley tied the scarf over his eyes. "May I have my last cigarette?"

"Now, just hold onto me," she said as I finished tying my scarf. "We'll arrive in just a moment."

I stepped tentatively onto a gravel path and then onto soft earth.

A few ducks quacked nearby. We took a few more steps forward.

"You may open your eyes!"

I pulled down my scarf and gave a little yelp. We stood in front of a small, rose-covered, sky-blue cottage with a vegetable garden in front and the canal to our right.

"Is it yours?" I squeaked.

"Come in, come in." She led us into the warm cottage, through a charming sitting room, and into a kitchen featuring a large cooking range and cheery red curtains.

Ruby picked up a tea kettle and turned on the faucet. "I'll give you the full tour soon, but I'm dying for a cuppa first."

"How did you manage to find this place?" asked Pixley. "You

haven't a bean! Neither do you, Fina. And I'm on the starving journalist's diet."

As the kettle began to hiss, Ruby opened a tin and handed it to me. "Biscuits with your tea?"

"Yes, please." I popped a Bourbon biscuit into my mouth, a marked improvement over those crumbs on the Paris barge.

My eyes ranged again over the cosy kitchen. "This cottage explains why you weren't in your rooms when I called last Thursday. And the Monday before?"

She nodded. "Madame Lafitte telephoned a few days after we left Paris. She still plans on retiring and wanted me to run the House of Lafitte on my own or for me to hire someone to handle the business, much like Yvonne did."

"That's splendid," I said. "Did you say yes?"

"I was touched, obviously, and I said I'd consider it. Before ringing off, she told me she'd severed ties with that dreadful factory and had taken steps to shut it down."

"Did she say who was responsible for House of Lafitte's involvement in the factory?" asked Pixley. "Or the copyist scheme, for that matter?"

"Madame Lafitte still suspected Yvonne was responsible, even if she were unaware of the appalling conditions. Because it cost so little to produce the gowns at that factory, it allowed Yvonne to hide her own accounting errors. As for the copyist scheme, it's clear Reggie and Virginie were involved, but Elizabeth Ryland's still searching for the mastermind." She waved her hand. "Unfortunately, even if they find this so-called mastermind, I'm afraid another will take their place – copying is now part of the fashion world."

I sipped my delicious tea and sat down at the small kitchen table. "And? What was your reply to Madame Lafitte's proposition?"

"After a sleepless night, I telephoned to say that I had to

complete my studies, especially for the sake of my parents. And not just for them. Chemistry and fashion are fascinating, and I want to pursue both. Though it's deuced difficult to study both at the same time."

"You've managed so far," said Pixley.

"You're a dear." Ruby smiled. "Fortunately, Madame Lafitte agreed and said we should revisit her plan later. In the meantime, she wanted a few designs a year – with my name attached – in exchange for purchasing this cottage. More than anything else, I need quiet and a space away from the bustle of Oxford to sketch and make designs."

Something tickled my ankle. I looked down at a plump grey shorthaired cat with golden eyes. The cat was munching on a biscuit by my foot.

"Hullo! Who gave him a biscuit?" I asked.

"I did," said Ruby. "He's been lurking around the cottage for the past few days, and we've become friends."

Pixley slapped his thigh. "You're friends with a cat?"

"Isn't he rather adorable? Though I still don't know his name."

I rubbed the cat's neck, surveying his chunky hindquarters and creased smile created from the folds of fat around his face.

"Pasty," I said.

"As in Cornish pasty?" asked Pixley.

"That's precisely what she means," said Ruby. "Plump and juicy, just like the best pasties."

"I say, perhaps they have pasties in that pub we passed earlier. We must inaugurate the House of Dove," said Pixley. "Fancy a celebratory dinner?"

"Perfect." She raised her teacup in a toast. "To old friends and new beginnings."

The End

Thank you for reading *Death in Velvet!*

Positive reviews help readers discover this book. If you enjoyed *Death in Velvet*, I'd be grateful for a review (Australia, Germany, United Kingdom, or United States).

If you want updates and goodies, please join my reader group!

MORE MYSTERIES

The Ruby Dove Mystery Series follows the early adventures of our intrepid amateur-spy sleuths:

Book 1: The Mystery of Ruby's Sugar
Book 2: The Mystery of Ruby's Smoke
Book 3: The Mystery of Ruby's Stiletto
Book 4: The Mystery of Ruby's Tracks
Book 5: The Mystery of Ruby's Mistletoe
Book 6: The Mystery of Ruby's Roulette
Book 7: The Mystery of Ruby's Mask
Ruby Dove Mysteries Box Set 1
Ruby Dove Mysteries Box Set 2

With many cases under their fashionable belts, Ruby and Fina are ready for more in *Partners in Spying Mysteries:*

Fatal Festivities: A Christmas Novella
Book 1: Death in Velvet

ABOUT THE AUTHOR

Rose Donovan is a lifelong devotee of golden age mysteries. She now travels the world seeking cosy spots to write, new adventures to inspire devious plot twists, and adorable animals to petsit.

www.rosedonovan.com
rose@rosedonovan.com
Reader Group
Follow me on Bookbub
Follow me on Goodreads

NOTE ABOUT UK STYLE

Readers fluent in US English may believe words such as "fuelled", "signalled", "hiccough", "fulfil", "titbit", "oesophagus", "blinkers", and "practise" are typographical errors in this text. Rest assured this is simply British spelling. There are also spacing and punctuation formatting differences, including periods after quotation marks in certain circumstances.

If you find any errors, I always appreciate an email so I can correct them! Please email me at rose@rosedonovan.com. Thank you!

Printed in Great Britain
by Amazon

84321173R00150